THE SU

ARE GOING

THROUGH

CHANGES

Written by:

Brandon Wilson

The Suttons Are Going Through Changes

Copyright © 2021 by Brandon Wilson

Written by: Brandon Wilson

First Edition: February 2021

Chapter 1

Brennan

BRENNAN CAME HOME from work feeling a little more drained than usual. He worked for a company called TransTech Global and was one of their senior IT consultants. He'd had a rough day at the office leading the team in putting out fires for a high-profile client. Unfortunately, the system that Brennan's team had set up encountered a security breach, and he spent the whole day dealing with the tirades of the client while also directing his team to get everything fixed. Brennan had to spend an extra hour at the office just to get everything sorted out before he could call it a day.

By the time he got to the house, he felt absolutely depleted of any energy. He walked through the front door wanting nothing more than to have some dinner and spend time with his family. As he entered the living room, he saw his two daughters, Amber and Riley, engrossed in their toys that were scattered all throughout the floor. Amber, who was three and just a year older than Riley, was fiddling with her toy cooking set while her younger sister seemed to be developing some kind of storyline involving a stuffed porcupine and a Barbie doll.

"Dada!" shrieked Amber as she saw her father. She immediately dropped the toy spatula that she was holding and scampered towards Brennan who was already waiting for her with his arms wide open. Riley couldn't be bothered as things were beginning to get really serious between the porcupine and the Barbie.

"Hey, babe," Brennan yelled loudly so his wife would be able to hear. "I'm home!"

"Hey, hun," echoed a voice from the kitchen. "Dinner's just about done. Help me get the kids set up at the table?"

"Roger that. Come here, you two!" he said, addressing the girls. "It's time to eat!"

"Could you also set the table after the kids are settled down?" asked Abigail.

"Sure, honey," said Brennan as he lifted Amber and Riley in his arms and carried them off towards the dining room. From the vantage point of the dinner table, Brennan caught a glimpse of his wife, slaving away over the stove in the kitchen.

"Anything I can help you with over there, babe?"

"No, it's all good."

Brennan put the girls down into their individual high chairs and made sure that they were secure. After giving them a toy each to keep themselves busy while waiting for dinner, he went over to Abigail and planted a kiss on her cheek. She continued to focus on dinner as Brennan pulled out the plates and utensils from the cupboard. Abigail had just pulled the roasted chicken out of the oven and begun to carry it over to the dining room table when she stopped midway.

"Brennan" she exclaimed. "I asked you to set the table! Where are the trivets? I can't put this chicken on the table without them. It'll damage the wood. And why did you bring out the regular plates for the kids?"

"Oh," said Brennan. "Sorry, honey. Let me get the

trivets right now."

Abigail was visibly frustrated as she was holding a very heavy baking dish in her hands while she waited for Brennan. She was usually the one who prepared the table for dinner. Once Brennan had properly set the table to Abigail's standards, she placed the chicken in the middle of the table then returned to the kitchen to get the vegetables and mashed potatoes. Brennan got up to grab a beer from the fridge and sat back down.

"Brennan! The girls' plates?"

"Oh, right."

"Nevermind," sighed Abigail as she stood up to get the children's dinnerware from the kitchen.

"I'm sorry, honey. I should know how to do this properly by now. I'll do better next time."

"Mmm."

"Alright, girls," said Brennan as he addressed Amber and Riley. "It's time to put those toys away and have dinner."

Brennan took Amber's toy frying pan and Riley's porcupine away from them which immediately triggered loud protests with corresponding screams.

"Brennan!" Abigail roared over the sound of two crying children. "Just give them the toys! We can feed them while they're playing."

A defeated Brennan returned the toys to the two toddlers. It took a while before the screaming stopped, but the fussy kids eventually calmed down.

"Right," said Abigail. "Let's just have dinner now, shall we?"

Brennan began carving into the chicken. All throughout their relationship, he had grown accustomed to her just instructing him on various things. That's just the kind of personality she had. She always played that role throughout the tenure of their relationship. It was probably because she was older than him by five years. Even when they had just started dating, she was already giving off a vibe of seniority over him whenever they interacted. But he didn't mind. He really liked Abigail. In fact, he was convinced that it was Abigail who taught him how to love. Before he met her, Brennan had a reputation in college for being quite a womanizer. He was notorious for having relationships come to an end due to his own infidelity. It was Abigail who had changed all of that.

Brennan first met Abigail fifteen years ago when he was an intern at TransTech Global. Abigail was working as an administrative officer at Perpetual Grace Hospital at the time. The hospital had hired TransTech Global to set up its hospital management system. Brennan was only tagging along as he shadowed his mentor who was assigned the Perpetual Grace account. It was during that initial meeting when he first laid eyes on Abigail in her powerful navy-blue pantsuit with her brown hair neatly tied up in a bun. He was noticing her slender frame as she listened to them talk about the many features that were included in the system. Brennan was immediately taken aback. The young twenty-three-year-old gazed in delight at the pretty hospital lady who was asking his mentor questions about the system.

She no longer looked like that feisty twenty-eight-year-old that she once was. After a decade of marriage and two kids, Abigail had packed on a few pounds and could no longer be considered slender. She never really got back to her pre-pregnancy body. But none of that mattered to Brennan. He was just as infatuated with her now as he had been when he first stepped into her office so many years ago.

"Crazy day at work today," Brennan lamented. "A disgruntled ex-employee over at McArthur Banking tried to hack into the bank's records and threatened to release them all over the internet. He got really close to doing it too. Good thing the team was on their 'A' game today."

Abigail didn't reply.

"It would have been a real disaster," continued

Brennan as he placed a few slices of chicken on Abigail's plate.

"Everything okay, honey?" asked Brennan. "You seem off."

"Yeah," she sighed unconvincingly.

"Listen, I'm really sorry about the trivets and the kids' toys. I didn't mean to irritate you. I promise it'll never happen again," said Brennan as he scooped smaller slices of chicken onto Amber and Riley's plates.

"It's not that, Brennan. I'm just really tired from doing chores and taking care of the kids all day."

"Sorry to hear that, babe. Looks like we've both had it rough today, huh?"

It was a relatively dull dinner for the Sutton family that night. Brennan continued to try to get Abigail to converse with him, but she just didn't seem like she was into it. Regardless, he went on to tell her about all the things that he had to do with his team today. In the middle of dinner, Riley started crying and was yelling for the iPad. After which, her sister started yelling as well. Brennan grabbed the iPad from his work bag and searched for a YouTube video that the girls would like. He settled on a video of Mickey Mouse and friends to keep the girls entertained as he tried to get his wife to talk to him. Much to his dismay, Abigail never got into the mood. She must be really tired, Brennan thought to himself.

After dinner was done, Brennan sat on the couch in the living room to watch some TV while Abigail prepped the kids for bed, but nothing interesting was on. Brennan flipped through the channels until he finally settled on a documentary about the dangers of social media data mining. This might be interesting, thought Brennan to himself. He tried his best to focus on the documentary, but he couldn't help but feel like something was off with Abigail during dinner. Of course, the two of them had gotten into rows and spats before. Being married for ten years meant that they've already seen their fair share of fights. Although, there was something about what happened during dinner that really bothered him. I really do love her, he thought. I love her just as much now as I ever have.

Brennan thought that he would try to get intimate with Abigail that night. He always wanted to make her feel loved and cared for. It had also been a while since the two of them had been together. Sad to say, it had been this way ever since Abigail first got pregnant with Amber. Then, when Riley came along, Brennan noticed that their sexual encounters really took a dip. Of course, he never blamed the kids. Heck, Brennan was thankful for his two beautiful girls. In fact, even when they had first gotten married, Brennan was eager to start a family with Abigail. However, the couple encountered a lot of issues with their pregnancy. Abigail had even experienced three separate miscarriages before finally successfully giving birth to Amber. Brennan knew that both of his two girls were miracles, and he wouldn't have traded them for anything in the world. Nevertheless, Brennan saw the toll that the years had taken on his wife. He never wanted to pressure her. He knew how tired she was having to be a stay-at-home mom to two incredibly energetic toddlers. Still, he loved her, and he craved her intimacy every once in a while.

Brennan shut the TV off and decided to start getting ready for bed himself. He figured that Abigail wouldn't be interested in getting intimate with him if he still smelled like the office, so he made his way to their bathroom for a quick shower. Brennan let all of the warm water just wash the stress of his day away. It had indeed been a long one, but he wouldn't let that get in the way of him expressing his love to his wife. He dried himself off and brushed his teeth to make sure that his breath smelled fresh. After exiting the bathroom, he lay in bed waiting for Abigail to finish up with the kids.

She walked through their bedroom door with the same

sad and tired look on her face that she had during dinner. As she was about to head straight for the bathroom, Brennan tried to stop her in her tracks.

"Honey," said Brennan. "Come here for a while. Rest up for a bit before you start getting ready for bed."

Abigail followed suit, she lay down on her usual spot beside Brennan and closed her eyes for a bit. He pulled her in for an embrace and planted a soft kiss on her cheek. Then he worked his way towards her lips to see if she was going to kiss back. She did. Brennan felt a rush of excitement as he gently nibbled on his wife's lips and tongue. Then he moved his lips downwards towards her chin and neck. He kissed her with varying intensities spanning mild gentleness and intense passion. Brennan could feel Abigail place her hands on his head as if it were a signal for him to go lower. Just as about he was going to start kissing her breasts, she pushed his head away from her body.

Surprised, Brennan withdrew himself and asked, "Sorry, was I being too aggressive?"

"I'm just not in the mood," she replied.

"Alright, hun," sighed a defeated Brennan. "I'm sorry. Is anything bothering you? Anything you want to talk about?"

"No," she answered. "Just get some sleep. I know you've had a tiring day."

Chapter 2

Abigail

I AM SO tired, Abigail thought to herself as she lay in bed beside her already-sleeping husband. She got up and plodded towards the bathroom sink and stared at herself in the mirror. I've gotten old, Abigail thought. She looked at her blue almond-shaped eyes and the dark half-circles that formed small caves underneath them. There were deep crevices in her forehead whenever she raised her eyebrows ever so slightly. Age spots were beginning to pop up throughout different parts of her face.

She looked at her breasts that were now starting to sag as a result of having to breastfeed two babies. Her belly showed off a muffin top at the sides to highlight her plump silhouette. I used to look good in whatever I chose to wear. Now, she was dressed in a white commemorative t-shirt that she got from a fun run organized by the hospital along with a pair of oversized fleece pajamas. Her hair was tied up in a messy bun, and she found it immensely difficult to love the person she was looking at.

She turned the knob on the faucet and splashed some water on her face as she prepared her facial cleanser. It's been a while since I last put makeup on, she thought. She missed the hassles of having to remove gunk off her face every day. She hadn't really needed to go out on a daily basis for three years now. Ever since she had gotten pregnant with Riley, both she and Brennan agreed that it would be best for her to avoid stress as much as possible. They didn't want to have to go through another miscarriage. She loved her job, but she loved the idea of being able to start her family more. When she was growing up as a little girl herself, she had always dreamed of eventually meeting the love of her life and having a family with him. Now that she had that opportunity, she wasn't going to waste it, and that meant taking every precaution.

Fortunately, Brennan was doing well at work and was rising up the ranks fairly quickly. He was earning enough financially to support the family and keep them comfortable despite Abigail not working. At first, she embraced the wonders of motherhood in lieu of her career. Every day was a real wonder watching her little infant grow into a beautiful toddler. Then, much to her and Brennan's surprise, she was pregnant again with Riley. She felt overjoyed at having two little girls she could care for and look after despite all of the previous pregnancy struggles she had to go through. This was her dream coming to fulfillment. Aside from having a beautiful baby girl, she also had an incredibly loving husband. Brennan was the kind of guy that most girls would deem as prototypically attractive. He had a tall and slender build with neatly cut hair and a strong jaw. He wasn't exactly a hunk in the traditional sense. Brennan didn't have bulging muscles and well-defined features. Rather, he had a more boy-next-door type of aesthetic. He had a very friendly face with a charming smile and soft blue eyes. Abigail had always been attracted to Brennan from the moment she first laid eyes on him. She had the kind of husband that most ladies would fantasize about. And for the first two years of Riley's life, she was really happy. Then it was almost as if her perspective began to change. Every day became a predictable routine for her. Yes, the girls were a wonder to behold. But Abigail also felt like she was attaching too much of her happiness to her children.

Something was off. And this was not a realization that she was making merely on that night. These were thoughts that had been percolating inside her head for quite some time now. She felt that there was a weight on her heart that she couldn't escape from. Slowly, bit by bit, it was crushing her every single day. But that wasn't the worst part. The problem wasn't so much that she was unhappy. Abigail was a problem solver. She was very much used to getting to the bottom of things and sorting them out. But this time things were different. She knew that something was wrong, but she couldn't say what. And all of that uncertainty only added onto the weight that was already pinning her down. She felt trapped and she tried desperately to grasp at whatever she could find that most resembled a solution. But there was nothing there.

She looked down at her skincare product collection and saw that Brennan had mixed in his soaps and shaving creams together with hers again. Abigail then proceeded to arrange her toiletries the same way that she always had. If she couldn't gain control over her emotions, then the least she could do was control her material things. Abigail took all of Brennan's stuff and put it back to the right of the sink with the rest of his toiletries. She then lined up all of her products to the left side of the sink and arranged them all in order of usage. Cleanser. Toner. Mask. Serum. Moisturizer. Sunblock. All of these products and I still look like I'm ten years older than I am, she thought.

Chapter 3

Brennan

SATURDAYS WERE ALWAYS a treat for Brennan. He knew how valuable he was to his company, and that's why he never really felt guilty about taking the weekends for himself to unwind. That Saturday night, he and Abigail were having their good friends over for dinner. Karen, Phillip, and Vince were all friends that Abigail met from her days working with the hospital, and Megan was Vince's wife of five years. These were the Suttons' closest circle of friends. Even though they had only met because of Abigail, they had all developed close friendships with Brennan as well. He was excited at the idea of having the whole group gather together for a night of good food and great conversations. He also thought that it would help with getting Abigail out of the slump that she seemed to be in.

The doorbell rang at just a quarter before seven, and Brennan got up from the La-Z-Boy to go see who it was. Megan and Vince were standing in the doorway holding a huge cherry pie and a bottle of Spanish red wine. Brennan welcomed them into the foyer, taking the cherry pie out of Megan's hands and giving both of them a half hug. Megan was dressed in a beautiful floral Sunday dress and cream colored flats. She was relatively shorter than the average woman, and she had a prominent curvature to her hips. Her shiny blonde hair flowed freely to the tops of her shoulders, and she smelled of lavender as Brennan drew her in for a hug.

"So nice to see you again!" said Megan as she removed her coat. "It's been quite a while since we've all been together."

"It really has!" agreed Brennan. "Abigail's already in the kitchen putting the finishing touches on dinner. I hope you guys are hungry!"

"Phillip and Karen aren't here yet?" Vince asked while also removing his coat.

"Not yet, but they shouldn't be far away. Let me take your coats and I'll just set this pie over on the dining table," said Brennan.

"Where are the little girls?" asked Vince.

"Abigail's mother came over today to pick them up. They're spending some quality time with their grandparents right now," Brennan answered.

Vince was always so fond of the girls, and he had quickly built himself up to become their favorite uncle. Perhaps it was because he reminded them so much of their own father. Like Brennan, Vince was also tall and had a slender build. However, that was where most of the physical similarities stopped. Vince was a blonde and offered a stark contrast to Brennan's brown hair. He had striking green eyes and very pronounced cheek bones that looked like little hills on the sides of his face. He was wearing a simple light blue poplin shirt underneath a navy blazer. Whenever he came over, he had always made it a point to greet the little girls first. Sometimes, he would even bring them random gifts or treats. Abigail and Brennan were always happy at how the girls had an uncle who loved them so much.

"I'll go over to the kitchen to see if Abigail needs any help," suggested Megan.

"And Brennan and I will pop this bottle open so we can get started on the festivities," added Vince.

Megan left the men by themselves as she rushed over to greet Abigail in the kitchen. Vince settled down at the kitchen table as Brennan hung his guests' coats on the coat rack. After grabbing a corkscrew, he joined Vince at the table and opened the bottle of wine.

"So," said Vince as he watched Brennan pour the wine into two glasses. "How have things been with you and Abigail?"

"It's been the same, man," replied Brennan. "Something's still off with her."

More than anyone else in the group, Brennan had always had a close affinity with Vince. He felt like he could relate with Vince on a much more fundamental level than the others. Perhaps it was because they were both working professionals whose whole lives revolved around supporting their families. Maybe they just had personalities that were destined to click. Whatever the case, Brennan always found comfort in being able to confide with Vince about whatever problems he was having, whether it was for work or with his family. When he was going through the initial miscarriages with Abigail, the Suttons had both sought the comfort of Vince and Megan.

"And she hasn't opened up to you about it yet?" asked Vince.

"Not at all," sighed a dejected Brennan. "I want to be able to help her, but she won't tell me how. I don't know what I'm doing wrong."

"Hey, man. I won't sit here and tell you that I know what's going on either. But sometimes, people just go through these emotional spells, and you just have to let them ride it out, you know?"

Brennan took a sip of his wine as he tried to process

what Vince had just told him. Was it possible that Abigail was really just going through an emotional spell?

"Either way, Vince. I miss my wife. I know that I see her every day, but I feel like she hasn't been around for a long time."

"I get what you mean, bud."

The doorbell rang again and Brennan rose up from the table to see who it was. Phillip and Karen had arrived together, and they each brought a bottle of wine as well. Phillip had a simple white t-shirt layered underneath a brown bomber jacket to go along with a pair of dark blue selvedge jeans. Karen sported a pink wool sweater and white trousers and sneakers. Her brown hair was wrapped up in a neat ponytail, and she wore a prominent dark crimson lipstick that contrasted against the paleness of her skin. Brennan gave each of them a hug and Vince stood up to greet them as well. By this time, Abigail and Megan were already transferring the food from the kitchen to the dinner table. Abigail had prepared quite a feast for the group. All afternoon, she had been busy with preparing a deliciously tender and juicy beef brisket. On the side, she had prepared a luscious looking lasagna and some roasted vegetables to round it all up.

"Damn, Abigail," exclaimed Phillip. "You really outdid yourself today!"

"Yeah," agreed Vince. "This is quite a spread."

"Hey, we're all rarely together these days. It was no problem at all," she replied blushingly.

Brennan saw that Abigail had a smile on her face and a twinkle in her eyes. Maybe Vince is right, he thought to himself. Maybe she was just going through an emotional slump.

"C'mon, everyone," declared Brennan. "This food isn't going to eat itself. Let's eat!"

Vince emptied the bottle of wine that he and Brennan had already started on. He then grabbed the bottle that Phillip brought and popped it open as well. After everyone's glasses were filled, Brennan began slicing the brisket.

"This really is quite a feast, honey," Brennan said as he began plopping slices of beef on to everyone's plate. "Thanks for taking the time to do this."

"You're welcome, honey," replied Abigail.

The group of friends immediately jumped into trying to catch up on each other's lives. Phillip had just received a promotion at work and was talking about how stressful his new position was. He worked as an impact consultant for a large non-profit that specialized in helping other companies with their social development efforts.

"Hey, at the end of the day, it's more responsibility, but it's also more money. I can't complain," he lamented.

"Then next time, dinner should be on you!" joked Abigail.

"I might be making more money now, but I'm not exactly swimming in the big bucks here! But yes, Abigail. Next dinner is on me, guys!"

"We really should be getting together more often," commented Megan. "I feel like I don't know what's going on in your lives anymore!"

The rest of the dinner went on as smoothly as could be. Abigail and Brennan spearheaded an animated discussion on parenthood and went into detail about funny stories involving the girls. They managed to get big laughs at the one about how Amber and Riley had just discovered the concept of vlogging and were arguing over what they should be talking about on their videos. Riley just wanted to talk about cartoons and her toys, but Amber was more interested in discussing fashion and cooking.

"It's amazing how smart kids are getting nowadays," commented Vince.

It was a night of great fun and love for Brennan. He really did enjoy being with his friends and had missed the joys of companionship. He hadn't really been getting much attention and love from Abigail lately, but he was sure that this dinner could turn things around. The group went on to talk about their lives over multiple bottles of wine late into the evening. Then, at around 11:00 p.m., they decided that it was time to call it a night. Brennan and Abigail had to wake up early the next day to get the kids from Abigail's parents' house.

"Listen, guys. It was great having you over. Thanks a bunch for taking the time," Brennan said as he and Abigail escorted their guests to the front door.

"It's a shame that we couldn't make this last all night like we used to," joked Karen.

"Speak for yourself, Karen," chimed Megan. "I love how we have an excuse to just head to bed earlier now that we're getting older."

"We really have to do this again soon, guys. Maybe we can make this a routine. Every last Saturday of the month, perhaps?" suggested Vince.

"Maybe we can make that work," said Phillip. "We can take turns hosting."

"And you've got next, Mr. Bossman!" chimed Abigail.

"You got it," Phillip said with a smile on his face.

All at once, each of them exchanged hugs and kisses as they said their goodbyes. Brennan and Abigail stood on the front porch of their suburban home as they waved their friends off while each of them drove away. Then it was just the two of them again. He turned to face her as she was looking at their friends drive away. She's beautiful, he thought.

"We better head back in," he said breaking the silence. "Get ready for bed so we can pick the girls up bright and early tomorrow."

Without saying a word, Abigail nodded her head and turned to walk back towards the door. Brennan followed her in and offered to clean up and do the dishes.

"No, it's okay," replied Abigail. "I can do it."

"Honey, you've been working all day with all of the cooking and entertaining. Let me clean up. It's the least I could do," Brennan insisted.

"Are you sure? Well, I could go and lie down for a bit."

"Please do. Go on upstairs and start getting ready for bed. I'll be up in a bit."

Abigail vanished into the second floor as Brennan immediately got right to work on cleaning up. He knew that Abigail must have been exhausted from preparing dinner that day, but he was hoping that she could rest up in bed for a bit to regain her energy. As he slowly transferred all of the dirty dishes and glassware into the washer, he decided to try to come up with a game plan. Should I ask her first? he thought. Maybe I should just get right to it and kiss her. He was feeling nervous. It was strange. He had never felt nervous about getting intimate with his wife - not since the two of them had just started dating. He felt like a kid. It was like the courtship stage of their relationship all over again. Brennan hated the fact that he had allowed his marriage to devolve to this.

After putting away the final plate of the night, Brennan switched off the lights in the kitchen and dining room before heading up the stairs to the master bedroom. When he opened the door, Abigail was already in bed reading a book. Brennan darted straight to the bathroom to brush his teeth to make sure that his breath smelled fresh. He decided that he was just going to start things off with a passionate kiss and see where things would go from there. After gargling some mouthwash and splashing some water in his face, he looked at his own reflection in the mirror. He definitely wasn't the young strapping man who had been able to woo Abigail in his early twenties, but he didn't look old either. The years had been kind to him. He was able to maintain a relatively svelte frame and there weren't too many nooks and crinkles on his face. In fact, one could have made the argument that he looked even better as he matured. He wiped the water off his face and went back into the bedroom where Abigail was waiting for something she didn't even know was going to take place.

He cozied up in bed beside her and just watched her read for a few seconds. She was already dressed in her silk nightgown, and she had her hair tied up in a half ponytail.

"Thanks for tonight, honey," said Brennan.

Abigail put her book down to look at him and replied, "You're welcome." She smiled at him and went back to reading her book.

Brennan took this as his opportunity. He leaned in close and planted a soft and gentle kiss on his wife's cheek. He immediately followed it up with another kiss on her jaw. Then he moved towards her neck in a series of soft and slow kisses, but she wasn't reacting. He continued kissing her neck while he planted his hand on her belly and slowly caressed her. Then he slowly lifted up Abigail's pajamas and slipped his hand into her panties until he felt Abigail resist and push him away.

"What are you doing?" asked Abigail with a distraught look on her face. Her brow was furrowed and mouth slightly ajar.

"Sorry, I was just thinking that the two of us could have some fun tonight, honey," replied a sheepish Brennan.

"I'm really not in the mood. I'm tired. I've been working in the kitchen all day, and we've had to entertain our guests. I'm absolutely drained."

"I know, hun. It's just that it's been a while since we last—"

"Brennan," interrupted Abigail. "I just want to read my book in peace and go to sleep early tonight. Weren't you the one who said we need to be up early to get the girls? I don't want to leave them over at mom's place too long. You know she's getting older."

"I'm sorry, hun," sighed Brennan. "You're right. Let's go to sleep."

At that, Brennan turned towards his side table and switched off his reading lamp. He could still see the shadows on the wall emanating from Abigail's lamp as she went on reading. It took another two hours before Brennan could finally fall asleep. It wasn't just the fact that she was refusing to be intimate with him anymore, he was restless because of her overall demeanor. She just didn't seem like herself, and it scared Brennan to his core. He was afraid of losing his wife — or worse — that he had already lost her entirely. Thoughts of better days consumed his mind as he stared blankly at a dark shadowy wall with his wife just behind him. There has to be a way to fix this, he insisted. There's no way that things are beyond repair.

Brennan was desperate to get to the bottom of things. He knew that one of the perks of being a stay-at-home mom was being able to save one's self from the stresses of a professional life. Obviously, Abigail couldn't be stressed over a job that she didn't have. Also, it's not like they were strapped for cash. Brennan wasn't exactly going to find himself on Forbes lists anytime soon, but they weren't poor either. He had always been able to provide for himself, his wife, and their children. Even when things got really messy at the hospital with Abigail's miscarriages and sensitive pregnancies, Brennan had always been able to pay those bills in full. Was it companionship that she was looking for? Brennan was always ready to provide that for her. In his mind, he had never failed to let his wife know that he was there for her. He rarely ever worked long hours at the office. He always made sure that his weekends were freed up for the family. Also, he knew that Abigail had friends who she could call on whenever she felt lonely. They were just here! Brennan thought to himself. She can't be feeling lonely after being surrounded by people who love her all of the time.

Chapter 4

Abigail

"YOU KNOW," SAID Abigail as she was having dinner with Brennan and the kids on a Monday night. "There's this new show that I've been watching."

"Oh?" replied Brennan. "What's that?"

"Well, it's not a new show, technically speaking. It's been around for a while, but I've only gotten around to watching it just now. It's called *Scandal*."

"Yeah, I've heard of that. Kerry Washington, right?"

"Yup. She got nominated for a couple of Emmys for this role."

"So, what's it about exactly?"

Abigail knew that Brennan had never really been fond of drama on television. Whenever he watched TV, it was usually sports, documentaries, or the news. Brennan wasn't the type of guy who got deep into shows like *Scandal*.

"It's a political thriller. It's about this lady, Olivia Pope, who runs a crisis management firm. Anyway, I know that you don't care so much and this kind of TV isn't really your thing. The story isn't important."

"It's okay, honey. Why did you bring it up?"

"Well," she hesitated. "Watching the show just made me think about a few things… about love, in particular."

"How so?" asked Brennan as he scooped spoonfuls of macaroni and cheese into Amber's and Riley's mouths. The kids were being particularly fussy with their dinner and Brennan needed to force feed them.

"Well, there's a lot of romance and passion in *Scandal* and it had me thinking… Do you ever miss the feeling of being in love?"

"What?" asked a confused Brennan. "Aren't we still in love now?"

"No, I mean, like the way that it is when two people first get together in a relationship," clarified Abigail. "You know how when two people are just falling in love for the first time and everything feels so perfect and magical?"

Brennan took a sip of his cold beer as he contemplated what Abigail had just asked him. She just continued to stare intently as she waited in anticipation for his answer.

"Well, yes, I guess so. But that's really all just a phase. It's the novelty of new love. All of it fades away over time," replied Brennan.

"What do you mean? You don't think that love can last?"

"No, that's not what I mean. I'm just saying that the tingly and perfect love that you're talking about is not sustainable. Love in itself has different shapes and forms. And that kind of love in particular… call it what you want, puppy love, honeymoon love, whatever… it just isn't built to last."

Abigail fiddled with the food that was still on her plate. "Do you really think that?"

"Think about it this way. Think of all the times you've bought a dress or a new pair of shoes. You love them instantly whenever they're new. You might tell yourself that you'll wear them three, four, maybe even five times a week if you could. But then, over time, the more you wear them, the more the novelty fades. Sure, you still love that dress or you still love those shoes. You're still going to want to wear them. Heck, you might even think that you're going to want to wear them forever. But it's never going to be the same kind of excitement as when you first bought them."

"I think the love that you have for another person is different from the love that you have for a shoe or a dress, though," argued Abigail.

"Of course," Brennan agreed. "But it's only different in degrees, and not by kind. It's all the same KIND of love and affinity. It's just that you tend to love people more than material things."

Abigail processed what her husband had just told her. It wasn't the answer that she was expecting from him, but it didn't surprise her either. Brennan always had a very practical and methodical way of looking at things.

"You're probably right," she admitted.

"For the first year or so in a relationship, everything's always bound to feel really magical. That's because the novelty hasn't worn off yet. The butterflies are still there. But eventually, they all go away over time."

Abigail took a while before she responded to really think about what Brennan was telling her. Maybe he was right after all. Maybe the love that two people had for one another in a relationship wasn't all that different from a woman falling in love with a pair of shoes. Everything might have seemed so amazing and magical at first, but it all eventually dies out.

"Yeah," she finally lamented. "You must think that I'm really silly for thinking about these things — talking to you about honeymoon loves and butterflies."

"No, I don't," replied Brennan. "Not at all. And to answer your original question, yes."

"Yes, what?"

"Yes, I miss the feeling of being in love… the butterflies and honeymoon phase kind of love."

So do I, Abigail thought to herself.

Chapter 5

Brennan

AFTER DINNER, BRENNAN told Abigail that he would do the dishes and that she could just help the kids get ready for bed. As he loaded the dishes into the washer, he wondered what was going through his wife's mind and what possibly could have prompted her to ask him about love and romance. Does she not love me anymore? Brennan tried to shake the idea of his wife no longer loving him out of his head. It can't be. Although, it may explain why she had been acting very strange and distant toward him lately. Has she fallen out of love with me?

Brennan felt himself on the verge of an anxiety attack. He rarely ever got anxiety attacks, but a lot of the time they came about whenever he felt unsure or uncertain about something. He used to get anxiety attacks waiting for test results as a student or performance reviews. But this was the first time he had ever experienced getting an anxiety attack as a result of his romantic life. He wasn't used to it, and he didn't know how to deal with it. I really have to get to the bottom of this, he told himself. He didn't want to wait any longer. He had been patient with his wife for long enough. It was time for him to confront her. Obviously, whatever she was going through was taking a toll on their marriage. It hadn't affected the way that they were raising their kids yet. But he was never going to allow their marriage to deteriorate to the point where it would affect the way that they were raising their kids. He might not have been the most emotional or sappy guy out there, but he adored Abigail, and he wanted to spend the rest of his life with her. This was why he decided on confronting her later on that night.

After putting the last of the dishes away, he decided to grab a beer from the fridge to help calm his nerves and give him some liquid courage. Before heading up the stairs, he wanted to take the time to gather his thoughts and really try to see things from his wife's point of view. He wanted to try to get inside her mind first before he confronted her about anything. He tried to examine her life from any conceivable angle that he could think of.

Brennan racked his brain. Unfortunately, the best that he could come up with was that she was no longer in love with him. The very thought of this frightened him, and he nearly talked himself out of having that conversation with her. If she's really fallen out of love with me, then I don't want to know, he thought. But then, his better judgement overcame him. He knew that the only way for him to stop being so anxious about it was to get closure on the matter.

After discarding the now-empty beer can, Brennan switched all of the lights off downstairs and began his slow ascent to their room. Before heading into the master bedroom, he decided to make a quick pit stop in the girls' room. He opened the door as slowly and as quietly as he could. Through the faint light from the hallway, he could see that both Amber and Riley were already knocked out on their beds. He deftly crept towards the side of Riley's bed which was closer to the door. Riley was always afraid of being in the bed near the window, and Amber had taken it upon herself as the big sister to take that bed instead. My sweet girls, Brennan thought. I don't know what I would do without you. He dreaded the idea of his wife falling out of love with him, but he dreaded the idea of breaking his kids' hearts even more. He knew that any strain on his marriage would also be a strain on his kids' lives. He planted a soft kiss on each of their foreheads before he crept outside the room and back into the hallway.

Before entering the bedroom, he took a deep breath. He didn't know what to expect and that scared him.

He walked in and saw Abigail seated at her vanity table in the corner of the bedroom. He took off his clothes and dumped them into the laundry hamper in the bathroom before grabbing a fresh pair of pajamas from the closet.

"Honey," said Brennan as he changed into his pajamas. "I need to talk to you about something."

"Can it wait until tomorrow? I'm kind of tired," replied Abigail as she sat in front of her vanity and brushed her hair.

"Sorry, babe. I don't think that this can wait any longer."

"What is it?"

Brennan walked over to the edge of the bed and sat down facing his wife whose back was still turned to him.

"What's wrong with you?" he asked her in as mild a tone as he could muster.

"What do you mean?" she replied as she continued brushing her hair.

"Honey, could you turn to face me for a while?"

Abigail put the brush down on her vanity table and turned to face Brennan. She had a meek, sad look in her eyes. She didn't respond and her silence prompted Brennan to ask her again.

"I know that something is off with you. You haven't been acting like yourself, especially when you're alone with me. It's weird because the changes in your personality are only evident whenever you're with me." His voice cracked towards the end, and he felt tears starting to well up in his eyes. "I know that something's wrong, and I'm just really scared because you're not letting me in."

"I'm sorry. It's not my intention to hurt you."

"Then please tell me what's wrong," Brennan pleaded. "That whole question about honeymoon love and the butterflies earlier... that wasn't a random question, was it?"

"No. It wasn't," she answered as she dropped her head down to stare at the floor.

"Do you not love me anymore?" Brennan struggled to stifle his tears.

It took a while for Abigail to gather her thoughts and answer. After what seemed like an eternity to Brennan, Abigail got up from her vanity and moved towards him. She took a seat beside him on the bed and looked him straight in the eyes.

"I'm forty-three years old now," she explained. "And I think that my beauty is fading away. That's why I've been really sad and down lately. I feel like I let myself go and that I wasted all of my energy. Now, my energy is gone, and it's making me look more and more drained every single day. I can literally feel myself age with each passing day."

"Oh, honey," said Brennan. "That's just foolishness. You're just as pretty now as the day that I first saw you."

"We both know that's a lie, Brennan."

"Listen." Brennan took her hands and cupped them inside his. "We're both getting older. Sure, you might have aged since we first met, but that doesn't mean that you're no longer beautiful. Aging shouldn't be a reason for you to be sad. If it's energy you crave, maybe you can try taking up a new hobby so that you can keep yourself busy."

She took her eyes away from his and looked down at her lap.

"Also," he continued. "You're married. You shouldn't feel pressured to be pretty anymore. You have a husband who thinks that you're beautiful. Isn't that enough?"

"That's not it." She took her hands away from his and cupped her face in them out of frustration. "It's not about that at all. You're missing the point here. Every time I look into the mirror, I see the face of a person I don't recognize."

Abigail stood up and walked across the room back to her vanity station. She stared at her reflection for a few seconds before she continued.

"I used to have so many dreams. I used to want so much out of life. I was a girl who thought that I could do anything and everything. Now, I look into the mirror and I see the face of a woman who dreams, wants, and believes so little." Her voice softened to a slight whisper as she continued to talk. "I used to wake up every day feeling so excited to live. Now, nothing excites me. Nothing at all."

She stood up and walked back to the bed, but this time, she stayed standing on her feet. "I think age has made me less excited about life. And my lack of excitement has made me much uglier and less attractive. No one flirts with me anymore. I used to walk down the hallways of the mall and men would always turn and stare. Some women too. I don't get that anymore."

"But, honey,"

"Don't interrupt me," she asserted. "Please just let me finish."

Brennan closed his mouth and nodded his head in agreement. She took a deep breath before continuing.

"I feel like I'm losing the part of me that makes me feel like a real woman. I know that this sounds really stupid to you. It sounds stupid to me. But it's what I feel. When I was younger, I always knew whenever certain people were attracted to me. I was always flattered and this knowledge gave me life. It made me feel like a real woman. I don't feel that anymore."

"Wait…"

"Brennan, please!" she shrieked. "Please just let me finish!"

"Okay, I'm sorry. Go ahead. I won't interrupt."

"I know that this all sounds so stupid to you. Trust me. I really do. But what you need to understand is that aging isn't the same for men as it is with women. Look at you. You've aged so gracefully over the years. You're just as handsome and as strapping now as you were back then. I still see it in public when girls look at you. You're still as charming as ever, Brennan. And I hate it! I hate it because you've managed to hold on to your youthful attractiveness, and I lost mine somehow."

She sat back down beside him and buried her face in her hands. She was weeping uncontrollably and Brennan didn't know what to do. He put his arm around her and beckoned her to lean on him as she cried some more.

"Honey, I still love you. I still find you incredibly attractive. What can I do to convince you of that?"

"You still don't get it," she said as she fought through her tears. "I know that you still love me. But that's only because I'm your wife. You are never going to understand what I'm going through because you're a man. You're still considered attractive even as you get older. It's not the same with us women."

"I don't know what to do to make you feel better, honey," replied Brennan. "Tell me what to do to make you feel better."

"I don't know," she said defeatedly. "If I knew, then we wouldn't be having this discussion anymore."

"So what happens now?" asked a dejected and desperate Brennan. He was eager to help his wife cope with her sadness, but he felt at a loss for words and actions. He didn't know how to help her.

"Nothing," she replied. "Nothing happens now. Let's just go to sleep, please. I'm feeling really tired."

"Okay." Brennan stood up and grabbed some tissues from the bedside drawer and handed them to Abigail. "I may not know exactly what you're going through. I also don't know how we're going to fix this. But I do know that I'm going to stay by your side throughout the entire process. You aren't going to be alone in this."

"Thank you," she said as she wiped her tears away. "It may not feel like it, but I'm thankful for how patient you've been."

"Of course." He sat back down beside her and gave her a big hug. Brennan waited for her to hug him back, but she didn't. He let her go and planted a soft kiss on her forehead. "Let's go to sleep, you sweet thing."

Abigail nodded her head and discarded the tissue that she dried her tears with. She turned her bedside lamp off and lay down with her back facing Brennan's side. Brennan also lay in bed, but he knew that he wouldn't be going to sleep anytime soon. His wife had given him a lot to think about. He stared blankly at the ceiling and thought about what he could do to try to break his wife out from her slump.

Had he not already been doing enough to make her feel loved? Were his sexual advances not enough to make her feel attractive? He still couldn't understand why it was so important to her that other people find her attractive. Sure, he had noticed whenever girls would look at him or give him double takes in public every once in a while. They were certainly ego boosters, but his sense of happiness wasn't reliant on chance encounters.

Chapter 6

Abigail

THE NEXT NIGHT, the entire family was hanging out in the living room after dinner to unwind. While Brennan sat on his lounge chair and watched another documentary, Abigail was on the sofa scrolling through her social media feeds on her iPad. The girls were in their play area with a mess of toys at their disposal. Amber was once again engrossed in her cooking set while Riley was busy with an Etch A Sketch toy. Abigail looked over at the documentary that Brennan was watching. It seemed to be about computers and she didn't really care for it that much. She diverted her attention back to her iPad instead.

While she was scrolling through her Facebook news feed, she clicked on an article that an old classmate of hers had shared. The article's headline was "Why Monogamy Is a Joke as Confirmed by Science."

She was immediately gripped by its opening line: Do you feel like the passion in your marriage is fading? The article talked about a study that looked into the lives of couples who were in long-term marriages.

"Brennan," she said as she continued to read. "Listen

to this article that I'm reading."

Brennan lowered the volume of the TV and turned his head towards Abigail.

"What's it about?"

"It's about real life couples who talk about how their sex lives change after getting married," she replied.

"Honey," said Brennan. "The kids!"

"Oh, don't worry about them," she said as she glanced over to where the girls were playing. "They're preoccupied."

"Okay, but hushed tones," lamented Brennan.

Abigail ignored his lament and continued using her regular speaking voice. "Anyway, it says here that on average, a woman's sex drive goes down drastically after one to four years of marriage."

"Is that so?" he replied. He didn't know where Abigail was going with this, and he shot her a look that encompassed both his curiosity and bemusement.

"Apparently, the women in the article all describe themselves growing tired of having sex with the same long-time partner. So, the researchers leading the study are saying that this may be a biological phenomenon."

"That seems… interesting," said Brennan.

"Wait, that's not all," she went on. "What they also found was that once these women were able to explore themselves sexually OUTSIDE of their relationship, their libidos went back up again."

"So, what does that mean?" Brennan was getting more and more anxious about the conversation.

"Well, the researchers say that perhaps women just aren't wired for monogamy, and that it's wrong for society to enforce such constructs on them," she explained. "They say that we need to be paying more attention to how women really feel in relationships."

"That's a stretch, though. What was the sample size for this study? How many women did they even interview? Where did you even find this article anyway?"

"A friend of mine shared it on Facebook."

"Be careful of the stuff that you find on the internet, dear," he cautioned. "They lure you in with these catchy headlines and feed you false knowledge on faulty assumptions. It's the era of clickbait."

"Whatever. I just found it interesting."

"You know what's interesting?" Brennan turned his head and pointed his hands towards the television and continued, "They're looking into the lives of athletes in different sports who are on strictly plant-based diets. It's pretty compelling stuff." He paused to turn back at her. "Maybe we should look into going plant-based too!"

"Maybe," sighed Abigail.

Chapter 7

Brennan

ABIGAIL CHOSE TO spend her Saturday at a friend's house to catch up with her closest gal pals. She asked Brennan to drop her off early and pick her up later in the afternoon. Brennan was already on his way to pick her up when he thought about what approach he could take to have a real conversation with Abigail about her feelings. Just as Brennan was pulling onto the street of Abigail's friend, he grabbed his phone and called to tell her that he was near. By the time he had the house in his sights, Abigail and two of her friends, Mary Alice and Joanne, were already making their way to the curb.

"Hey," said Abigail as she climbed into the front seat. "Is it okay if Mary Alice and Joanne hitch along? I told them it was fine since they live along the way."

"Sure, no problem," replied Brennan.

Mary Alice and Joanne hopped into the backseat of Brennan's SUV and strapped on their seatbelts.

"Thank you so much, Brennan," said Mary Alice, a middle-aged blonde who Abigail had known since she was in high school. "You're a real gentleman."

"A gentleman like Jessie?" chimed Joanne.

The three girls burst into laughter as Brennan turned to look at Abigail and the two girls through the rearview mirror.

"I don't get it," sighed Brennan. "Who is Jessie?"

"Oh, he's no one," replied Abigail who was still giggling.

"She's Darlene's new boyfriend!" offered Joanne.

"Wait," said Brennan. "So, Darlene and John are broken up?"

"NOPE!" replied Mary Alice without skipping a beat as if she were already anticipating the question.

"Darlene and John are having an open relationship now," explained Joanne.

"Open relationship," Brennan paused. "What does that mean exactly?"

"It's this thing that a lot of couples are doing these days," Joanne went on. "It's when two people are still technically in a romantic relationship, but are also seeing other people."

"So, in this case," chimed Mary Alice, "John and Darlene are still together… but so are Darlene and Jessie!"

The three girls burst into laughter once more as Brennan felt his grip on the wheel get tighter. He took a quick glance back at the girls through the rearview mirror. He turned towards Abigail who had the giddiest expression on her face. He couldn't even remember the last time he heard her laugh like that.

"Doesn't that defeat the whole point of being in a relationship?" he finally lamented.

"Well, Darlene says that she's as happy as she has been in a long time," said Mary Alice. "She claims that Jessie is pretty happy too."

Once more, the three girls giggled in unison at the idea of Mary Alice having two boyfriends.

"I bet he's not as happy as Darlene is, though," offered Abigail who had been relatively quiet up until that point.

"Imagine what it would be like to choose who you get to go home to at night."

"Honey, if I had that luxury, then I would be sleeping in a different bed every night of the week," joked Mary Alice with a sly grin on her face. Again, this cued a chorus of laughter from the three women.

"I couldn't do a different one every night of the week," offered Joanne. "Maybe one for the weekdays and another one for the weekends would be good for me."

The car filled up with the sounds of laughter from the three ladies with the noticeable silence of the lone male in the vehicle.

"Oh, come on, Brennan, have a little fun!" urged Mary Alice. "It's funny!"

Brennan shifted his focus from the chorus of laughter to the music that was blaring through his car's speakers. He had no interest in participating in this discussion and made no efforts to contribute to it. The soft hum of gentle jazz music slowly took over his senses as he tried his best to divert his attention away from the conversation that was taking place in his car. He was the kind of guy who subscribed heavily to the belief that if one had nothing nice to say, then it's better to not say anything at all.

Chapter 8

Abigail

IT WAS A loud and animated Sunday morning in the Sutton home. The little women of the household were up early as was customary every weekend. They had always looked forward to Sundays where their mom and dad would take them out for lunch at a nice restaurant and then to the ice cream parlor for their favorite scoops. Riley spent most of the morning singing along to some of her favorite YouTube music videos. Abigail lay in bed staring up at the ceiling. She had been up for at least a couple of hours now but hadn't moved one bit. She didn't even bother to check her phone. When she woke up, Brennan was still sleeping, and she didn't bother to wake him. In fact, she didn't feel compelled to do anything up until she started hearing her kids' voices echo through the hallway.

"Mommy!" groaned Amber. "Let's take a bath, please!"

She was already walking through the bedroom door and making her way to Abigail. Riley was struggling to keep up with her big sister with a huge iPad in her tiny little hands. "Let's go to lunch now, Mommy!" Amber said again.

"Okay, honey," said Abigail. "Let's get back to your room."

She scooped Riley up into her arms and followed Amber as she led the way back to their bedroom. Abigail picked out a couple of outfits for the girls and laid them down neatly on their beds. She looked as if she were functioning on autopilot. Abigail usually put a lot of attention and detail into dressing her kids up to go out. This time, she didn't care so much. She just grabbed the first easy dress that she could find for each child, told the girls to undress, and went to fill the tub.

Amber was quick to remove her pajamas, but Riley was struggling to take her top off. Abigail helped her younger daughter get undressed and carried both of them off to the bathroom.

"Are you guys excited to go out to lunch today?" asked Abigail. There was a plainness to her voice that wasn't typical of her whenever she was talking to the kids.

"Yes, Mommy!" replied the two girls in unison. They had the biggest smiles on their faces as they splashed around in the water.

"Don't play around too much. Mommy doesn't want to get wet," said Abigail. "Listen, Mommy isn't going to be joining you for lunch today, okay? Daddy will take you out, but Mommy is going to stay at home."

"But why, Mommy?" asked Amber.

"Mommy isn't feeling too well," she replied. "I think it's best if Mommy just stayed at home to rest."

"Are you sick, Mommy?" asked Riley.

"Maybe you can take some of the medicine that you gave me before when I was sick, Mommy," suggested Amber. "Maybe you'll feel better and can go get ice cream with us."

"I'm not sick, my dear," said Abigail. "Mommy is just feeling a little tired, and she has to take a nap to feel better. Is that okay? I'll tell Daddy that you can have an extra scoop for me."

"Yay!" yelled Riley.

Abigail went on to bathe her kids, asking them what flavors they were going to get. Amber was dead set on getting a scoop of cookie dough while Riley just started enumerating every single flavor that she knew. After the kids were done, Abigail dried them off with their individual towels and helped them get dressed. Once their clothes were on, she grabbed the iPad and gave it to Riley.

"Alright, girls. You're ready. I'll go tell Daddy that you're ready to go, okay?" She gave each of them a kiss before leaving the room. The staleness in her voice was still there, but the girls seemed to not have noticed the lack of her usual charm and enthusiasm. Abigail made her way back to the bedroom where Brennan was already fully dressed and ready to go.

"You better start getting ready, honey. Let's go before the girls get all fussy," he said.

"I'm not going," replied Abigail. "I already told the girls that you'll be taking them out today.

"What?" replied Brennan blinking rapidly. "Why not? You know how much the girls always look forward to our Sunday lunches out."

"They were fine with it. I told them that they could have an extra scoop of ice cream for me."

"But why aren't you going?" he asked again. He looked at her as if she had been caught doing something that was completely unforgivable.

"I'm just not feeling well." She sighed.

"What?" He lowered his voice, trying to comfort her. "Are you feeling sick? Should we call a doctor?"

"No. I just don't feel like I can go out today is all."

"Is there anything I can do?" asked Brennan with his voice rising with concern. "Did I do something wrong?"

"Brennan! I just don't feel like going out, okay? I just want some time for myself to rest up. Just please take the girls and go. They're already dressed and waiting for you."

Brennan didn't make any moves right away. He just

stood there looking at Abigail for a while as if he were struggling to figure out what to do next. He opened his mouth as if he was going to say something, but no sounds came out. Abigail walked over to the bed and lay down without waiting for Brennan to say anything else. She closed her eyes and focused on the sound of her breath. Then, she heard the door close and when she opened her eyes, Brennan wasn't standing there anymore. She lay her head back and closed her eyes once more as she listened to the sound of footsteps coming from the hallway. The next sounds she heard was the thud of the front door closing and the rev of the car engine. And then, complete silence.

She turned her face towards the bedside table to check the time. 11:00 a.m. Abigail closed her eyes and focused on nothing but the sound of her breath going in and out. In. Out. In. Out. She opened her eyes and turned towards the clock again. It was 1:37 p.m. It was already the afternoon and she hadn't done anything other than help the girls get dressed. She could feel her stomach caving in on itself as it let out a prominent grumble. For the first time that day, Abigail went downstairs and headed straight to the kitchen. She scoured the fridge for anything that she could just heat up in the microwave, but she ended up settling on a bowl of the girls' favorite cereal instead. Abigail brought the bowl with her to the living room where she curled up on the couch and turned on the television. She flipped through different channels without seeing anything she particularly liked. She eventually settled on a reality show that was centered around the lives of housewives who lived in Beverly Hills. Her eyes were glued to the screen, but she wasn't absorbing any of the information.

She decided to change the channel and chanced upon a showing of *Notting Hill* starring Julia Roberts and Hugh Grant. She smiled and got comfortable in her seat as she shoveled even more cereal into her mouth. Abigail watched intently as Hugh Grant's character tried desperately to woo Julia Roberts's character. Then, seemingly out of nowhere, tears began to well up in her eyes. Her nose became runny and before she knew it, she was already in a full sob. The sound of actors and actresses delivering their lines on the television couldn't drown out the cries emanating from Abigail. She put the now-empty bowl of cereal down on the coffee table before her and grabbed the nearest pillow that she could reach. Abigail hugged that pillow as tightly as she could as she gradually descended into a fetal position on the couch. She hadn't cried like that for as long as she could remember.

Chapter 9

Brennan

BRENNAN WAS JUST getting back home with the kids after their Sunday afternoon at the park when he saw Abigail sitting on the couch. He noticed that the television was on, but Abigail wasn't watching it. Rather, she was staring blankly into space. Her eyes were all puffy and swollen and her nose was blushing red. Abigail eventually got up to welcome the kids, but there was still a certain deadness in her eyes and a flatness in the tone of her voice.

"Hi, girls," she said as she knelt down to hug Amber and Riley. "Did you eat an extra scoop of ice cream like Mommy told you to?"

"Yes!" replied an eager Amber who proudly flashed her missing teeth with an unforgiving smile at her mother. "We also got to play with a dog at the park, Mommy! Can we get a dog too?"

"Yes, Mommy! Doggy!" urged Riley.

"We'll talk about it, honey. Why don't we go to your rooms to get you cleaned up and changed into a fresh set of clothes?"

"Okay," said Amber as she grabbed Riley's hand and

dragged her towards the stairs.

"Honey," whispered Brennan. "What happened? Have you been crying?"

"No," she replied without looking at him.

"Yes, you have. What happened? Why are you crying?"

"We'll talk about it later." She turned away from him and helped the girls up the stairs and to their bedroom.

Brennan didn't know what to make of his wife choosing to stay home for no reason on a Sunday. His anxiety was only exacerbated by coming home to her crying on the couch. He took off his shoes and slid into his slippers before he went to the kitchen. He opened the fridge and grabbed an ice cold bottle of beer, leaning his back against the kitchen counter as he took a sip. He felt the cold beer sweating against his fingertips.

He thought about following the rest of his family upstairs but decided against it, instead bringing his beer with him to the couch. He mindlessly flipped through the channels looking for something to watch but wasn't able to focus on anything. His mind was too clouded.

He looked at the television, and it reminded him of when his wife had brought up *Scandal* and how exciting the idea of young love was. Brennan also recalled the article that Abigail read on Facebook and shared to him, the one about how women lose their libidos over time in a long-term relationship. This led to him having thoughts about Mary Alice, Joanne, and Abigail all giggling in the car because one of their friends had taken on another boyfriend. Brennan didn't necessarily know where his thoughts were taking him, but he didn't like it.

He lay his head back on the couch and closed his eyes to try to focus on his breathing instead. He didn't want to think about his wife anymore. What he needed at that time was a clear mind. Brennan took a few deep deliberate breaths and paid attention to how slowly they filled his lungs. That's when he heard footsteps coming from the second floor. He kept his eyes closed as the footsteps became louder. He knew that Abigail was already making her way down the staircase.

He saw her descending the steps with a dejected look in her eyes. They were dead and unspirited. There was no way for him to possibly determine what she was thinking or feeling. She drew nearer to him in the living room and sat down beside him on the couch.

"We need to talk"

Brennan took a deep breath and cleared his throat. He focused his eyes directly on hers and said, "About what? What's on your mind?"

"There's no easy way to say this," she said as she stared straight into his eyes.

Brennan braced himself for the worst. "Then just come right out and say it."

"I want to take on another lover."

Brennan took a deep sigh and lowered his gaze to his feet. He tilted his head back and closed his eyes as he muttered under his breath, "I knew it."

"Knew what?"

"I knew it. You want out of this relationship," He thrust his face into his cupped hands and let out a stifled scream. He sobbed and wailed. A pool of tears began forming in Brennan's hands when Abigail spoke again.

"Brennan, no," she said. "You're misunderstanding. I don't want to put an end to our relationship."

"But you said that you want another lo-" he said, cutting himself off. "Another L."

"Yes," she said nodding her head. "But I still want us to be in a relationship. I want us to be in an open relationship."

"What?! You think that I would willingly still be in a relationship with you while you make love to other men?"

"Honestly, I hoped that you would. I still hope that you'll consider it."

"Ugh," he grunted. "I can't even imagine the idea of you taking on another... L. I can't even say the word,

Abigail!"

"Then don't say it," she insisted. "But consider my proposal nonetheless."

"No." He shook his head. "That's just plainly out of the question. How can you expect us to still be in a relationship if you're going to be with another I? With other men?"

"That's the whole point of this." She tried putting a hand on his arm.

"What's the point?" His nostrils began to flare and a visible vein emerged on his temple. Brennan felt his body running hot and his face gradually eased into the color of a ripe tomato.

"Hear me out, please?" pleaded Abigail. "I've been doing a lot of thinking and soul searching over the past few weeks. I haven't been happy, Brennan. I haven't been happy in a long time. I've found myself questioning why I'm still even in this relationship, even if it isn't making me happy anymore." Her voice began to break and her eyes were welling up. "But I'm not ready to give up on us. I want to be able to find the love and passion that I once had for you, for us. I think I can find it again. But in order to do so, I need to see what's out there for a while. I know I'm not making much sense to you right now—"

"You're right," he interrupted. "You're not."

"Please," she asked. "Please just let me finish. I know that this is very hard for you to accept. It was a difficult idea for me to accept too at first. This is why it took me a lot of time to really think about it. But I honestly can't see any other way to fix what we have. If we continue on the road that we're on now, then I'm afraid that I'll eventually end up hating you and giving up on this relationship altogether."

"You can't possibly have me believe that you think that you're going to fix this relationship by sleeping with other men, can you?" he demanded.

"I don't know whether you believe it will work or not.

Even I don't know that. I just need you to trust me when I say that I think that this is the best course of action for the two of us right now. If we are ever going to have a chance at fixing our marriage, you need to let me do this."

"Marriage," said Brennan who had risen to his feet and was deeply animated by now. "I'm glad you brought up that word because that's exactly what we have, Abigail. A marriage. An eternal union of man and wife."

"See!" said Abigail who had also risen to her feet at this point. "That's the problem right there! Just because we're married doesn't mean that I'm your property, Brennan! It's that kind of mindset that's led to me feeling so suffocated all the time when I'm with you."

"What are you talking about?" argued Brennan. "I don't own you!"

"No, you certainly don't! But because you're a man, it's so easy for you to feel like your wife is your property."

"Well, call it whatever you want. But I don't think it's unfair for me to hold you to the promise that you made when you married me. Your promise to be committed to me!"

"Just because we're married doesn't mean that you get to choose what I do and what I don't do. That's what you fail to understand."

Brennan didn't respond right away. He looked at his wife who was standing right in front of him with a stream of tears rolling down her face and a look of desperation in her eyes. He thought very carefully about what he would say next.

"Abigail," he sighed as he sat back down on the couch. "Please think really hard about what you're asking of me."

"I have," she replied as she took a seat beside him. Both of them had calmed down somewhat and had lowered their voices. "I really have. And I know what I'm asking of you. This is why it's taken so long for me to open up about it."

"This is really big. There's a reason why couples rarely

ever do this kind of arrangement. This will break our marriage."

"And I'm telling you that our marriage is already broken, Brennan. Staying on the same path is just going to break it beyond repair. Can you understand that?"

"But what happens if you fall in love with someone else? What will happen then? What will happen to our family?"

Brennan's voice began to break. He couldn't even dare entertain the thought of his wife falling in love and being in the arms of another man.

"I've read about plenty of couples who went through the same thing and became stronger as a result of it. Don't you want that for us? You say that you want us to be happy again, but you're letting your need to ALWAYS be in control get in the way of that. Can't you see?"

"I think that you're being very unfair right now. You're asking for too much."

"I may be unfair or I may not," she replied. "But it's how I feel."

Chapter 10

Abigail

ABIGAIL WATCHED AS Brennan stormed out of the living room without saying anything else. He didn't even take the time to turn the TV off before storming out. Brennan just walked straight out of the living room, grabbed his car keys from the foyer, and darted towards the front door before slamming it behind him. Abigail was left alone with her thoughts as she watched her husband walk away from one of the most important conversations they had ever had as a couple. She knew that she was asking a lot from him, but she didn't expect him to have that kind of reaction.

She sat down on the couch in disbelief.

"Maybe I'm being too selfish," she whispered under her breath. No, she told herself. He's the one who's being selfish here. Abigail grabbed the throw pillow next to her and hurled it towards the television. Not once throughout our marriage have I ever asked him for anything. I willingly gave up my job and career for this family. I didn't even think twice about it.

She stood up and started pacing the room. Her

eyebrows were scrunched up together and her lips were curled up into a light snarl. What makes him think that he can assert his ownership over me like that? He's such a chauvinistic pig, just like the rest of them.

After she calmed down a bit, she went to get her journal and pen. She wrote, "I really don't know what to do. I want us to still be a family, but the way Brennan is behaving I really don't know…" She continued, "I can't believe he's such a baby. I'm sure that he wouldn't mind sleeping with other women but of course he 'has issues' when I want to do it. 'Issues' because of his antiquated ideas of what a marriage is. I should never have married him in the first place." Abigail sighed.

Chapter 11

Brennan

BRENNAN HEADED STRAIGHT to his car after slamming the front door of his home. He got into his SUV and pulled out of the driveway. Before he knew it, he was already speeding along the empty streets of his suburban neighborhood. Brennan was cruising along without any destination in mind. All he knew was that he needed to escape that conversation and get out of the house. "WHY ME?" he screamed at the top of his lungs. "WHAT THE FUCK IS WRONG WITH HER?"

The car was slowly exiting the suburbs and approaching the main highway. Brennan didn't know where he wanted to go and just followed the road in front of him. Is this the thanks I get after everything I've done for her all these years? he thought to himself. Did I not love her enough? He pictured Abigail's cold and dead face once more in his mind as she brought up the idea of being in an open relationship. His entire body grew hot with rage, and he slammed his fist onto his car's dashboard. How ungrateful can she be after all of the years I've given her?

Then, tears began streaming down his face just as he was getting onto the freeway. The rage that was so fiery within him just a few moments before had now turned into anguish. There was a heavy weight that filled his heart as he obsessed over the idea of being unable to make his wife happy.

Am I really that bad of a husband that she requires another man to fulfill her needs? Then, he thought of what she was really asking from him. In his eyes, it went against the very oaths that they swore to one another when they got married. That's when his thoughts started drifting towards random mental snapshots of their wedding day. They were both so happy then. He wasn't making so much money yet, but he always said that they were rich in love. At the time, Brennan couldn't give her the house, the kids, or any material item. And yet, he knew that he made her happy. He was confident that she was happy to be with him. That's why he couldn't understand why things were any different now. He had given her a house. He helped her birth two beautiful girls. He made sure to spoil her with occasional luxuries like vacations and jewelry. Yet, somehow, she thought that he still wasn't giving her enough. He also recalled how she used to tell him that her friends were jealous of what the two of them had in their marriage. "They're frustrated that their husbands aren't as great as you," she used to tell him.

He saw that he was running out of gas as he felt himself grow calmer. He decided to turn onto the next exit on the freeway and head back home. "This might just be a phase," he tried to convince himself. "She's going to come to her senses eventually." He thought about when they had been on vacation and walked hand in hand on the beach. They had been so happy then.

On the drive home, Brennan's thoughts gradually shifted from his wife to his kids. "What would they think?" he asked himself. "Open relationship…" He knew that his kids were far too young to understand what was going on.

Heck, even he didn't know what was going on.

"It's out of the question. This is going to rip our family apart." Then, he thought of what everyone else would think. "I will not allow our family to be turned into a laughingstock," he told himself.

Chapter 12

Abigail

IT WAS WEDNESDAY and Abigail was in the middle of bathing her kids and helping them get ready for bed. As she helped scrub and shampoo both Amber and Riley as they splashed around in the tub, her mind was elsewhere. She thought back to that Sunday night when Brennan came back home after just abandoning her in the middle of a conversation. She was absolutely fuming at him for leaving so abruptly like that. He knew how important this was to her and he just left.

"Where have you been?" demanded Abigail. "We were in the middle of a serious discussion. You can't just walk out on me like that."

"I went for a drive. I needed time to think," he replied.

"Well, have you thought about it?"

"Yes, and my sentiments haven't changed."

"So, it's really true, isn't it?" She stood up.

"What?"

"You think that you get to decide what I do or don't do."

"Of course not. Of course I don't think that."

"Then what's the problem?" She walked up to him and got in his face. "Why won't you let us become an open relationship?"

"Because I think it's going to destroy our marriage! That's why!"

"You know what's destroying our marriage? This! Right now. This is destroying me. I don't feel happy anymore. How can you expect this relationship to survive when one of us isn't happy in it? All I'm asking for is a chance for us to see what's out there for a while."

"You're asking for way too much," sighed Brennan. He approached her in the living room and took a seat back on the couch where they had begun the conversation. "What you're asking me for is that I share you with other men."

"That's the thing," she said as she took a seat beside him. "I'm not yours to share. I am my own person."

"I know that you're your own person, honey. I do truly understand that, even though I don't fully understand why you feel the way you feel right now."

"Then can you just trust that this is what I need? This is what the relationship needs. This is what you need."

"You're the only one I need." Brennan looked away from her and down at his feet. Tears began to form in his eyes again. "I don't want an open relationship because there's no one else I would rather be with than you."

"How would you even know what you want or don't want? You're so close-minded! I tried talking to you about it and you just walked out the door! You're just so resistant to change."

Brennan looked at his wife's desperate eyes and placed his hand on hers. "Maybe you're right. Maybe I am being close-minded. But I can't give you a decision right now. I'm sorry."

"Okay, that's fair," she said. "But I don't want to be kept waiting either."

"Just give me time to think," he replied. "I promise you that I'm not putting an end to this conversation. I love you, and I'm willing to do whatever it takes to make this work. I just need time to really think about it. Can you give me that, at least?"

"How much time, Brennan?"

"I can't say for certain." He kissed her on the forehead and looked straight into her eyes once more. "But I just need time to think." He held her face in his palm and just stared at her for a moment. Then he stood up and disappeared into the bedroom upstairs.

That was the last time that either of them had even discussed the subject. Abigail was growing antsy while waiting for him to talk to her about it again. He's avoiding talking to me about it. She noticed that he never spent any alone time with her. Whenever she walked into the bedroom after getting the kids ready for bed, he was already fast asleep or on his phone answering work emails. Whenever he was awake, it always seemed like he made sure that the kids were around so that Abigail could never bring the subject up. She felt as if Brennan was merely trying to delay the discussion in the hopes that Abigail would eventually just forget about everything. But she wasn't intending on letting him off the hook so easily.

She asked Amber and Riley to tilt their heads back as she rinsed their hair. "Look at you, girls," she said with a huge smile on her face. "Do you know just how beautiful the two of you are?" The two toddlers giggled at their mother and resumed the water splashing. Each of them had a bathroom toy that their father had given them as a bribe for baths. Riley had the traditional squeaking rubber duck while Amber had a toy boat that she splashed around at will. Seeing her kids so happy gave Abigail a melancholy that she had never encountered before. At that moment, thinking about Brennan and how he had completely shunned her feelings, she was absolutely livid.

"Girls," she said to her giggling kids. "Do you love Mommy?"

"Yes!" the siblings replied in unison.

"And do you know how much Mommy loves you?"

"Yes!" they replied again.

"You're the best part of my life, girls," said Abigail as she joined in the splashing party.

As she was saying this, Abigail couldn't help but find the irony in it. There was a time before she met Brennan where she didn't even want children. She could still recall the day that he had completely changed her mind on the matter. They had already been dating for a few months and were getting serious as a couple. A lot of her friends were already settling down and tying the knot with significant others. She had never really prioritized marriage before, but things had changed now that she and Brennan were dating.

It was just another usual date night for the two of them. They were in a mid-tier Italian restaurant that was near the hospital where Abigail used to work. After devouring a whole pizza and a bunch of pasta just between the two of them, the two decided to unwind by ordering a bottle of wine. That's when Brennan brought up the topic of marriage and families.

"I don't know," said Brennan. "With the way things are going at work and with you, I feel like I have some real direction in life now."

"That's good," said Abigail. "I'm happy for you."

Brennan took a sip of his wine and hesitated for a bit. "How about you? How do you picture your future turning out?"

"Honestly, I'd never really given it much thought."

"You mean that you've never thought about eventually just settling down? Getting married? Having kids? Starting a family?"

"Well," this time Abigail hesitated, "I've never really pictured myself having kids. It's not that I don't like kids. I do. It's just that I've never really considered it to be a priority."

"Okay," muttered Brennan. "That's fair."

He left it at that and took another sip of his wine. He looked at Abigail, smiled, and then turned his head to look around the restaurant. Abigail knew that he was trying to think of something to say.

"Go on," she said.

"What?"

"You have something on your mind. Just say it."

He laughed and took another sip of his wine before topping his and Abigail's glasses up for another serving.

"You're really smart. Nothing gets by you," he said.

"You got that right," she replied with a sly smile on her face.

"Well, I know that we've only just started dating and all, but I really like how things are going."

"Awww," she said. She reached out and grabbed his hand across the table. "I really like how things are going too."

"I'm really happy to hear you say that," he said with a boyish smile. "It's just that I'm not that kind of guy who gets into relationships for the heck of it. I used to be, but I don't want to be that guy anymore. And I feel like I can really picture a future with you." He paused and hesitated for a bit. Before Abigail had a chance to reply, he went on, "Is it too soon? Am I moving too fast? I don't want to pressure yo—"

"Brennan," Abigail interrupted. "It's okay. No, you're not pressuring me. I feel like you and I have a real shot at the future too. I like being with you. I like who I am whenever I'm with you."

"Really? His face light up.

"Really. Now tell me more about this future that you're envisioning," she teased.

"Well, I still picture myself at TransTech. I feel like I have a lot of upward mobility there. In a few years' time, I'll be making so much money that I wouldn't even know what to do with it. Of course, I'll be getting my own place. A house in the suburbs. A nice neighborhood where I can start a family. Wife. Kids. The whole shebang."

"Wow, you really know what you want, huh?" she asked.

"Yeah," he said. "Don't you?"

"I honestly hadn't given it much thought. I've always just been a lone wolf, I guess."

"Well, do you still see yourself as a lone wolf now?" He flashed a big confident smile her way.

"No." She gave a sheepish grin. "I don't."

That was when she realized that she really liked Brennan. She had never considered starting a family with any guy until she started dating him. He was the one who managed to change her mind and convince her that she wanted to start a family after all. Now, she was looking at her two kids in adoration and playing with them in the tub as she thought back to that moment in the restaurant.

"Come on, kids," she said. "Bath time's over. We have to dry you two up."

She helped the kids out of the tub and rubbed a towel over their heads one by one. Still, as she was helping the girls get ready for bed, her mind was still on Brennan. I'm not going to let him off the hook, she kept repeating to herself. This was not the life I envisioned for myself.

"Mommy!" said Amber, breaking Abigail's train of thought. "Can you ask Daddy to read us a bedtime story to sleep?"

"Bedtime story!" added Riley.

"I think Daddy is really tired from work, honey." She shook her head. She just didn't want to talk to Brennan unless it was about her proposal for an open relationship. She didn't feel like talking to him about anything other than that. "If you want, Mommy can read you a story."

"But we want Daddy, Mommy," cried Amber. "Daddy, please!"

"Maybe tomorrow, dear," soothed Abigail. "Daddy isn't feeling well, but he'll be okay tomorrow. And he'll read you a bedtime story, okay?"

"Okay," sighed a dejected Amber.

Abigail helped them dress into their pajamas and tucked them each into their beds. She grabbed a storybook from their bookshelf and asked, "Are you sure that you don't want Mommy to read you a story?"

"It's okay, Mom," replied Amber. "We'll ask Daddy tomorrow."

"Okay, honey. Good night, you two."

"Good night, Mama!" the two girls chorused.

Abigail turned their night light on before switching off the main lights in the bedroom. She closed the door quietly and stood in the hallway for a while. Then, she let out a silent burst of tears. Abigail knelt down in the hallway just outside her children's bedroom door and wept. She wept because she felt like she had been cheated out of a life that she wanted. She felt guilty about not being content with her life, and that guilt only added to her being unhappy. Most of all, she felt suffocated. She never wanted to be locked down in any kind of relationship before she met Brennan. She wasn't even sure that she wanted to be tied down with him. Abigail only agreed to marry him because it felt like the logical thing to do at the time. Yet, now she realized that she merely forced herself into believing that she could be happy with this kind of arrangement.

She walked towards her bedroom door and tried to gather herself. Abigail wiped away the last of her tears and took a deep breath. She turned the doorknob and swung the door open only to see her husband in bed, seemingly asleep.

"You know," she said, "your kids wanted you to read them a bedtime story tonight."

"Mmm," grumbled Brennan.

"Whatever, Brennan."

She headed straight towards the bathroom and cried in front of the mirror once more, hyperventilating as she struggled to fill her lungs with air. This was what it was like for her in the relationship. Her emotional struggles were now being manifested into physical pains. She splashed some water on her face and knelt down in front of the sink.

Abigail stood up and stared into the mirror at her own reflection and saw the face of a woman who was growing tired and weary. The circles under her eyes looked a shade darker, and she could see new strands of silver hair in places that she hadn't seen them before. Her eyes were puffy and her nose was red. I look horrible, she thought. I need to breathe. I need air. I need to get out of here.

Chapter 13

Brennan

BRENNAN WAS WATCHING his wife from the dining room as he finished his dinner. Abigail had already begun doing the dishes even though Brennan was still eating. The girls were left at the table with him watching a Mickey Mouse video on the iPad. Brennan sliced off a chunk of beef and chewed it slowly as he peered at Abigail. It was Friday now, and the two of them had barely spoken to one another since that heated discussion they had on Sunday night. Brennan tried to initiate conversation with her, but he was always greeted with non-responses or one-word answers. In fact, Abigail never really talked to him unless it concerned the children. It was obvious to him that she was upset.

Maybe this isn't a phase after all, Brennan thought to himself as he chewed on his vegetables. Maybe she's forcing my hand here. He looked at his two kids and wondered how they would feel about their parents separating. He knew that separation was a very real possibility if he and Abigail couldn't work through their issues. Brennan had paid witness to so many friends of his whose relationships came to a tragic end. Somehow, a thought occurred to him that if it weren't for the girls, Abigail would have already left him. He didn't want them to have to grow up choosing between their father and their mother. Brennan for one knew what it was like to grow up without a father. He thought back to this vivid memory of his when he was just six years old. It was his first week of school in first grade and he came home crying to his mother.

"Brennan," said his mom who wrapped him in her arms. "What's wrong?"

"My friends made fun of me, Momma," he replied, barely comprehensible as he tried his best to fight back his tears.

"But why?" said Corrine, Brennan's mom. "What did they say?"

"All my friends have a daddy, and they told me that my daddy left because he didn't love me," he said before letting out a full wail. "Why doesn't my daddy love me, Momma?"

"Oh, Brennan. He had many problems in life, and that's why he's not here anymore. That's not your fault, okay?" She caressed his head. "Who are these kids? Tell me their names."

Brennan didn't reply and just kept on crying, screaming for his absent father. Corinne helped usher him to the couch and cradled him until he calmed down. After he stopped crying, Corinne told him something that would stick with him for the rest of his life.

"Brennan," she said, "one day, you're going to become a dad too. And when that happens, make sure that you never leave your kids behind. Make sure that they will never feel lonely. Make sure that you always make them feel loved."

"Okay, Momma," he replied as he struggled to catch his breath.

"You know how much Momma loves you, right?"

"Yes, Momma."

Corinne hugged him tighter and gave him a kiss on the forehead. "Good," she said. "Love is important in family, Brennan. And we never leave family behind. That's not what we do to people we love."

"Okay, Momma."

I'm never going to leave, Brennan thought as he watched his two girls. He looked at Abigail who was still in the kitchen with her back turned to him. I'm never leaving you either.

"Abigail," he said. "I'm done eating. How about I be the one to help get the kids ready for bed tonight?"

"Huh?" replied Abigail as she turned to face him. "Oh, yeah. Okay. Sure. Just leave those dishes there and I'll get to them later."

"Hey, girls," he said to Amber and Riley. "How about Daddy helps you change into your jammies and then I'll read you a bedtime story after?"

"Yaaaaay!" said the two girls together.

Brennan put the iPad away and lifted the two girls out of their booster seats with ease. He carried them up the stairs to their bedroom as they laughed and held on to his shoulders.

"What do you girls want me to read tonight? Sesame Street, maybe?"

"I want Winnie the Pooh, Daddy!" replied Amber.

"Winnie the Pooh?" replied Brennan. "Is that okay with you, Riley?"

"Yes!" Riley agreed with her sister.

"Winnie the Pooh it is then."

Brennan set them down on the floor of their bathroom and filled Amber's toothbrush with toothpaste.

"Amber," he said as he held the toothbrush out to her. "Can you show Daddy how to brush your teeth?"

"Okay, Daddy!"

She grabbed the toothbrush from him and started brushing her teeth on her own.

"Riley, how about Daddy helps you brush your teeth like your big sister?"

Riley looked at Amber and nodded her head. Brennan adored how much Riley wanted to be like her big sister. He took Riley's toothbrush and gently began brushing her teeth in slow circular motions.

He brought the girls to their beds and sat in between both of them. Riley chose the book that they were going to read with much excitement. As Brennan narrated to them Christopher Robin's adventures together with Pooh, Tigger, Piglet, and the rest of the gang, the girls slowly drifted to sleep. He stopped talking to check and see if they had truly fallen asleep. When he was sure that both of them were knocked out, he put the book down and sat there for a while. He brought his thoughts back to Abigail and her proposal. Brennan already heard her go into their bedroom, and he didn't feel like being alone with her just yet. He stayed in the girls' room a little longer to think about what he was going to do about their marriage.

Passion, he thought to himself. That's what she's looking for right now. Maybe I need to give this to her just so she'll realize that she's never going to find a man who will love her like I do. He understood that in order to save their marriage, he needed to really grasp where Abigail was coming from. She'll grow to appreciate me more if I give her what she wants.

Then Brennan felt his pulse intensify and his blood grow warmer. He was beginning to really entertain the idea of giving into Abigail's request. That's when a sudden rush of fear and anxiety overcame him. He tried his best to steady his breathing. There he was, alone with his two kids, in a dark room thinking about whether he should let his wife see other men or not.

He thought back to the day of their wedding. In his mind, he was looking straight into the loving eyes of Abigail. She wore a simple ruffled wedding gown that draped her slender shoulders so elegantly. He recalled lifting her veil and seeing her mouth the words "I love you" to him just before they shared their first kiss as husband and wife. He chuckled to himself in irony as he thought about where that version of Abigail had gone.

That Abigail would have never asked him to enter an open relationship under any circumstance. He felt a binding sensation in his stomach as if his intestines were attacking one another. Maybe this really is something that we both need to go through.

He thought about her accusation of him being misogynistic. There was no way that he would ever consider himself a misogynist. But Abigail had planted that seed in his head and he just couldn't shake it. The very idea of him being a misogynist sat with him and fermented over time. Could it be true? he thought as he began to doubt himself. He felt his heart sink and a huge wave of guilt overcame him. Brennan wanted nothing more in life than to make his wife and children happy. It was killing him to know that he was the source of his own wife's unhappiness.

Maybe she's right, he thought as tears began to form in his eyes. He took a deep breath and leaned his head back against the wall behind him. Perhaps this is the only way out for us. But why does it feel like this is just the beginning of the end?

The tears were streaming down his face uncontrollably now. He tried his best to compose himself so that his kids wouldn't wake up and see him crying. Suddenly, a grim thought overcame him. Brennan wanted her to feel the guilt of his current sorrow as well.

For a brief moment, he thought about killing himself and putting a stop to everything right there. Maybe then Abigail would realize how unreasonable she was being and how she had driven him to take his own life. He turned his head to face Amber and watched her looking so peaceful as she slept. He turned the other way to see Riley with her mouth wide open and both arms clutching onto a teddy bear. I can't leave the girls behind, he thought. They need a dad. They need their mom and dad to stay together.

Chapter 14

Abigail

SATURDAY MORNING CAME around and Brennan was busy packing his belongings to go away for the weekend on a business trip. Abigail woke up to her husband walking back and forth between his suitcase and the closet He saw that she had woken up and gave her a smile.

"Hi," he said. "Did I wake you? I'm sorry. Heading to Colorado for a conference with the team for the weekend. Might also meet some potential investors and clients. I'll be back late on Monday."

Abigail didn't say anything and just continued to look at her husband as he filled his suitcase up with dress shirts and trousers.

"Please," he continued, "get some more sleep if you want. I'll be quieter now."

Abigail got up without saying a word and went straight to the bathroom. As soon as she closed the bathroom door behind her, she burst into tears. How could he be so stupid and selfish? She let out a full scream as tears rolled down her face and snot began to build up in her nose.

"Honey? Abigail?!" yelled Brennan bursting through the bathroom doors. "What happened?"

"You're so stupid!" she replied. She was absolutely hysterical at this point. Abigail's face was a mess as she knelt down on the tile floor in utter frustration.

"Why?" he asked. "What's wrong?"

"You know what's wrong! I've been telling you, but you haven't been listening. You're selfish and you're only thinking about yourself!" replied Abigail. She had gotten back up on her feet and was regaining her composure now. "I've told you what I wanted, and you've just been dodging me. You've been ignoring me and keeping to yourself."

"Abigail—"

"No!" she demanded. "You don't get to interrupt. Now, more than ever, you have a chance to save our marriage. And what do you do? You're leaving! You coward."

"Abigail, please," Brennan pleaded. "I have to go on this trip for work. But if you really want me to stay so you can yell at me some more, I'll do it. I'll do it if that will make you happy. I don't care if I lose my job."

"Please," she said. "Don't patronize me. Spare me that, at least."

"I don't get it," said Brennan. "I just need to go away for a while for work. What do you want?"

"What I want, Brennan, is to stop suffocating." She had stopped crying at that point, but the tears came flowing out once more. "I feel so trapped and alone. We're in a marriage, but I feel like I'm on my own to fend for myself. Why can't you see that?"

"I've always been there for you. That's not fair," he defended.

"No, you haven't. You're there physically, but when was the last time you have made me feel like you could be there for me emotionally? Sexually?"

"I've always made my love known to you. Isn't that enough?"

"You just don't get it!" she said as she raised her voice again. "You're either too selfish or too stupid to see! You don't understand how I feel."

"That's enough, Abigail. I will stay here and fight for our marriage, but I won't stand here and let you tell me that I'm stupid over and over again,"

"Whatever," she said, turning his back to him as she faced the bathroom mirror. She placed her hands on the counter for support and looked down at the sink. Slowly, she turned her head upwards and looked at his reflection right in the mirror and said, "If it weren't for the kids, I would have left you a long time ago."

Chapter 15

Brennan

BRENNAN LEFT THE bathroom and zipped his suitcase up. He didn't care that he wasn't finished packing yet. He just needed to get out of that house as soon as possible. He grabbed his phone and booked an Uber to drive him to the airport. Brennan finished getting dressed as he waited for the driver to arrive. The app had told him that a driver was nearby and would be there for him in just two minutes. He put on the first jeans and button-down shirt combo that he could find and paired it with his usual pair of travelling sneakers. To him, the most important thing was getting away from Abigail as quickly as possible.

Before heading down the stairs, he went over to the girls' room to see if they were awake. Both of them were still sleeping, and he decided against waking them up to say goodbye. He made his way downstairs, grabbed a protein bar from the pantry, and headed out the front door. According to the app, the driver was making the final turn towards their street. Brennan looked up and could see the car driving down to where he was standing on the curb. He waved the car down and got into the backseat.

"Brennan?" asked the Uber driver. "Good morning! We're headed to the airport?"

"Yeah," replied Brennan.

"Do you want to choose our route for today?"

"It's up to you. Let's just get going."

The driver followed the route that was suggested to him by his phone's navigation system, and they were on their way. Brennan was red in the face and fuming at this point. He opened the protein bar and took a big bite out of it. How could she say that to me? he thought.

"Hey, man," said Brennan, addressing the Uber driver. "What's your name again?"

"Dave," replied the driver.

"I hope you don't mind my asking, Dave, but are you in a relationship right now?"

"Yes, sir. I have a girlfriend. We've been together for a couple of years." Dave was a brown-skinned man who looked as if he were in his mid twenties. He had the appearance of someone of either Latino or Asian descent. He wore thin wireframe glasses and had a small goatee.

"Good for you," said Brennan. "Mind if I ask you another question? A hypothetical?"

"Go ahead, sir. We've got a few more minutes to kill before we get to the airport anyway," replied Dave.

"Please. Just call me Brennan."

"Alright, Brennan."

"Let's say your girlfriend just comes out of the blue and tells you that she wants an open relationship. What would you do?"

"Open relationship?"

"Yeah. It's when the two of you stay together, but you also date other people at the same time."

"Oh, yeah. I've heard of those! Like a relationship without the commitment, right?"

"Yeah," affirmed Brennan. "Exactly."

"Damn." Dave hesitated. "I don't know, sir. Seems like things could get really messy."

"Right?"

"Yeah, but I guess some people just aren't wired for being in long-term relationships, sir."

"What do you mean?" Brennan leaned forward in his seat.

"Well, I have this friend of mine. He's a stand-up guy. Really great guy. He's the kind of guy who would be a good samaritan to anyone in need. You know what I'm saying?"

"Yeah, go on."

"Okay," Dave continued. "So he's really nice, and he's the kind of guy that a lot of girls could really fall for because of how nice he is. Although, in every long-term relationship that he's been in, he's cheated on his girl. Every. Single One."

"What?" said Brennan. "But I thought you said that he was a nice guy?"

"He is. He really is. Heck, even his ex-girlfriends would still probably say that he's a nice guy. He's really generous. Helpful. He's thoughtful. It's just that he can't commit to a relationship. His mind and heart aren't built for staying with one girl forever, you know?"

"Huh." Brennan sat back. "That's interesting."

"Yeah. I'm not like that because I don't have any trouble with commitment at all. But I can see how some people just can't be locked into relationships like that. It doesn't mean that they're bad people per se. They might just love differently than others. I don't know if I'm making any sense." He met Brennan's eyes in the rear-view mirror.

Brennan stayed quiet for a while as he absorbed what Dave was saying. He thought about Abigail and how he would feel if she had just cheated on him without telling him. Would that be better than what she's asking from me right now? he thought.

"You've given me a lot to think about, Dave," said Brennan. "Can I have your take on another hypothetical?"

"Go ahead, Brennan."

"Would you rather that your girlfriend asked you for permission to sleep with another guy? Or would you rather that she just did it behind your back?"

Dave turned the radio volume down.

"Hmmm, that's a tough one, Brennan," replied Dave "But my gut is telling me that I would rather she ask my permission first. Either way, I would hate for her to be getting it on with another guy. But if she tells me about it beforehand, then at least I know that the trust and respect is still there."

"Yes, trust and respect is important."

"Very important," he said. "A relationship is practically nothing without those two things, don't you think?"

"You're right," Brennan replied. Brennan changed the topic and asked Dave about his life. He learned that Dave was indeed a second-generation immigrant whose parents were both Filipinos. Dave was also in the process of completing graduate studies and his job as an Uber driver was just something to help him pay the bills. Brennan also discovered that Dave had plans of going into the tech industry. He explained to Dave where he worked, and the two of them bonded over industry trends and emerging technologies.

Just as they arrived at the airport, Brennan offered Dave his card and told him to give him a call once he graduated from school.

"We might have a place for you over at TransTech," he said.

"Wow, thanks, Brennan!"

"No worries at all. Thanks for the car ride and the conversation."

"Thanks as well, man. Oh, and I don't know if I'm overstepping my bounds here, but whatever you're going through, I hope that you figure things out. If it makes any difference, I think that love is the one thing that's always worth fighting for."

"Thanks, Dave," said Brennan as he gave off a slight chuckle. "I'll keep that in mind."

"Have a safe flight!"

Brennan grabbed hold of his carry-on and alighted from Dave's car. He gave him a wave through the window and turned to make his way towards the departure gates. Love is always worth fighting for, he thought to himself. He's right.

He checked into his flight and headed towards his assigned boarding gate. Brennan was still hungry, so he decided to order a cup of coffee and a sandwich and found himself a seat. He had been thinking long and hard about everything that has happened so far between him and Abigail. He also thought about his conversation with Dave for some outside perspective. Brennan came to a decision and reached for his phone, starting to write text message. His heart was pounding deeply and rapidly as he tapped on send. He was getting anxious again, and he knew that the coffee he was drinking wouldn't help that situation, but he drank it anyway. It was done. He had made his decision.

Chapter 16

Abigail

ABIGAIL LAY DOWN in bed waiting for her kids to wake up after Brennan had left. She was still feeling the weight of her emotions and didn't feel like doing anything that day. Her earlier argument with Brennan only exacerbated the situation and she didn't know what to do anymore.

Suddenly, the phone on her side table rang. She didn't want to pick it up at first as even that would require so much energy from her. Yet, Abigail decided to check who the message was from, at the very least. Once she read that the message had come from Brennan, she thought twice about opening it. She didn't want to get into another fight, not especially through text message. In the end, her curiosity overcame her, and she decided to open the message anyway.

Hey, the message read. I've thought about it. You win. Let's give this thing a try. Talk more when I return home.

She reread the message once and then another time just to make sure that she didn't misread anything. Did he really agree to this? she thought. She set her phone down and stared at the ceiling for a while. Things seemed a little lighter to her now. The next thing she knew, she gave in to an immense urge to get on her feet and start preparing breakfast for her family.

Chapter 17

Brennan

BRENNAN RETURNED HOME from his business trip late Monday night. When he arrived home, the house was already dark. The only light that was on in the first floor was the one in the dining room. On the dining table, he found a note from Abigail:

There's some spaghetti in the microwave. Just heat it up if you're hungry or place it in the fridge if you're not.

Brennan had already eaten dinner at the airport in Colorado while waiting for his flight, but he still took this gesture from his wife as a good sign. He took the plate of spaghetti out of the microwave and placed it in the fridge. His heart started racing again as he thought about the talk that he was about to have. In the back of his mind he hoped that Abigail was already asleep.

He grabbed his carry-on and trudged up the stairs as lightly and quietly as he could, then made his way to the bedroom door and placed his hand on the doorknob. He took a deep breath and closed his eyes before turning the knob to open the door.

Abigail was in bed, reading a book when Brennan

walked in. She was already dressed in her nightgown and her hair was wrapped in a towel.

"Hey," said Brennan. "I thought that you would already be asleep."

"Couldn't sleep," replied Abigail. She stood up and removed the towel from her head, tossing it into the laundry hamper. "How was the trip?"

"It was okay," answered Brennan as he unfastened his tie and began to unbutton his shirt. "We were able to close a couple of big clients over there. It'll be stressful at work, but at least there will be more money coming into the company."

"That's good," said Abigail with a dead half-hearted tone. "I'm happy for you."

"Listen," His heart was racing really fast now. "I think we have to talk."

"Yes, that's why I couldn't sleep. I feel like we needed to talk things out first."

"Maybe we should sit down for this?" suggested Brennan.

"Let's go downstairs. I'll make us a pot of tea," said Abigail.

Brennan nodded and followed Abigail. She went straight to the kitchen and poured some water into a pot for boiling. Brennan studied her movements closely. She moved with a certain grace and elegance that infatuated him the very first time he met her. He opened his mouth to say something but changed his mind. He waited for her to finish her tea-making ritual and have a seat at the table.

Abigail brought two cups of hot tea with her on a tray together with the large teapot and settled it down on the table. She took a seat across from Brennan and had a sip of her tea. Finally, she cleared her throat and took a deep breath before looking him in the eyes.

"So, you've thought about my proposal?"

"I have. I've given it a lot of thought actually." He took a sip from the tea and recoiled. It was too hot and nearly burned his tongue.

"Sorry," she said as she saw him wince. "Forgot to tell you to wait a while. The batch I made ran a little hot."

"That's okay." He sat back in the chair. "Okay, so let me just tell you about where my head is at. Is that okay?"

"Of course," she said. "The floor is yours."

"Alright. I love you. I love you more than life itself. I love you more than I could possibly love another person, save for our two girls. And the only reason I have them is because of you. So I love you even more for that," he explained.

"Oh, Brennan. I know you love—"

"Please. I have the floor now, remember?"

She nodded her head and motioned for him to go on.

"I really want to make this work. I want to make us work. I can't envision a future where you and I aren't together and happy with our kids. And if you think that the only chance for us to have that future is if I let you do this, then okay."

"But Brennan, this isn't just for me. It's not just about me doing this alone. You have to do it with me. That's the whole point. It's an open relationship for the BOTH of us."

"I understand. And I wanted to talk to you about that." Brennan took another sip of his tea. It had cooled down by then, and he could tolerate the heat without getting burned. He was stalling because he knew that what he was about to say was going to upset Abigail. However, he knew that there was just no getting around it.

"I'm open to us exploring the idea of an open relationship. But I need us to come to a compromise on this. I feel like there have to be ground rules in order for me to really be on board. Can you at least respect that?"

She squinted her eyes at him and took a while before responding. "Okay, I can respect that. But what kind of ground rules are we talking about here?"

"One of my biggest fears about this is that you end up

meeting a guy who you might eventually leave me for. You can understand why that would make me apprehensive, right?"

"Of course," she said, rolling her eyes. "Stop patronizing me."

"I'm not. I'm really not. I just want you to understand where I'm coming from before I tell you about the rules that I want to establish. So, to give me better peace of mind about this, I only want you to date younger guys."

"What?" she said. She was growing visibly frustrated now. "Why?"

"Well, I just feel like you would be less likely to run off with someone young. He wouldn't be able to offer you the kind of stability that I'm already giving you right now."

"Uh huh," she said with a sarcastic tone. "Any more of these ground rules?"

"Yes," replied a stern Brennan. "You can only date guys who don't live here in Minnesota."

She opened her mouth to protest, but Brennan didn't allow himself to be interrupted.

"Another one of the biggest reasons as to why I was so against this to begin with was that I was afraid of what the public would say. I didn't want our friends and family finding out about you and I having this kind of setup. It didn't help that you and the girls were always giggling when you were talking about John and Darlene or John and Jessie or whatever."

"They were just joking around!"

"Exactly!" Brennan felt himself becoming more enraged now. "I don't want our marriage to end up as a joke. I don't want our relationship to be somebody else's punchline."

"That's not fair!" she complained. "How would I be able to go on proper dates with guys who don't even live in the same state as me?"

"Abigail, please…"

"No, Brennan. You've had your turn to talk. Now it's

mine. First of all, I'm not interested in dating younger guys. That's really stupid. I wouldn't be able to handle their immaturity."

"But I thought all you were after was the lust and passion?"

"You really don't get it, do you? And even if that were the case, where would I find a young man who would want to date someone old and fat like me, huh?"

"Honey, you're not o—"

"Shut up, Brennan. I'm still talking. Also, how would I date someone who lives in another state? How expensive would that be for me to travel away for a single date? Think of the time that I would have to spend away from the kids!"

Abigail was turning red in the face and was stuck in a very intense scowl. Her one hand had a very tight grip on her tea cup while the other was clenched in a tight fist.

"I don't know." He held her stare with a cold glare. "But those are my terms."

"Well, your terms are shit!"

She got up from her chair and stormed off towards the stairs.

"Find another place to sleep tonight," she said as she walked away. "Those are my terms.

Chapter 18

Abigail

IT WAS A WEDNESDAY afternoon and it was her birthday. Abigail was driving back home from spending a day at her mother's house with the two children. While most people tended to be happy and optimistic about their birthdays, Abigail had very little reason to celebrate. She was stuck in a crumbling marriage that was suffocating her. She hadn't talked to her husband in days, and she felt more alone than ever. At the very least, she would be spending her birthday with people she loved and who she knew loved her. However, she knew that she had to get back home because Brennan had texted her that they needed to have dinner together as a family to celebrate her birthday. He didn't want the kids to think that there was something wrong. Abigail agreed with him and told him that she would be home from her mother's house by 7:00 p.m.

"Did you kids have fun at grandma's house today?" she asked.

"Yes!" said Amber. "I love Grandma, Mommy!"

"I love Grandma too!" chimed Riley.

As she pulled onto the street of their house, she

noticed that a bunch of cars were already parked outside.

"What is going on?" she said aloud to herself. She pulled into the driveway and parked the car. "Did your dad tell you anything about a party tonight?" she asked the kids.

"Yay, a party!" said Riley. "Is there going to be cake, Momma?"

Abigail didn't answer, but she recognized the cars that were parked along the road. She helped her kids out of the car and walked them both to the front door. Abigail walked through the door to a loud cheer of "surprise!" from a bunch of familiar faces. It was almost like everyone she knew was there at the house. She saw Karen, Phillip, Vince, Megan, Mary Alice, Joanne, Darlene, and a bunch of her other friends from the hospital. She also saw Brennan standing on the other side of the room with a huge grin on his face as he mouthed the words "surprise" to her.

The kids were excited to see that their home was filled with so many people, and they rushed forward to say hi to everyone. After the initial shock, Abigail welcomed everyone who was there and gave each of them a big hug as they wished her a happy birthday.

"Come on, everyone," said Brennan as he suddenly emerged with a birthday cake and led them all in a chorus of the birthday song. The kids ran towards Abigail, eager to be the ones to blow the candles out. After finishing the song, Brennan said, "Go ahead, honey. Make your wish."

Abigail closed her eyes, but before she could open them, Amber and Riley blew the flames out, which prompted a chorus of cheers and laughs from the guests. "Alright, everybody," announced Brennan, "now, I didn't cook this feast, but I did pay for the catering company that did. Grab a plate and dig in, everyone!"

The night was filled with a lot of friendly chatter and casual conversation. There was an energy in the house that hadn't been there for a long time. A steady flow of soft jazz music filled the first floor all throughout the night, which served as the perfect backdrop to delicious food, great wine, and fulfilling conversations. Even Abigail couldn't help but smile the whole night, being surrounded by people she deeply cared about. When it was getting later in the night and the kids were growing sleepy, Brennan told Abigail to stay downstairs and have fun while he tended to the girls. "It's your night, honey," he said. "Let me do all the work."

Brennan had really gone the extra mile, booking her favorite catering company and inviting all of her closest friends, even the ones he wasn't particularly fond of. It was as if he wanted to show her that she really was still worth all of the effort. She gave him a smile and told him, "Thank you. I didn't expect this, but thank you."

"Don't thank me yet. I've got another gift for you. But I'll give it to you later when everyone leaves."

"I wonder what that could be," she said with a sly grin on her face.

It was the first time that she and Brennan had had that kind of playful banter in the longest time.

As the party journeyed deeper into the night, guests began to trickle out bit by bit. Before they knew it, the clock had struck eleven, and it was just the two of them again in the middle of a quiet house.

"Let's finish off this bottle of wine," said Brennan, holding up a half-empty bottle in his hands. "It's practically good enough for two servings anyway. What do you say?"

"Okay, pour me a glass," replied Abigail. The two of them sat across one another at the dining room table as they had for many years. Brennan poured wine into their glasses until every last drop of the bottle had been emptied. He took a big sip and stared at his glass for a while.

"So, did you have fun tonight?" he asked her.

"Yes, I did. Thanks for that. I wasn't expecting it."

"No problem at all. Everyone was happy to swing by for you. Everyone loves you," he said as he flashed a gentle grin at her. "Anyway, as promised, I still have one more gift for you."

"And what would that be?"

"Well, I've given even more thought to everything that we've been talking about. While I may not be too comfortable with it, I love you too much to not give you what you want."

"What does that mean?" asked Abigail as she placed her wine glass down on the table.

"I'm ready to give you what you want. Everything. No ground rules. No terms. Let's do it. Let's have an open relationship," he said with a blank face.

"Are you sure, Brennan? You're not just kidding around?"

"Actually, I do have one rule. I don't want to know about any of the details. I wouldn't be able to handle it."

"What do you mean? You don't want to talk about it?"

"No. Let's say we adopt a 'don't ask, don't tell' kind of policy."

"Well," said Abigail with a confounded look on her face. "I guess that's okay with me. But I think it might be a lot of fun for you and I to be talking about our experiences. I think that we could both learn from each other in the process. Don't you agree?"

"Please, honey. I'm already doing my best here. Don't force me to talk about it with you when you know how all of this makes me feel," he pleaded.

"Okay, I won't force you to do anything. But I really don't have a problem with talking about it because it isn't a big deal. We're just going around and meeting other people. Let's see what's out there."

"Thank you. I'm also willing to let you date other guys within the state. It was stupid for me to suggest otherwise. I'm sorry about that. But can we still find a way to make sure that other people won't know about our arrangement? That's still something that makes me really uncomfortable."

"You're right," she agreed. He looked up at her with his eyes wide open. "I also think that not a lot of people would understand or be too accepting of this new arrangement. Heck, even I don't really understand how I feel yet."

"Thank you. So, what did you have in mind? Any ideas on how we can keep this on the down low?"

"Well," she said. "I imagine that we'll exclusively be meeting people online on dating sites. It's not like we can ask our friends to introduce us to new people, right?"

"Yes, that sounds about right."

"Okay, so what if we just try to discreetly hide our identities on social media?" she suggested. "We could use blurred or low resolution photos. Maybe we can use aliases. What do you think?"

"That sounds like it could work." He nodded. "We should also have a series of standard questions to ask them just to make sure that they're not friends or family with anyone we might know."

"Okay, I think we can work that out," she agreed. "Anything else?"

"Well, if word ever does get out there about what we're doing, I think it's best that we try to spin it as if we're just cheating on each other. That would be easier to explain, don't you think?"

"Wow," said Abigail with her mouth wide open. "You're really getting into this, huh?"

"Like I said, I'm willing to do whatever it takes to make you happy."

She smiled at him and saw the sadness in his eyes. It was obviously eating him up inside to be having this conversation with her. That's when she felt a warmth of adoration for her husband. It was a feeling that she had not experienced for a long time, and she even found herself second-guessing her desires for an open relationship.

"Thank you so much for this," she told him. "I want you to know that I truly understand how hard this is for you. I really do. I know that I'm asking for a lot from you. But this is the only way I can see us being happy together again."

Chapter 19

Brennan

THAT SATURDAY, BRENNAN felt like he needed to get out of the house. Even though he told Abigail that he was willing to engage in this new arrangement of theirs, he was still uncomfortable with it. He had managed to convince Abigail that he never wanted to talk about their adventures. Every once in a while, Abigail would slip and tell him about her signing up on dating sites or messaging new people. Then Brennan would just prompt her to stop and tell her that he didn't want to know anything.

He exited the bedroom and headed downstairs where Abigail was preparing lunch for the family.

"Honey," he said. "I'm going to go out for groceries, okay? If I get home late, just go ahead and have lunch without me. I had a big breakfast anyway."

"Okay," she replied. "I'll text you some of the stuff I need for the house too. Be on the lookout."

"Alright."

Brennan got out of the house and into his car. As he pulled away from his driveway, he felt a sudden urge to cry. He hadn't really gotten a chance to express how uncomfortable he felt about the whole situation. He knew that if this was going to work, he needed to portray to Abigail that he was fully invested in the process. She needed to feel like he was supportive, and he was struggling to constantly tiptoe around her feelings.

"I just need to get out of the house, man," he told himself. "I'm the one who needs to breathe now."

He tapped on the guided meditation app on his phone and allowed it to talk him through mindful breathing as he drove to the grocery store. As he pulled into the store's parking lot, he saw that it was rather packed. He circled around the lot a couple of times in the hopes that he would be able to find a spot nearby. After the second tour around the lot, he decided that he would settle on a slot far away from the entrance. As he walked over to the front door of the supermarket, he saw a bunch of other guys walking to and from their cars as well. In spite of his better efforts, he couldn't help but picture these guys as potential mates for his wife.

"Brennan," he muttered under his breath. "Get a hold of yourself. Mindful breathing."

He tried his best to focus on his breathing. But he couldn't control it. Every single guy who passed him was a viable sexual companion for Abigail. He even started picturing them having sex with her one by one, and it made him sick to his stomach.

Brennan's heart was racing at this point. He looked down at his smartwatch and saw that his heart rate had indeed bumped up by a few beats per minute. He suddenly felt as if he were about to faint, and he had difficulty breathing. He got the sense that he was in the early stages of a panic attack, but he shrugged it off.

Brennan proceeded to walk to the front door of the supermarket, but the nausea he was experiencing only got worse. His breathing was even more labored now, and he could feel his skin growing hot. I need to get inside, he thought. He shuffled towards the door and thrust it open.

He felt somewhat relieved by the cool air-conditioning from the supermarket, but he still felt like his world was spinning.

Brennan scampered towards a spot on the wall where there were less people. He leaned his back against the wall and closed his eyes as he tried to focus on his breathing. No matter what he tried, the situation wasn't getting any better. The glare from the bright lights inside the supermarket hurt his eyes, and he felt his knees begin to buckle underneath him. He slowly slid down to a seated position with his back and head still leaning against the wall behind him. Brennan was sure at this point that people were staring at him, but he didn't want to open his eyes to see. All he wanted to do was focus on his breathing. His heart rate was still erratic, and he struggled to get oxygen into his lungs.

Brennan sat on the floor for a good five minutes before he felt any signs of improvement. His breathing wasn't as labored anymore, and his heartbeat began to regulate itself. However, he still felt an immense pain in his chest. It was as if someone had kicked him right in the middle of his sternum. There was a part of him that thought that he was having a genuine heart attack, but he threw that thought out of the window as his breathing slowly improved. Once he was able, he got back up on his feet and made his way back to the car to isolate himself from people. He was right. There were people who were staring at him. One person had approached him and asked, "Are you alright, sir? Should I call an ambulance?"

"No," replied Brennan. "I'm fine. I'm fine."

Once he was already inside the car, he turned the engine on and turned the AC to full blast. Brennan grabbed his phone and dialed Abigail. He was already crying at this point, and he didn't even realize it.

"Honey," he said dejectedly once she had picked up. "I don't feel too well."

"What? Brennan? What happened?"

"I don't feel well," he repeated. Brennan cried and tried his best to slow his breathing again. Once he had been able to regain some sense of calm, he recounted everything that had happened to him.

"Brennan," she said with a soothing voice. "Just breathe. You had a panic attack. Things are going to be okay. You just need to breathe."

"Talk to me, please. Tell me something. Take my mind off how I'm feeling."

"Okay," she obliged. "Uhm, I've been thinking lately about taking a trip one of these weekends. Would you be okay if I left you alone with the girls? I just thought it would be fun for me to get out of town on my own, even for just a bit."

"I don't think that I want to be hearing about your sexual adventures right now. In fact, it's the last thing that I want to hear." He squeezed the phone harder. "I've just had a panic attack thinking about all these hypothetical men sleeping with you. Hearing you plan things out for real is only going to add to my stress."

Abigail didn't say anything. There was a long silence between the two of them, and Brennan thought that the line had gone cold.

"Abigail?" he said. "Are you still there?"

"Okay," Abigail replied in a cold voice.

"Thank you. I think I'm getting better now. Can you continue to talk about something else?"

"You've really got some nerve, Brennan," said Abigail. She had taken a completely different tone now from when the phone call had started. "You manipulative and controlling bastard. This was all a part of your plan, wasn't it?"

"Abigail," said a flabbergasted Brennan. "What are you talking about?"

"You really didn't have any intentions of doing this with me, did you? You just made me believe that you were ready. Then, at your first opportunity, you would fake a panic attack to make me feel guilty about all of this. Brilliant plan you've got there, mister. Unfortunately for you, I'm not buying any of it. I'm a lot smarter than you give me credit for!"

"That wasn't my intention at all! I really wanted to give this a try! I didn't fake this panic attack to guilt you!"

"That's kind of hard to believe considering how controlling you've been since we first started having this discussion. Why would I ever believe that you've just suddenly had a change of heart?"

"Abigail, please. I'll come home and we can talk about this," he pleaded.

"Oh no you don't. You stay there and finish the grocery shopping. Panic attack or not, follow up on a promise for once."

The phone line went dead, and Brennan was left open-mouthed at what had just happened. His panic attack had gone away for sure, but now he was dealing with another set of complex emotions entirely.

"What just happened?" he said to himself out loud.

Chapter 20

Abigail

"THE NERVE OF that guy!" yelled Abigail as she threw her phone across the coffee table. She turned the TV off and cradled her head as she closed her eyes.

"What did you say, Momma?" asked Amber.

"Nothing, honey," she replied. "Momma just has a headache."

Abigail got up and walked over to her two kids, giving them both a bear hug. She kissed each of them on the forehead and went straight to the kitchen. She reached for a bottle of wine and poured herself a glass. He better remember to get some more wine, she thought. Abigail rested against the kitchen counter as she thought about Brennan and how angry the thought of him made her feel. If there was one thing she hated most in the world, it was being made out to look like a fool.

She closed her eyes and tried to keep her anger in check. At least I have some good wine to comfort me.

Chapter 21

Brennan

BRENNAN RETURNED HOME a couple of hours later. He took the grocery bags out of the car and headed towards the front door. When he opened the door, he didn't see anyone. They must have eaten lunch already.

He brought the grocery bags in one batch at a time and managed to unload everything after just a couple of roundtrips to the car. As he came back with the final batch of grocery bags, Abigail was already there in the living room.

"Can we talk?" he said.

She looked at him and said nothing. She merely stood there and stared at him for a good while before turning her back and making her way up the stairs. Brennan then heard the slam of their bedroom door.

I guess she doesn't want to talk, he thought to himself. He always hated it whenever they would get into arguments like this. Brennan was the kind of guy who was normally comfortable with conflict. He always wanted to find a resolution to problems whenever they presented themselves.

Now he felt as if his heart sank at the sight of his own helplessness. A wave of emotions overcame him right on the spot as he stood in his tracks. He closed his eyes again just as he had numerous times during that day and tried to breathe. Brennan never liked knowing that someone felt anger towards him, most especially his wife. He didn't want to just stand there and do nothing.

Brennan went back out of the house and into his car. He decided to visit a nearby strip mall and buy a few things for Abigail. He pulled into a parking slot and made a mental note of everything that he needed to buy while he was there. In a span of just thirty minutes, Brennan had managed to return to his car with a huge teddy bear, a bouquet of flowers, and a blank card with a romantic theme to it. He grabbed a pen out of his bag and began writing a note.

"My love," he wrote. "I'm sorry for making you mad. This new arrangement is completely new to me, and I'm still adjusting. I promise I'll be better. For you. For us. For always. Love, Brennan."

He stuffed the card into its accompanying red envelope and taped it on the bouquet, then drove back home and pulled into the driveway. He wanted to play it cool and surprise his wife with the gifts, so he walked in the house without making a sound. He quietly crept to the second floor hallway with all of her gifts and left them right outside their bedroom door. He crept back downstairs and sat on the couch to catch his breath. Brennan grabbed his phone and sent a text to Abigail.

"Honey, I left you a peace offering outside the door. Please check if you're ready."

After sending the text, he sat for a while and waited for any signs of movement from upstairs. Nothing happened at first, but Brennan continued to sit in silence as he waited for Abigail to bite. Around ten minutes passed without any signs of movement and Brennan was getting restless. Just as he was about to go upstairs to check, he heard the sound of the bedroom door opening. He sat there and waited for what Abigail's next move was going to be. After a few seconds of waiting, he heard the bedroom door slam shut.

Then his phone lit up with Abigail's name flashing on the notification screen.

"I don't want a stupid teddy bear! You better return it!"

Chapter 22

Brennan

A FEW DAYS had passed and Brennan was in the middle of a shower when he heard Abigail giggle from inside the bedroom. He knew what she was doing and why she was laughing. In fact, she had been giggling and laughing like that the whole week.

On Monday, he had arrived home to a wife whose face was completely covered in makeup. On Tuesday, he walked in on her watching makeup and style tutorial videos on YouTube. On Thursday, he saw her used workout clothes in the laundry hamper. He couldn't even recall the last time he saw his wife do any sort of exercise.

But more than just the changes in her behavior on her own, he also noticed that there was a change in the way that she treated him as well. On Monday, she apologized to him for overreacting with the teddy bear, and she told him that she found the note to be sweet. She even gave him a soft kiss on the forehead before he left for work. Abigail appeared to be a lot kinder to him now, and she was smiling a lot more than she had been over the previous weeks.

There truly was something different about her, and Brennan knew that it was all the result of their new arrangement. There were times throughout the week where he would hear her conversing on the phone over hushed tones so that he couldn't make out what she was saying. Her phone was also constantly abuzz with message notifications, especially during the night when the two of them were already in bed. It had been that way all week, and he knew it was what was responsible for the uptick in her mood. During these moments, Brennan had never felt lonelier.

Brennan let the water from the showerhead rain all over him as he accepted that this was going to be the new normal for their relationship. He felt a heavy weight in his heart as he pictured his wife laughing while talking to another guy. And yet, there was another feeling that was tingling inside him as well. He felt his heart rate quicken and become more pronounced. Then he looked downward and saw that his manhood began to gradually rise in rhythm with his heartbeat. He felt his body get really warm as he slid down and grasped his erection with his right hand and gently stroked it in a soft pumping motion. He gradually picked up speed until his leg muscles stiffened and his knees buckled. Brennan then reached for the soap and washed his groin area thoroughly to get rid of any residual sticky substances. He felt a huge wave of satisfaction sweep over him, but then it was immediately followed up by a wave of awkward sadness.

He turned the shower off and grabbed a towel to begin drying himself. As he patted himself dry, he thought about what kind of marriage he had allowed his relationship to become. He had never envisioned himself as being in a marriage with this kind of arrangement. In spite of his reputation during his more juvenile years, Brennan had really grown up to embrace a monogamous lifestyle so long as it was with Abigail. The irony didn't escape him that a younger version of himself would have jumped at the opportunity to get into an open relationship with a beautiful girl. But he was no longer the young man that he once was. He had had a change of perspective, and he didn't like the road that his marriage had taken.

None of this was what he wanted. He felt his brows stiffen as he thought about what his wife had talked him into agreeing. He felt violated and manipulated, but he couldn't do anything about it. Brennan was growing hot with rage at the idea of allowing Abigail to bully him into agreeing to this kind of setup for their family.

He changed into his sleepwear and walked out of the bathroom. Abigail was seated at her vanity station with her head down over her phone. She was texting with someone again, and Brennan forced himself to not pay her any attention.

He headed straight to bed and closed his eyes. He knew that he couldn't go to sleep angry and so he decided to start focusing on his breath again. Before he knew it, he was knocked out cold.

That night, Brennan had a dream. He dreamt that he was an old man and already on his deathbed. He looked up and saw a bunch of tubes and wires all hooked up to various parts of his body. He could see from the window in his room that the sun was slowly setting and that night was coming soon. His nurse walked into the room and told him that there was someone outside who wanted to see him.

"It's your wife, sir," said the nurse. "She says that she wants to talk to you."

"Well," replied Brennan, "tell her that I don't want to talk to her. Tell her that I never want to see her ever again."

"Are you sure, sir? You might not know when she'll come back."

"I hope she never comes back. I never want to see her again."

Brennan woke up the next morning with an unusually

high amount of energy. He looked over and saw Abigail was still in a deep sleep. That's when he realized that the anger he felt towards her wasn't anger at all. It was jealousy. He was jealous at how much she was enjoying this whole process while he remained miserable. Although he got the feeling that this day was going to be the start of a big change for him. He wasn't going to be content on just playing along and allowing Abigail to have all of the fun on her own. If she was going to go around having fun with other guys, then he thought he might as well make the most out of the opportunity to have fun as well.

He told himself that he should stop thinking about Abigail sleeping with other men and instead focusing on how it would feel to be with another woman. He got excited by the thought. He hadn't felt another woman close since before he met Abigail. He started thinking about undressing another woman and touching her body. He smiled.

He grabbed his razor and put some extra time into carefully shaping his beard to accentuate his jawline. Once he was content with the outcome, he put the razor away and reached for his facial soap.

He looked over to his wife's arsenal of skincare products and compared it with his. He realized that he had never paid much attention to his looks since he had gotten married and that it was time to change that. Brennan made a mental note to look up skincare products for men later on in the day. For the first time in the longest time, he was the one with some pep in his step now. He felt excited about starting the day and going to work.

After washing his face, Brennan dried himself off and went downstairs to make breakfast for the whole family. He decided to cook up a bunch of pancakes to go together with some classic bacon and eggs. While waiting for the bacon to finish frying, he hopped on his phone and started researching skincare products he could use to treat the lines that were forming on his face. Once he settled on a few products that he thought would work for him, he placed an order for them right away.

Breakfast was ready, and Brennan finished preparing the table with placemats, plates, and utensils. Then he ran upstairs and woke Abigail up.

"Good morning, honey. I made breakfast. Get your butt down there. I'll wake the kids and get them ready."

"Hi, good morning," she replied. "You made breakfast, did you? So that's why it smells so good."

"It'll taste just as good as it smells, I guarantee that. Now get down there while I go get the kids."

Brennan planted a kiss on her forehead and made his way towards the girls' room. He gently nudged Amber first as she was the easier one to wake up.

"Good morning, Daddy," she whispered with her eyes still half-closed.

"Good morning, sunshine," he whispered back. "It's time for you and your sister to wake up. Daddy has a surprise for you."

"Surprise?" she said, now fully awake. "What surprise?"

"Daddy made your favorite. Pancakes for breakfast!"

"Yay!" rejoiced Amber. Riley heard the commotion in the room and began to stir herself.

"Riley!" Amber yelled at her sister. "Wake up, wake up! Daddy made pancakes!"

Riley couldn't be bothered as she turned away from them and drew her blanket tighter.

"Oh, come on, honey. You're going to love Daddy's pancakes," Brennan said as he scooped a defiant Riley and a giddy Abigail up into his arms. "Mommy's already downstairs. Remember to give her a kiss when you see her."

Brennan and the girls descended the staircase to find Abigail already seated at her place at the table.

"Momma! Momma!" exclaimed Amber as she ran towards Abigail. "Daddy said he made pancakes!"

"He sure did, sweetie," replied Abigail. "Daddy put a

lot of effort into breakfast this morning. Have you girls thanked Daddy already?"

"Thank you, Daddy!" said an excited Amber. Riley was still drowsy but was beginning to regain consciousness from the aroma of freshly cooked pancakes.

There was an unusual level of energy at that breakfast table that had not been there for a long time now. Brennan could see the difference and it was palpable. Abigail was happy and smiling, not just at their kids but towards him as well. He felt a certain warmth from her that was missing from their marriage for as long as he could recall. He smiled back at her and mouthed the words, "I love you."

"So what is everyone waiting for?" asked Brennan. "Dig in!"

The girls got straight to work on their pancakes as Abigail helped both of them squeeze some maple syrup onto their plates. Brennan helped himself to a hefty serving of bacon and eggs. He had worked up quite an appetite working on breakfast that morning.

"Listen, girls," said Brennan as he struggled to talk in between chews. "Daddy can't stay too long for breakfast, okay? I have to go to the office now. I hope you enjoy breakfast. Do you like the pancakes?"

"Yeeeeaah!" replied the two little girls who were now both wide awake.

"I enjoyed them too," added Abigail.

Brennan got up from the table to go back upstairs, brush his teeth, and change into his work clothes. While picking out his outfit, he decided to sit and pause for a while. He usually just grabbed whatever he thought would pair best at first glance. This time, he paid attention to how the colors of his shirts and trousers would complement each other. Brennan also contemplated throwing on a nice blazer since he knew that it was going to get chilly that day.

He finally settled on a crisp white poplin shirt paired with a pair of navy chinos. He layered a matching navy blazer over his shirt and completed his look with his favorite pair of Oxfords from his shoe rack. Before leaving the room, Brennan eyed himself in the mirror and felt strange. It was like he was looking at a man he had never met before. He couldn't even recall the last time he had taken a few seconds out of the day to look into a mirror and admire how he looked.

Brennan made his way back downstairs to say goodbye to the girls before heading off to work.

"Wow," exclaimed Amber. "Daddy, you look so handsome!"

"You look so handsome, Daddy!" repeated Riley.

"They're right," agreed Abigail. "You look really good. What's gotten into you this morning?"

"Thank you, family. Although, does this mean that I've never looked handsome before?"

"You're always handsome, Daddy," replied Amber. "You're just a lot handsomer now!"

"I'll take it," said Brennan with a sheepish grin on his face.

"No, really," said Abigail who had been smiling the entire time. "What's gotten into you?"

"I don't know," said Brennan. "I guess a change of perspective."

"Well, whatever it is, it suits you," replied Abigail.

Just as he was about to leave, he heard Abigail's phone ring. He took a final glance at her before exiting the door and saw that she was reading a message. Brennan knew that it was probably from some guy that she was talking to. He refused to acknowledge it. He pushed the thought out of his head and instead started to think about any cute girl he had seen lately.

"Bye, girls!" he yelled from the front door. "Have a good day today and see you after work!"

Brennan walked over to the car and caught his reflection again in his windows. He couldn't help but stop to admire how he looked one last time before stepping into the driver's seat. This was as energized as he had felt in a very long time.

On his commute to work, he encountered the usual rush hour traffic, and not a single frown or snarl crossed his face the entire time. The positive energy of the morning stayed with him throughout his commute.

He parked his car in his usual slot at the office's indoor parking lot on the fourth floor and made his way to the elevators. His office nested on the twenty-fifth floor of the thirty-story building.

The building served as a home to a variety of companies including a law firm, a marketing agency, a media agency, and an accounting firm. As he entered the elevator, he locked eyes with a young brunette dressed in a sleek navy blazer and matching pencil skirt. Underneath her blazer was a pastel pink blouse that was unbuttoned at the collar. She wore smokey eye makeup and let her wavy brown hair fall down onto her shoulders. The girl looked at Brennan and gave him a smile. He smiled back at her as he noticed that the lanyard around her neck had the logo of the accounting firm in the office building.

"What floor?" the girl asked him.

"I'm sorry, what?" Brennan replied.

"What floor are you going to?" she reiterated. "You didn't press a button on the elevator."

"Oh, right," Brennan gushed.

He tapped the number twenty-five on the elevator control board and situated himself beside the woman.

She smiled at him again and said, "Twenty-fifth floor. I'm guessing you work for that tech company, right?"

"TransTech Global, yes," replied Brennan. "And you work for SGB accounting," he said as he gestured towards her company ID.

"Yup," she nodded. "My name's Kate."

"Hi, Kate," he replied with an outstretched hand. "Brennan."

They shook hands and smiled at each other. Brennan couldn't help but notice the softness of her palm against his as they shook. "Listen," he said. "If SGB needs to upgrade its accounting systems, you give us a visit upstairs."

"Will do," she giggled.

The elevator stopped at the seventeenth floor and the doors slowly swung open.

"Well," said Kate. "This is me. Maybe you can give me your card in case we do need a new IT firm to handle our software needs?"

"Oh, right," replied Brennan. "Where is my mind at today?" He took out his wallet and handed Kate his business card. "Give me a call anytime."

"Alright," she said with a smile. Brennan smiled back while Kate walked away as the elevator doors closed behind her.

Chapter 23

Abigail

ABIGAIL PULLED HER phone away from her face and checked how she looked on the screen. She tilted her head at a slight angle and rounded her eyes before clicking on the shutter button. After taking a couple of shots at the same angle, she checked her phone to see if she would be happy with the results. Her face sulked as she reviewed the output of her efforts.

Somehow, Abigail knew that the photos were less than pleasant and that they didn't do her much justice. She raised her phone once again but from a different angle now. This time, she exaggerated the tilt of her head even further and lessened the rounding of her eyes. She smiled, snapped the photo a few times, and immediately went back to review the results. Again, she wasn't happy with what she was looking at.

Maybe it's the lighting, she thought to herself. Her facial expression seemed okay, and the head tilt improved how she looked to a certain degree. But she thought the photo was all pixelated.

Abigail ran to the living room where she knew she

could get the most natural light for her shots. Much better, she thought as she tilted her head and puffed her lips and snapped another photo. When she reviewed the photos she took, she realized how pale she looked against the natural light.

Abigail ran back upstairs to the bedroom and sat at her vanity table to put on a little makeup. She applied just a thin layer of foundation before highlighting her lips with a light rosy tint. After that, she grabbed a darker shade of rose and lightly smeared it on her cheeks. She rubbed the tint into her cheeks and spread it out evenly so that it looked like a natural blush. After she was done, she took a glance at the mirror and liked what she saw, then ran back down the stairs and into the living room to test out a few more shots.

She sent some of her favorite photos out to the different guys she had been communicating with and felt her heart racing with excitement and a slight bit of anxiety. She had been anxious about putting herself out there like this, but she knew that this was what she had to do. Every few seconds or so, she would glance down at her phone and refresh the page to see if she had gotten any replies. She decided to put the phone away for the meantime because her heart was beating uncontrollably fast from all the anxiety.

Brennan was still at work, and the kids were taking their afternoon nap. Abigail thought about doing a quick yoga session while the house was quiet. She had been consciously trying to get in better shape, but she lacked the time to get in a proper workout during the day. Just as she was about to hop on YouTube to search for some instructional yoga class videos, she saw a notification pop up from one of the guys she had been messaging.

"Looking good," wrote Martin, a guy from Nevada. He owned his own contracting company, but she knew that the distance between them would make it difficult for them to get serious. Although she still enjoyed the fact that

Martin was persistent in messaging her. She felt her face turn hot and giggled to herself as she read and reread Martin's message over and over again.

"Thank you," she replied. Abigail placed her phone back down and then got another beep. Assuming that it was Martin again, she was eager to see what his follow-up message would be. Instead, it was Maverick, a real estate agent from Minnesota. She never found him attractive and wasn't interested in meeting him even though they were in the same state, but she still liked the attention he gave her.

"Did you get your hair done? You're gorgeous!" he wrote her.

She gushed and smiled as she reread Maverick's message over and over again too. "No," she replied. "Didn't get my hair done. Just lounging around the house."

"Wish I could come over," he replied.

"Oh, stop!"

Abigail had completely forgotten about searching for yoga classes. It seemed that her efforts to take better pictures of herself were paying off. She was floating and getting high off the praise she was receiving. I haven't felt this beautiful in a long time, she thought.

Abigail grabbed her iPad and opened the YouTube app. Instead of searching for yoga classes, she typed how to take the best selfies. She was greeted with a variety of videos, a vast majority of them from female content creators giving their various takes on how to take the perfect selfie.

Abigail first settled on a video from an influencer named Jessica who had more than a million subscribers to her channel. The first thing that Jessica started talking about was the importance of lighting in taking photos. By watching the video, Abigail learned that if she didn't have access to professional lighting equipment, then natural light was the way to go. She wasn't interested in spending too much money on buying professional-grade light, so this was a valuable tip for her.

She continued watching the video and learned more tricks about capturing selfies, like making sure that she was always centered and different apps that she could use to edit her photos after the fact. Abigail hadn't even realized that she could manipulate her photos after taking them. She clicked on another video entitled "Top Photo Editing Apps for Selfies." Abigail spent the rest of the afternoon practicing her editing skills on the photos that she had taken earlier that day.

Around a few minutes before 4:00 p.m., Abigail could hear the girls calling for her from their bedroom. She put her phone down and checked the clock, doing a double-take just to be sure about the time. She darted up the stairs and went straight into the girls' room. Riley was already crying, and Amber was asking for a particular toy that she couldn't find. Abigail rifled through Amber's chest of toys looking for her stuffed porcupine while Riley's cries had regressed to mere sniffles. She found the porcupine and handed it to Amber.

"Thank you, Momma," she said.

Riley let out a whimper as if she were about to start crying again, and Abigail swept her up into her arms before she could do so.

"Why don't we go downstairs for a snack?"

Both girls nodded their heads enthusiastically, and Amber jumped straight into her mother's free arm without letting go of her toy porcupine. Abigail carried both of her girls down the stairs and set them up on the kitchen table, then went over to the stove and began heating up some milk for some hot chocolate.

As she waited for the milk to get hot, she browsed through an article on her phone about makeup tips that she could use on her future selfies. The article said that men were more likely to message girls who looked like they put a little bit of effort into their makeup. However, that same article also mentioned that men tended to stay away from women whose faces were completely covered by thick makeup because they felt like these girls couldn't be trusted. Abigail had her eyes focused on her phone screen until Amber caught her attention.

"Momma!" she yelled. "The milk!"

Abigail looked down at the pot on the stove and saw that the milk was already boiling and starting to overflow. She quickly turned the stove off and grabbed a rag to clean the milk that had spilt over, then Abigail waited for it to cool a bit before serving it to the girls in their cups. She also laid out a plate of animal crackers.

As the girls were kept busy by their snacks, Abigail started reading an article about filters that were built into certain camera apps. She learned that these filters would enable her to manipulate her photo in real time as it was being taken.

Abigail quickly downloaded some of the recommended apps and tried them out. She saw that some of the filters were fun and quirky, but she was afraid that the men who saw them wouldn't take her seriously. She also saw that there were a few features that exaggerated her looks and made them seem too fake. It was a learning process for her, and she was having a lot of fun exploring this new world that she had never ventured into before.

Checking the clock once more, she put the phone down after realizing that she needed to start getting dinner ready. Brennan would be home in a couple of hours, and she hadn't even started defrosting any of the meats. It dawned on her that she had just spent an entire afternoon figuring out how to take photos of herself, and she couldn't help but let out a chuckle.

"Why are you laughing, Mommy?" asked Riley.

"Oh, nothing, darling," she replied. "Mommy just thought about a joke. Do you girls want to go to your play area now?"

"Yes, please!" cried an exuberant Amber who was eager to get back to her toys. She had been eyeing the playpen the whole time she was drinking her milk.

Abigail lifted her girls out of their booster seats and brought them to their play area. She stood there for a while and watched as Riley hobbled over to the dollhouse. She felt a warmth of affection sweep over her as her girls played with the toys. They're so beautiful, she thought. And they came from me. Abigail felt a tear forming in her right eye and quickly wiped it away before it could fall. For the first time in a long time, she was proud of herself for giving birth to two beautiful girls. More importantly, she was proud of coming around to believe in her own beauty as well.

Brennan arrived shortly after 6:00 p.m., and Abigail was putting the finishing touches on dinner. She turned around to take a look at Brennan as he entered their home. He was still just as cheery and as energetic as he had been when he left for work that morning.

"Hi, girls!" he said as he bent down to give Amber and Riley a hug. "What did you do today?"

"I drew a picture!" declared Amber as she held up a sheet of paper for Brennan to examine.

"Wow, that's beautiful, sweetheart!" he replied. "And what have you been up to, little princess?"

"I played with the dollhouse and helped Barbie decorate her bedroom!"

"Wow," he said with excitement. "Can Daddy see?"

"No!" replied an adamant Riley. "It's not done yet."

"Oh, okay. Well, when it's done, let Daddy see it, okay?"

"Okay," replied Riley.

"It looks like Mommy's been pretty busy too," he said loud enough to make sure that Abigail could hear him. "It smells really good in here, hun!"

"Thanks, Brennan," she replied from the kitchen. "Dinner will be ready in a few. Go ahead and get settled down first."

Brennan went up the stairs and into their bedroom as

Abigail slowly drizzled gravy over the meatloaf that she had just pulled fresh from the oven and topped with bits of fried garlic. By the time Brennan came back down the stairs, all of the food was already on the table, and Abigail was opening a bottle of wine.

"Oh," said Brennan. "We're having wine tonight, are we?"

"Just to keep the positive energy going," she replied. "So how was work today?"

"Same old. This one client has been a real hell-raiser, and a bunch of my team members are really on edge. What about you?"

"Well, I've been learning a lot today actually. But we can talk about that later. Tell me more about this client of yours."

After what had seemed like many eons, the Suttons had a regular family dinner with just themselves that didn't involve awkward silences or forced one-word answers. Abigail asked Brennan lots of questions about the stuff that he had been dealing with at work while she filled him in on her adventures with the girls. Eventually, the wine ran out, and the two of them were laughing about a funny remark that Riley said. Riley told her family that she wanted to be a cow when she grew up, so that she could just keep giving herself milk whenever she wanted. The entire family laughed alongside her as she continued to justify her dreams of becoming a cow.

Brennan lifted both girls out of their high chairs and into his arms as he disappeared onto the second floor. Abigail began gathering the dishes and placed each of them into the sink. She then propped her phone up on the shelf just above the sink and streamed an instructional video on YouTube about natural makeup techniques. While she scrubbed the oil and grime away from the dinner plates, she was also focusing on the nuances of matching lipsticks to eyeshadows.

After putting away the last of the dishes, she darted up

the stairs and headed straight to her vanity table to try out some of the techniques that she had just learned online. One of the videos taught her a particular technique that would make her cheekbones look more prominent. She got right to work on contouring her face and following every instruction that she could remember from the YouTube video.

Brennan suddenly walked into the bedroom and saw her putting makeup on. He had a puzzled look on his face and asked, "You heading out?"

"No," she replied. "I told you that I spent the whole day just learning about new stuff. I'm putting all of those lessons into practice now."

"So, you've been learning how to put on your makeup? Haven't you always known how to do that?" he said in a teasing manner.

"The learning never stops, Brennan," she replied, playing along with his joke.

"Well, as much as I would love to sit and watch you apply what you've learned today, I have to go back to the girls' room. I promised I would read to them," he said.

"Go ahead," said Abigail as she continued to contour her cheeks. "Don't worry about me. I'll keep myself busy."

Abigail placed her contouring brush down and examined her own work. Not bad, she thought to herself. She didn't have the same exact tools that the person in the instructional video was using, but she made do with what she had.

She smiled at her own reflection, admiring her work as she tilted her head from one angle to the next, then took a few photos of herself to document her new skills. Once she was content with the shots that she took, she walked to the bathroom and washed all the makeup off her face.

As she was cleaning her face, her phone started buzzing on the counter. She picked it up and saw that another one of the guys she'd been messaging with finally replied to her selfie photos.

"Looking forward to seeing this pretty face in person," replied Greg. He was another guy from Minnesota in a town that wasn't too far from Minneapolis, where Abigail lived. Out of all the guys she had been messaging, Greg was the one she felt she was most likely to actually meet in person. A huge smile swept across her damp face as she drafted a reply.

"Maybe soon," she texted back with a winking emoji.

She reread Greg's message and giggled to herself as she stood in front of the bathroom mirror. Abigail put her phone down and stared at her barefaced reflection. You're still beautiful after all, she told herself.

After doing her usual bedtime skincare routine, she lay in bed with her iPad and watched more makeup tutorial videos, taking note of all the makeup tools and gear that were being recommended. Before going to sleep, she hopped onto Amazon and ordered a bunch of the makeup that she had written down. Just as she was finishing up her online purchase, Brennan walked through the door and saw her smiling at her phone.

"What are you so giddy about?" he asked.

"Just buying some stuff online. I'm excited for them to get here," she replied.

"Oh no. What stuff?"

"Makeup," she replied, still smiling.

Brennan laughed and started walking towards the bathroom.

"What?" she asked. "Why are you laughing?"

"I don't know," he said. "I've never seen you this happy about buying makeup I guess."

"Well, maybe you just haven't seen me this happy in a long time."

"You're right," he said with a more serious tone. "And you're really pretty when you're happy."

She smiled and looked at him for a moment before he continued his walk towards the bathroom.

"I need to take a bath. You don't have to wait up for

me," he said.

"Okay," she replied. "I think I'm going to turn in. I feel so sleepy all of a sudden. Goodnight, Brennan."

Abigail woke up the next morning and turned on her side only to find that Brennan wasn't in bed. She dragged herself of the bedroom and went to check on the kids. Both Amber and Riley were still fast asleep in their beds. She quietly made her way down the stairs and into the kitchen to find a note on the table. It was from Brennan.

"Had to leave for work early. I made pancakes. They're in the oven."

The morning was quiet. In a home that housed two female toddlers this was a very rare occasion. Abigail felt unsettled at how quiet it was and decided to play some music on her phone. She didn't know what she wanted to listen to, in particular, but she just wanted something to fill the gaps between the noise.

The Spotify app recommended an 80s playlist for her to listen to. Suddenly, the intro to U2's hit song "With or Without You" came on. Abigail took a breath and closed her eyes as she listened to Bono's soothing voice serenade her over breakfast. She took a bite of the pancakes that Brennan had prepared and couldn't believe how fluffy they were. It was like taking a bite out of a marshmallow. She washed the pancakes down with a good swig of orange juice.

After the strums of The Edge's guitar gradually faded away to signal the conclusion of the song, on came the prominent sound of a saxophone. This was a song that Abigail was very much familiar with. Her eyes lit up as she grabbed her phone to increase the volume. The voice of Glenn Medeiros suddenly came to life and began serenading her with a classic ballad from her childhood. Abigail was jolted with memories of her pre-teen self hearing this song on the radio and listening to it with her family. As if from instinct, without her even realizing it, she began singing along with Glenn and was surprised to discover that she still knew all of the words. This aroused a feeling of nostalgia in her that she rarely ever entertained.

Abigail thought back to the younger version of herself who used to listen to these songs on the radio on Saturday mornings with her family. She thought about how happy and full of energy she used to be.

Remembering the vitality of her younger self brought a sudden surge of energy to Abigail's morning. She ate the last of her pancakes and downed what was left of her orange juice, then brought the dishes to the sink and felt a certain melancholy as the water touched her skin. She was happy for having built the life that she had, but she also yearned for the innocence and vigor that accompanied her youth.

She felt herself becoming separated from her body. Abigail imagined her own spirit hovering above her as she did the dishes. She felt like she was being judged and observed by her own subconscious. As a child, whenever she would watch television shows that depicted female characters as housewives who were relegated to doing laundry, cooking meals, and washing dishes, she always laughed. She swore to herself that she would never allow herself to have that kind of life. Yet, there she was, washing the dishes and being the housewife Maybe this is why I've been so unhappy, she thought to herself. Maybe not everyone is cut out for this. Abigail continued to do the dishes as a tear slowly rolled down her face with Glenn Medeiros crooning in the background.

Chapter 24

Brennan

IT WAS A Thursday night, and Karen, Vince, Megan, and Phillip were all coming over for dinner. Brennan had to leave work early because Abigail asked him to pick up a few last-minute items from the supermarket. "As always," Brennan groaned to himself as he drove to the store. "She always puts so much pressure on herself when hosting dinners like these."

By the time he got home, he saw Abigail already slaving away at the kitchen counter. She was slicing up the vegetables and spices while a stew was simmering on the stove. A wave of 80s music was streaming through the entire first floor while the kids were locked in their play area. "Hey, guys!" Brennan declared. "Dad's home!"

"Hi, Brennan," said Abigail without taking her attention off the kitchen counter.

Brennan proceeded to the kitchen and unloaded the bag of groceries. Abigail grabbed hold of the carrots that Brennan brought and immediately began slicing them.

"What are you making anyway?" asked Brennan.

"Beef casserole," replied Abigail. "And I'm nowhere

near finished. Did you get the bottle of wine like I asked?"

"I got three," proclaimed Brennan as he held up the wine. "Just in case we need more."

"Thanks."

She went right back to focusing on slicing vegetables, and Brennan went to say hi to the kids.

"Hey, girls," he said as he crouched over to give them both a hug. "Did Mommy tell you that we're going to have a party tonight?"

"Yes," said Amber. "But Mommy said that it's going to be a grown-up party and that there won't be any clowns or magicians."

"That's right," replied Brennan. "It's going to be a boring grown-up party. Will you girls behave yourselves?"

"Yes, Daddy" replied both girls who had lost interest in the conversation the moment Brennan confirmed that there wouldn't be any clowns.

He headed upstairs to change into a nice dinner-party outfit, putting on a light-blue Oxford shirt to go along with a pair of black jeans. Brennan did a quick head-to-toe of his outfit through the bathroom mirror and thought that he looked presentable enough for dinner.

He checked his watch and saw that their guests would probably start arriving in a few minutes. Quickly spraying some cologne on his wrists, he rubbed them together before smearing the sides of his neck. He did another quick glance at the mirror and headed back downstairs.

Abigail had done wonders in the time that he was gone. The kitchen counter was a far cry from the mess that it was when Brennan first arrived. In lieu of a jungle of chopped vegetables and spices, the kitchen counter now housed clean plates of assorted cheeses and cold cuts.

"Good job with dinner, honey," remarked Brennan. "Can I start bringing some of these to the dinner table?"

"Yes, please," replied Abigail. "I'm just putting some finishing touches on the casserole and the pasta. They should be arriving any minute now. You can open a bottle of wine and keep them company. I have to go upstairs and change after I finish cooking. I smell like tomatoes and garlic."

"Alright, honey," said Brennan. He noticed that she was rambling, something she often did when she was nervous.

Brennan could feel the tension building up in the household as well. This was going to be the first dinner that they would host ever since they made their agreement. Neither of them had any plans to reveal their situation to their friends. Still, being in this new setup in their marriage was like being in a new relationship altogether. There were a lot of things to be nervous about.

At Abigail's suggestion, Brennan opened up a bottle of wine so that it had time to breathe before the guests would arrive. He poured himself a glass and sat on the living room couch as he observed the girls playing. It seemed like they were in the thick of a romantic drama involving their dolls and stuffed toys. Amber was calling all of the shots while she struggled to get Riley to cooperate with her storyline. Brennan laughed as he tried to follow along when he heard a car approaching their house. He peeked outside the window and recognized Vince and Megan's car gradually pulling into the curb.

Brennan placed his wineglass down on the coffee table and told Abigail that Vince and Megan were already there. Abigail, who had just finished plating the food, removed her apron and ran upstairs to change. Brennan put on his dinner jacket and opened the door to greet his friends. Surprisingly, Brennan only saw Vince step out of the car, and there was no sign of Megan.

"Hey, man!" said Brennan as he held his arms out for a hug. "Is it just you? Where's Megan?"

Vince hugged Brennan and replied, "Yeah, it's just me. Megan's got some stuff to do tonight. Out of the blue. You know how it is."

"Aw, that's a bummer," remarked Brennan. "Well,

come on in. I've just popped open a delicious Spanish cabernet from 2002."

Vince and Brennan stepped through the door and into the foyer where Brennan offered to take Vince's coat. Vince then went over to say hi to the kids as Brennan poured another glass of wine.

The two men situated themselves on the living room couch and talked about work as they waited for their other friends to arrive. After a few minutes of talking, Abigail descended the stairs looking like she was dressed for a fancy cocktail party. She had her hair tied up in a neat bun and she wore a black cocktail dress that accentuated her curves.

"Wow," exclaimed Vince. "You're looking gorgeous, Abigail!"

"Hey, that's my wife, buddy!" joked Brennan. "But he's right. You look stunning, hun."

"Oh, Vince. Don't mind Brennan. It's nice for a woman to receive a compliment every once in a while," gushed Abigail. She went over to Vince and gave him a hug before making herself comfortable on the couch with the boys. "Where's Megan?" she asked. "Isn't she joining us tonight?"

"She sends her apologies," replied Vince. "She had some stuff pop up that she can't ignore. She said she was sorry and that she was sure you had cooked up a feast."

"As always," chimed Brennan.

"So, what's on the menu tonight?" asked Vince.

"Beef casserole, aglio olio, and cold cuts," replied Abigail.

"My stomach's grumbling already," said Vince just before the doorbell rang.

"Oh, that must be Karen and Phillip. They said that they were coming together," commented Abigail. "They should just date already."

"It would never work," joked a laughing Vince. "They'd kill each other."

Brennan went to the door to welcome their final guests for the night. Karen was dressed in a plain white t-shirt that she tucked into a pair of striped trousers. Phillip looked like he had just come from the office with his hair slicked over to one side and a bottle of red wine in hand. He wore a blue gingham shirt that was tucked into a pair of navy chinos that went along with his dark chocolate Derbies.

"Hey, everyone!" said Karen. "Are we late?"

"Yeah, sorry! It's my fault. Got a little caught up at the office tonight," said Phillip.

"No, not at all," replied Brennan. "Come in!"

"Before anyone asks," said Vince as Karen and Phillip made their way over to the living room, "Megan couldn't come tonight. She had something pop up out of the blue. But she sends her best wishes."

"Aw, that's a bummer!" remarked Karen.

"Hey, it's alright. Let's all have fun tonight, shall we?" said Phillip as he held up his bottle of wine.

"Put that down," said Brennan. "I've just uncorked a bottle here."

"Damn, Abigail," said Phillip. "If we have these dinners too frequently, I might have to start buying bigger pants! I always overeat when it's your cooking."

"That's the goal, Phillip." She smiled mischievously at him.

Phillip, Karen, Vince, and Brennan all made their way towards the dining table as Abigail got the girls and fixed them up in their high chairs. She gave them the iPad to keep them distracted as she prepared their mashed carrots and thin slices of beef.

Brennan topped up everyone's glasses with red wine and offered to make a toast.

"That's a great idea!" said Abigail. "I'd love to make a toast."

Brennan, puzzled at his wife's enthusiasm, kept quiet and let her have the floor.

"In life," Abigail began as she held her wineglass up, "it's important that we always hold on to who we truly are. However, at the same time, it's also just as important to venture outside our comfort zones to see what else we can be. We have to be willing to go out and do things that frighten us because sometimes our fear can help reveal our true selves." She paused and looked around the room. Brennan had a dead and expressionless face while all their other friends were smiling and nodding in agreement. "May we all continue to have adventures that frighten us, adventures that show us who we really are inside... to adventures!"

"To adventures!" replied everyone, except for Brennan who forced a smile and took a swig of his wine.

The rest of the night went on like a blur for Brennan. He struggled to keep track of the conversations and felt like he was on autopilot. Three times during dinner, Vince asked him if he was feeling okay. Brennan could merely nod and pretend that he was fine.

As the night went on and the group of friends shared what was going on in their lives, Brennan found himself just nodding along. At one point, Abigail shook his arm and said, "Brennan, snap out of it." But that didn't work. By the time he came to his senses, it was already half past nine and people were starting to leave.

Brennan got up from his seat and hugged both Phillip and Karen goodbye. Phillip mentioned that he would bring more bottles of wine next time as one obviously hadn't been enough for them. Puzzled, Brennan realized that they had finished four bottles of wine over dinner.

He leaned over to give Karen a kiss on the cheek and waved both of them goodbye. Vince didn't leave right away, staying for a bit to help Abigail clean up. Brennan also joined to help put the dishes away.

"Hey, Abigail," said Vince. "Let Brennan and me clean up here. You can go take care of the girls. They look like they're about to pass out."

"Oh, really? You don't have to—"

"I insist."

"Thank you," replied a grateful Abigail as she removed her apron and went over to the girls. She scooped the two tired souls into her arms and carried both of them off to bed. Brennan and Vince were now left alone in the kitchen to put the rest of the dinnerware away.

"You okay, Brennan?" asked Vince. "You seemed off during dinner tonight."

"What?" asked Brennan. "Oh, yeah. Honestly, just some stuff going on between Abigail and I. No biggie."

"Sorry to hear that. Is it anything serious?"

"No. I don't think so. We're just in a really weird place right now."

"I hear you." A long pause of silence drew on between both men until Vince said, "Megan isn't really busy with work tonight."

"What?" asked Brennan.

"Yeah. We're going through some things too."

"Oh, man. That sucks. What's the problem?"

"I don't know." Vince shook his head as he takes a bite. "She just says that something is off between us somehow."

"Seems to be a lot of that going around these days." He subconsciously looked towards the stairs where his wife disappeared. "Women."

"Women. The things we do for them, huh?"

You have no idea, thought Brennan.

Chapter 25

Abigail

ABIGAIL WOKE UP the next day to find Brennan without the energy and positivity that he had been exhibiting in previous days. It was so weird for her last night when they were getting ready for bed after everyone had left. She was enthusiastic to talk to him about everything that she'd been learning, but he didn't seem interested. All she got from him were one-word replies and a few nods of the head before he dozed off. At first, she thought that he was just tired and that work was stressing him out. But somehow, she knew that it had to do with the toast that she made over dinner.

It was early in the morning, and the kids were still asleep. The two of them sat across from one another at the dining table as Brennan munched on undercooked oats and Abigail smeared butter on her toast. After a while, the silence began to get on her nerves.

"What's wrong?" she asked.

"Nothing."

"Don't make me ask again." She put the knife down.

Brennan sat in silence for a few seconds before finally

replying, "You know what's wrong."

"It was the toast, wasn't it?" she asked. "It made you uncomfortable."

"You knew that it would."

"Is there anything wrong with wanting adventures, Brennan? Was there any malice to what I said?"

"Adventures are fine when we go on them together, Abigail. But we both know you want to go off on adventures without me. With other men. I tried to be okay with it. I really did. And I even thought that I was for a while. But it turns out that I'm not."

Brennan put his spoon down and rubbed his forehead. Abigail watched as Brennan put his spoon down and rubbed his forehead. For the first time, she heard the support and sincerity in his voice and saw how much he was hurting. Suddenly, a feeling of guilt swept over her as she watched her husband try to cope with his pain.

"I won't see other men if you're going to continue being like this," she said.

"Being like what, Abigail?"

"Like this!" she said with her arms outstretched towards him. "Being all sad, depressed, and mopey. It's taking the fun out of it."

"Well, I'm sorry that my feelings are getting in the way of your fun," said Brennan.

"Stop being so overdramatic, Brennan. Can't we have an adult conversation here?"

Brennan stopped and looked at Abigail with an apologetic expression on his face.

"I'm sorry," he sighed. "Yeah. My emotions are all over the place right now, and I really can't put them into words. It's only adding to my frustration. That's not your fault."

"I don't understand why you have to overcomplicate everything, Brennan!" Abigail was crying and her voice was starting to crack. "Any other man would jump at the opportunity to have sex with other women with their wife's approval. Why do you have to be so difficult?"

She stormed off to the living room and he followed after her. Abigail was about to make a turn towards the stairs, but Brennan grabbed her arm and stopped her in her tracks.

"Hold on," he pleaded. "I'm sorry, okay? I'm just finding all of this too difficult. But I'm really trying here!"

"I know you're trying, Brennan, but it's not enough! You make me feel so suffocated and trapped! You've only been feeling bad for a few days, and you already want to quit. Think of how much I've been struggling for the past months!"

Abigail was barely comprehensible as she struggled to talk in between her gasps for air. Brennan sat her down on the couch and got her a glass of water.

"I hate my life, Brennan," she said after calming down a bit. She took a sip of water and gathered herself. "I think it's very annoying how emotional you are being over all of this. All of the misery and sadness that I've kept quiet about all these months, I blame it all on you. You are the cause of all of this!"

"I think you're being very unfair." He shook his head.

"You just don't get it, Brennan!" she continued on as if he didn't even say anything. "If you really loved me and cared about me like you always say you do, then you would be on board with this. You would know that this is the only way to make me happy and able to smile again. Aren't I deserving of happiness, Brennan?"

"I can't stand the thought of having another guy make you happy!"

"And I can't stand the thought of having sex with you ever again! What do you have to say about that?"

Brennan stayed silent, leaning back into the cushion of the couch and staring at the ceiling.

"I can't change how I feel," he said.

"No. But you can change how you think. And maybe that will change how you feel," she suggested.

"I have to get ready for work," replied Brennan.

He stood up and disappeared onto the second floor as Abigail remained on the couch. She took a deep breath, closed her eyes, and cried.

Chapter 26

Brennan

WHILE BRENNAN WAS driving home from work, he realized that he hadn't been very productive that day. All day long, his mind was on the argument that he and Abigail had that morning. He considered whether he was really being unfair with her or not. He knew that he loved his wife and he wanted her to be happy. But was she right in saying that if he truly loved her, then he would be more on board with this? I might as well give it a real try, he thought to himself.

He arrived home and immediately went to the kitchen where he knew Abigail would be busy preparing dinner. The kids were in their play area and were fully occupied. Still, he spoke in hushed tones when talking to Abigail to make sure that the kids wouldn't hear.

"I'm sorry," he said. "You're right. I haven't been fully on board. But I am now. Are you still willing to give this another try?"

"For real, this time?" she replied with no hints of nonsense or irony in her voice.

"For real."

"Okay. So, have you been messaging any girls lately?"

"What? No. I've only just decided that I'm really going to be serious with this thing."

"Okay, well, you better catch up. I've already been talking to a bunch of guys."

He gave her a spiteful look that made her laugh.

"I'm only teasing," she said. "But seriously, don't be afraid to just go in there. I was a little hesitant and self-conscious at first myself. It really took a little getting used to."

"One step at a time," he said. "I'll go upstairs and freshen up."

"Okay. Dinner will be ready in a bit."

Dinner was as calm and as wholesome as could be. One would have never been able to guess that the two of them were at each other's throats just that morning.

That night, after the two kids had been put to sleep, Brennan was lying down on their bed as he watched Abigail at her vanity table. He expected to feel sad and mopey over seeing her happy like that. Instead, he grabbed his phone and opened the app store.

"So, what app do you use to meet people online?" asked Brennan.

"Really? You're seriously asking me that question?" Abigail had a look on her face that was half surprised and half intrigued.

"I told you I was ready to really give it a try." Brennan smirked.

"Okay," said Abigail, nodding her head as if in approval. "Well, there are two popular apps: Tinder and Bumble. Though, I've found that most people I meet on Tinder are just guys who want to have sex. You get higher chances of having a more meaningful conversation with people on Bumble."

"Duly noted," replied Brennan. He downloaded both the Tinder and Bumble apps on his phone and got to work on setting up his profile. "Now, what photo should I use as my profile picture?"

"Remember that it can't be one that would make you easily recognizable. Just take one right now with the dim lighting of the bedroom."

"Okay. If you say so."

He put his phone out in front of him and took an expressionless photo of himself. Abigail, who was watching in, chimed in and said, "No, no. You're doing it wrong."

"What?"

"You don't want to be recognized, but you don't want to look like a creepy lurker either. At the very least, you should smile."

Brennan took another photo of himself, this time with a smile, and settled on it as his profile picture.

"Okay, I've set up my profile," he said. "Now what do I do?"

Abigail put down her phone. "Well, you browse through the girls on the app and you message the ones you like. Then, you wait to see if they'll message you back."

"So, that's it?" he asked.

"Yeah," she answered. "And if you're comfortable, you can send each other pictures too. This is just so you know what you both really look like. You can never trust a profile picture alone."

"Right," he agreed. "So, guys have been sending you pictures of themselves?"

"They have," confirmed Abigail. She paused and hesitated before continuing. "And they aren't always so wholesome either."

"Ugh," grunted Brennan. "That's enough. I don't want to know."

He tried browsing through the different profiles of the girls on Bumble in an attempt to get his mind off the idea of guys sending his wife pictures of their privates.

"Oh, come on." Abigail gave him a cold look. "You said you would be mature about this."

"I said that I would be on board. I didn't say that I wanted to talk about it with you."

"Well, you can't have one without the other, Brennan!" she reprimanded. Her face had turned sour. She turned to face him and continued, "You have to accept that I'm going to eventually end up sleeping with someone else! I might even sleep with a few of these guys!"

"Abigail, please shut up!" Brennan rubbed his eyes as if to rid them of the visions of his wife in bed with other men.

"I will not!" said Abigail. "I want to be able to share this with you properly! Being in an open relationship means the two of us also being open with one another, Brennan. What don't you get about that?"

"It's one thing for me to know that you're sleeping with other guys. That's already been difficult for me to accept," he replied. "But it's another thing entirely for me to hear all the details from you!"

"You are so selfish!" she said as she rose from her seat. "There are dozens of men who are dying to fuck me, Brennan. And here's a newsflash for you, I'm going to sleep with them. You're going to have to accept that and be comfortable with it!"

"I already told you that I'm on board, haven't I?" He was also growing more agitated now. He felt his heart rate quickening and his breaths becoming shorter and shorter.

"No, you're not! You're still in denial. You're still pretending like this isn't for real and that it isn't happening. If you were truly comfortable with it, then you would be willing to talk to me about it."

"Just let me take it one step at a time, Abigail," he pleaded.

"You can take it as slow as you want, Brennan," she said. "But I'm done waiting."

Chapter 27

Abigail

WHEN ABIGAIL WOKE up the next morning, Brennan was already off to work. She grabbed her cellphone from the bedside table and went downstairs to brew herself a cup of coffee. After settling down at the dining table to enjoy her fresh brew, she checked her phone for messages.

She was surprised to receive a notification from Andre after not hearing from him for days. Andre was a guy that she met on Bumble and had been incredibly fond of. He was a doctor, and she had always thoroughly enjoyed the conversations that they had. Abigail especially liked the fact that he never made any indications that all he wanted to do was sleep with her. It seemed like he was also in it for the emotional connection.

Unfortunately, Andre was married and had to delete the app from his phone every so often in order to hide his online escapades from his wife. This meant that he would often go for a stretch of days without replying to Abigail. In a way, this added a layer of value to their conversations whenever they did get the chance to connect with one another. Due to the fleeting nature of their connections, both of them seemed to cherish it even more.

"Sorry that it's been a while," he messaged her. "The wife's been extra suspicious lately."

"I understand," she typed back. "I have to say that I'm quite impressed with how careful you're being."

Abigail put her phone down and took a sip of the coffee. She closed her eyes and enjoyed the quiet morning, smiling to herself as she waited for his reply.

"It's been challenging. She's been cracking down on me really hard. In fact, I can't talk long right now," he said. "I just wanted to let you know that I'm still here and that you haven't scared me off."

"Yeah," she replied. "Me along with a bunch of your other girls, right?"

"There are no other girls," he replied with a winking emoji. "Talk to you again soon. Hopefully longer next time."

Abigail pouted as she typed out her goodbyes to Andre. "I wonder when that'll be. Talk soon!" she wrote. She finished up her cup of coffee and got to work on preparing some waffles for the kids. Abigail wanted their breakfast to be ready by the time they got up.

As she mixed the batter, she decided to play her favorite Spotify playlist in the background. The rhythmic bass beats of Michael Jackson's Billie Jean began echoing through the kitchen as she loaded the batter into the waffle maker. While the waffles were cooking, she went upstairs to wake the kids.

When she opened the door to the girls' bedroom, she found Riley still fast asleep in her bed while Amber was going through her chest of toys.

"Good morning, little one," she said as she knelt down beside Amber. "What are you looking for?"

"I can't find Doris, Momma!" cried Amber. Doris was Amber's stuffed giraffe toy.

"Oh, you know," comforted Abigail. "I think I remember seeing Doris in your playpen downstairs. Why don't we wake your sister up so we can all go down together and check?"

"Okay," sighed Amber. She walked over to Riley's bed and gently shook her little sister. "Riley. Riley. Wake up. It's time to go down."

Riley slowly opened her little eyes and let out a big yawn as she stretched her arms out to the sides with clenched fists. "It smells really good, Momma," she said with her eyes half open.

"Mommy's making waffles for breakfast," said Abigail. "Why don't we go down and have some waffles together?"

"Okay," said Riley. "Where's Daddy?"

"Oh, Daddy's already off to work, honey. But you'll see him tonight, okay?" she affirmed.

"Can we put maple syrup on our waffles?" pleaded Amber.

"Of course, dearest," said Abigail. "What are waffles without syrup?"

She gathered a drowsy Riley up into her arms and held Amber's hand as she led them both out of the room and down the stairs to the kitchen. Abigail propped both of the girls up on their high chairs and checked on the waffles She had overcooked the first batch and discarded it.

"Looks like Mommy burned the first batch, girls. Not to worry. I'll make some more right away. In the meantime, who wants orange juice?"

Abigail was smiling and happy as she enjoyed breakfast with her kids while her favorite music played in the background.

After the girls had finished with their breakfast, she set them up in their play area as she did the dishes. While loading the dishes into the washer, she noticed an unread notification on her phone from the Bumble app. It was a message from Chris.

Chris was a guy that she had been messaging with over the past week or so. She wasn't all that interested in him; definitely not as interested as she was with Andre.

However, she still indulged him with her replies to his messages. Just like Andre, Chris was also married in an unhappy relationship. Somehow, Abigail was attracted to these kinds of men, not because of who they were, but because of their stories. She indulged Chris purely because she was interested in learning more about what he and his wife were like. She asked him a lot about his marriage and why he was on dating apps even though he had a wife.

Over the past week, he opened up to her about how he didn't have the same connection with his wife as he used to. The two of them had met in Europe where she was originally from while Chris was vacationing there after graduating from college. They fell in love and he convinced her to move to the States with him where they were both sure that they could build a life of happiness together. Unfortunately, things didn't go as planned as his wife struggled to adapt to American culture. Her personal struggles took a toll on their marriage and made Chris very unhappy.

"Hey," he texted. "Good morning!"

"Hey," she replied. "What's up?"

"Can I call you?" asked Chris. "My wife's not here."

"Sure," said Abigail as she stepped away from the kids to the other side of the living room so they wouldn't hear.

"Not having the best morning," said Chris when Abigail answered his call. "Got into a fight with my wife again last night. Had to sleep on the couch and my back is killing me."

"Well, that makes two of us. Didn't sleep well last night either," she said. She thought about explaining that she had gotten into a fight too but opted against it.

Chris tried to extend the conversation to the best of his abilities, but Abigail continued to feign disinterest. She dignified him with responses, but she never made an effort to engage with him in a more intimate capacity. To her, he had a very bland personality.

"So, what do you do in the house all day?" he asked

her.

"Well, I have the two girls. Sometimes I'll let them play while I read a book or watch some TV. There are days where the older sibling asks me to help her with coloring and reading."

"Oh, so what books do you read?"

"Any kind, really. Hey, listen. I gotta go. The girls seem a little fussy."

"Oh," he said, seeming startled and disappointed. "Okay. Thanks for talking to me."

"Yeah," she answered. "Sure. Bye."

She put the phone down and rested her chin on her palm. Why can't I find any interesting guys? she thought to herself.

Chapter 28

Brennan

THE SITUATION HAD improved in the Sutton household. Abigail apologized to Brennan for pressuring him too much, and he apologized for not trying harder. The two of them managed to stay civil enough to not fight during this weird transitory phase of their relationship. Brennan had even slowly started to get the hang of online dating. He was already talking to a few girls whose profiles had caught his attention. There were even a few girls who messaged him themselves, but he didn't care so much for them. However, there was this one particular girl he struck up a conversation with whom he found quite interesting.

Her name was Sheila, and she was just twenty-seven years old. That made her more than a full decade younger than Brennan, but she didn't mind the age gap. In fact, that's part of what attracted her to Brennan in the first place.

"I'm so tired of dating guys my age," she told him during their first conversation. "I need more maturity in my life. So, don't worry about the age difference."

Brennan found her to be quite smart and mature for

her age. She worked as a lawyer for a big corporate firm and was on her way to being one of the youngest partners in the company's history. This meant that she didn't really have the time to go out and date guys in a traditional sense. Her work schedule demanded too much of her time. This was why she resorted to online dating.

"It's really weird," he told her one time when they were chatting. "I've met a lot of girls my age on these sites and they're a mess. You would think that the older you get, the more put-together you are, but that's obviously not the case."

"Does that mean that you're a mess too?" she asked.

"Maybe," he replied. "That's a chance you're going to have to take."

"I'll take it," she texted back.

The two of them had really gotten into deep conversations with one another. Sheila shared with Brennan about her struggles of keeping up with the timeline that she set for herself.

"When I graduated university, I wrote down a list of things that I needed to accomplish by the time I turned thirty. I fully expected to be a partner at a big law firm, and I'm already ahead of schedule on that front. In fact, my career is going really well. It's my personal life that's lagging behind."

"Really?" asked Brennan. "How so?"

"Well, I also wrote down that I expected to be married with two kids before thirty as well. I'm twenty-seven now and you're the closest thing I have to a serious relationship. Obviously, it doesn't look like I'm going to meet my deadline."

"Don't put too much pressure on yourself," he told her. "We all go at our own individual paces. I expected to be in the thick of a happy marriage at this point in my life and look how that turned out."

"I guess."

"The point is that you can make plans for yourself all

you want. But sometimes, life is going to throw you a curveball, and you're just going to have to adapt."

On his lunch break one day, Brennan decided to check his messages. There were a few emails that he set aside for after lunch. He also had a message from Phillip asking him about a particular wine that they drank during their last dinner.

As he scrolled through his notifications, he eventually found what he was looking for. Sheila had texted him and asked him if he wanted to meet that night. She was going to get off work earlier than usual and she had a free night.

Brennan felt the pace of his heart quicken. Taking the step into online dating was already a big enough deal for him. But living in the digital space still kept things somewhat fantastical for him. He eventually became okay with just conversing with these girls online, assuming that he would never have to meet them in real life. He felt that meeting Sheila in person would really legitimize the open relationship he had with Abigail.

"Sounds good," he texted back, trying to make it seem like it wasn't a big deal. "There's something I have to tell you, though."

"What's that?" she replied. "You're being weird."

"Yeah, sorry. It's just that when me and my wife agreed to start seeing other people, we also agreed that we would do it discreetly so that our friends or family wouldn't find out."

"Alright. And this means that you can't be seen in public with me, I assume?"

"Yeah, I'm sorry. I totally understand if you're upset."

"I'm not upset. Is this just your way of getting me to invite you straight to my home without buying me dinner first?"

"I wish it were. But yeah. Are you okay with that?"

"No problem. Come over after work. Maybe around 7:00? Bring a bottle of wine," she said. "I'll send you the pin to the address of my condo in a bit."

Brennan felt like his heart was about to leap right out of his chest. This current version of Brennan was more anxious than excited. He knew that he should have been happy at the idea of him having the chance to get intimate with a girl. But he also knew at the back of his mind that if he was getting intimate with someone else, then so was Abigail.

The rest of the afternoon went by like a daze. Brennan struggled to focus on his work as thoughts of meeting Sheila occupied his mind. He thought a couple of times about coming up with some kind of excuse to get him out of meeting her. But he also knew that Abigail would get upset if he didn't take this open relationship arrangement seriously. He was at a crossroads, and before he knew it, he was already dropping by the liquor store and picking up a bottle of wine as he made his way to Sheila's condo.

Sheila lived in a high-rise right in the heart of the Minneapolis central business district. After parking his car, he rode the elevator up to her floor with a bottle of wine in his hands. Not even the jazzy elevator music could calm his rapidly beating heart. The higher the floors went, the more anxious he became. He got off the elevator and made his way towards Sheila's unit. Brennan took a deep breath and knocked on her door.

"Coming," he heard a voice say from the other side of the wall, followed by a series of footsteps. The door opened, and there stood Sheila. She was a lot taller than he had initially imagined.

Standing in front of Brennan was a beautiful brunette with light mocha skin. Her wavy hair fell all the way down to her shoulders, and she was dressed in a fitted blouse and the bottom part of a pantsuit. She had a small flat mole just above the left part of her lip, and her eyes crinkled when she smiled.

"I see you have good taste in wine," she said as she eyed the bottle.

"Only the best," replied Brennan.

"Please come in."

He stepped inside her minimally decorated, two-bedroom condo. The walls of the hallway were painted a cream white and were all lined with minimalist abstract paintings. All of Sheila's furniture carried very similar visual themes. Her tables and chairs were all in muted colors and had very boxy aesthetics. There were a few strategically placed potted plants here and there just to break up the monochromaticity of the space.

"Beautiful place you've got here," Brennan commented.

"It's bigger than what I need, but I got it at a good price. So, I just pulled the trigger. I'm glad you like it." She took the wine from him and brought it to the kitchen. "Please, have a seat on the couch. Make yourself comfortable."

Brennan took his seat on the couch and heard her uncork the wine bottle from the kitchen. Then he heard the clinking of glassware before Sheila came back with two glasses filled. It was then that Brennan noticed that an appetizing smell of garlic and basil filled the air.

"It smells really good in here," he said. "What are you cooking?"

"I'm making spinach lasagna to go along with some tenderloin tips," she replied. "Oh, I hope you're not lactose intolerant."

"I'm not," he confirmed. "I can't wait to dig in. It reminds me of my wife's cooking. She's really skilled in the kitchen."

"We're not going to be talking about your wife all night, are we?" she asked with a raised eyebrow.

"No," Brennan replied apologetically. "We're not. I'm sorry. Tonight, let's focus on us."

His heart wasn't racing as fast anymore, and he had somewhat calmed himself down now. Sheila raised her wine towards his as she clinked their glasses together before taking the first sip.

"Well," she said. "I'm really good in the kitchen too. The food will be ready in just a few minutes. I hope you can wait."

"How can I when it just smells so damn good?" he replied with a smile.

They got to talking about their days at work. Brennan didn't have much to talk about as his work day practically ended at noon, but he didn't mention that to her. Sheila went into great detail about a case that she was handling for a big client. A pharmaceutical company that Sheila's firm worked for was being sued for medical malpractice, and it was really stressing her out.

"We've honestly got all of the best lawyers that we have on this case, and we're still not sure that we can win."

"I don't know much about the law, but I'm sure you'll be able to figure things out."

"I don't know," she said. "I don't want this to go to trial."

Just as she said that, the ding of the oven timer went off, which signaled that the lasagna was ready.

"Alright," she said. "I've already set a place for you at the dining table. Just make yourself comfortable as I go get the food."

Brennan took a seat at the glass dining table and noticed the elaborate chandelier that was situated just above him. It was as peculiar a lighting fixture as he had ever seen. It closely resembled wiry tree branches that stretched out into various directions that eventually concluded in a small source of light.

"This is a really unique chandelier that you've got here," he said.

"Oh, thanks," she replied from the kitchen. "It was a gift from the firm when I first moved in. It was made by some fancy Italian designer."

She brought the lasagna over to the table and set it down. "Speaking of things Italian, I present to you my masterpiece."

"Wow. It looks really good."

"Thanks," she said. "But don't dig in just yet. I've got to go get the tenderloin tips and the rest of the wine."

After Sheila brought out the tenderloin tips and topped up Brennan's glass, the two of them dug into the lasagna. Brennan was impressed at how good it tasted. He had never had lasagna as creamy and as delicious as that.

"Where do you get the time to learn how to cook?" he asked her.

"Oh, I've always been fond of cooking. Even before I knew I wanted to be a lawyer, I already had a few skills in the kitchen," she replied.

"Then I imagine that you're quite the foodie."

"If by foodie, you mean someone who enjoys good food, then yes," she said with a chuckle.

The two of them ate in silence for the next few seconds as Brennan savored the delicious lasagna paired with the exquisite wine. He looked at Sheila and smiled. He just couldn't believe that he was in the situation that he was in.

"Brennan," said Sheila, breaking the silence. "I never asked you, what led to you being in an open marriage anyway?"

"I thought we weren't going to talk about my wife."

"We're not. We're talking about you and your marriage."

"Okay, well, the answer to that question has more to do with my wife than it does with me."

"How so?" she asked placing her chin in her palm leaning towards him.

"It was her who wanted it. I never did. In fact, even now, I'm still quite iffy about our arrangement."

"What made her want to do it?"

"I guess she was just unhappy in our marriage but didn't have the courage to just leave me outright. As you know, we have kids. That complicates things significantly."

"Right, I understand," she said. "It must be really hard to just leave a marriage when you have kids to think about."

"Exactly," he replied. "She did tell me that if it weren't for the kids, she would have been long gone by now. So, I guess this new arrangement is just a way for her to see what's out there without untethering herself from this family completely."

"And how's she been doing so far? Has she been dating?" she asked.

"So, we're really talking about my wife now, huh?"

"I guess we are." She stabbed another tenderloin with her fork and chuckled.

"I honestly don't know how she's been doing. I don't like talking about it. She tries to bring it up every now and then, but I change the subject."

"It makes you feel uncomfortable thinking about your wife being with other men."

"Yes." He nodded his head. "It does."

"Now, does it also make you uncomfortable to be here with me?" she asked with a stern look in her eyes.

She wasn't trying to be coy or witty here. She was genuinely asking. He paused for a while to make it seem like he had given a lot of thought to his answer.

"No," he said, shaking his head. "It doesn't."

"Good," she replied. "I'm glad." She held out her hand and grabbed his. She gently stroked her fingers against the back of his hand and looked softly into his eyes.

The rest of the dinner went by as smoothly as could be. Both Brennan and Sheila shared similar taste in music, particularly, the blues. The two of them bonded with discussions over the best Stevie Ray Vaughan records and the revolutionary career of Ray Charles. Sheila had a vinyl record player in her living room and put on an old Jimi Hendrix Experience record called *Electric Ladyland*. The sounds of Jimi's electrifying guitar riffs resonated through the condo as the two of them continued talking and sipping their wine. Eventually, when dinner was over, the two of them made their way to the couch with a freshly uncorked bottle of wine.

"I really shouldn't be drinking so much," said Brennan. "I have to drive home tonight, and I'm already feeling the last bottle."

"Well," whispered Sheila, "what if you don't have to drive home tonight?"

Brennan turned to look at her and realized that her face was awfully close to his. He could practically feel her breath on his neck. Just then, as if helpless to her gravitational pull, Brennan felt himself leaning in . He closed his eyes and felt her soft supple lips against his.

Sheila gently nibbled at his upper lip as she grabbed the right side of his face. He felt her smooth palm caress the side of his cheek as she softly slid her tongue into his mouth and tickled the front of his teeth. . He grabbed a hold of the back of her head and pulled her closer as he thrust his tongue into her mouth.

Brennan lay her head softly on the couch's armrest and mounted her carefully. As he was atop her, he looked straight into her eager eyes and caressed her face, trailing his fingers all the way down to her neck and breasts. He methodically unbuttoned her blouse as she unzipped his pants.

The slow rhythmic sounds of blues music continued to fill the air as Brennan removed his shirt while Sheila took off her pants. They were both completely naked now and he straddled her on the couch taking the top position. He leaned in to kiss her passionately on the lips and felt Sheila kissing him back with the same intensity.

He moved down to kiss her neck and chest as Sheila let out a light moan as if to signal for him to keep going. Brennan moved to her breasts and sucked on her nipples, feeling her heart race and realizing his was doing the same After lingering on her breasts for a few seconds, Brennan slid his face further down to her abdomen and kissed his way to her groin while listening to Sheila's moans grow more and more intense. She grabbed him by the head once more and said, "Let's take this to the bedroom."

Brennan got up from the couch, and Sheila wrapped her legs around his waist. She directed him towards the bedroom and then began kissing his neck. "You taste so good," she whispered into his ear.

He carried her all the way to her bed and lay her down gently. She turned to dim the lights before laying on her back.

Brennan stood there and looked at her naked body for a moment. He thought about Abigail and what he was doing, and he expected to feel some kind of way about it. Strangely enough, everything felt so fine and natural, as if he was doing exactly what he should have been doing.

"Hold on for just a moment," he told her before running back into the living room where his pants were. He quickly grabbed a condom out of his wallet and put it on before returning to Sheila's bedroom.

"Where did you go?" she asked.

"Oh, I just needed to put this on really quick," he replied.

"To make sure you don't get pregnant and we both stay protected."

"Ugh," she said with a smile. "How many guys do you think I've been with?"

"I don't know," he said. "I just wanted to keep us both safe here. There's no way for you to know if I've been getting around either."

"Oh, just shut up," she said with a laugh. "You're nervous. Now come on over here and kiss me."

Sheila smiled at him and slowly opened her legs as she bit her lip and motioned for him to come closer. Brennan felt his muscles stiffen as he walked forward and situated himself between her legs. He kissed her again, alternating between her mouth and neck as he slowly slid himself inside of her. She let out a light moan as he rhythmically rocked back and forth in a very slow and methodical manner. She grabbed his shoulders and flipped them so that he was now on his back and she was straddling his hips. Sheila put her hands on his chest to support herself as she slid back and forth like waves coming into and away from the shore. Then she took her right hand and placed it firmly around Brennan's neck, slightly choking him as she increased her pace. She then grabbed both of Brennan's hands and placed them on her hips.

Brennan grasped her hips firmly and helped her push and pull, and every single thrust of their hips evoked uncontrollable moans from both of them.

He once again felt Sheila's hand grope his neck, impairing his breathing and making his heartbeat just a little bit faster. Brennan sensed that he was about to climax as he clenched his buttocks and thrust his hips upward to get deeper inside of her. He grabbed a hold of her hips and helped her move back and forth until he felt his legs stiffen and then suddenly relax as he felt a wave of euphoria sweep over him. Sheila collapsed onto him and rested her head on his chest. He could feel her heart beat against his lower abdomen as he tried to catch his breath.

"Wow," she muttered under her breath. "That was amazing."

She pulled away from his chest and gave him a kiss on the lips, gently nibbling on his upper lip once more before pulling away as if to restrain herself. "I think I'm ready for another round." She continued kissing him passionately as she was now alternating between his lips, neck, and chest.

Brennan lay there and focused all of his attention on every sensation that Sheila's kisses were arousing in his body. It was as if her lips were setting off tiny little shockwaves every time they made contact with his skin. He felt his body getting hot again before grabbing a hold of her head and saying, "Wait, wait. No. Stop."

"What?" she said, smiling at him. "Not ready for round two yet?"

"No, it's not that." Brennan sat up straighter now on the bed. "I'm totally up for another round. That was amazing."

"Then what's the problem?"

"That was my last condom. I should have brought more, but I honestly didn't think that I was getting any action tonight."

"What did you think was going to happen with me inviting you over here?"

"I didn't think much about it, to be honest. I haven't been on a first date in a long time," he sighed.

"You're cute," she said, smiling. She leaned in closer to him and started kissing him again. "It's okay, I don't mind. We can do it without a condom. I trust you."

Brennan could feel the little shockwaves that her lips were sending down his spine, and it took every ounce of willpower for him to pull away and resist. She was being very aggressive and was wearing down his resistance bit by bit. He knew that it was all wrong, but everything about it just felt so good.

"No, I'm sorry," he said. "I can't take any chances."

"Come on," she said with a more aggressive tone. "Stop being such a wuss."

Brennan gave in to Sheila's advances and kissed her. Sheila turned her back towards Brennan as she positioned herself on her hands and knees atop her bed. He approached her slowly and placed both of his hands on either side of her hips. He leaned over to kiss the back of her neck as he gradually slid himself inside her.

"Doesn't it feel so good?" asked Sheila.

"Yeah," he said. "You're right."

He could feel the sweat dripping down his face as he gradually quickened the pace of his thrusts. Sheila grabbed a pillow and stuffed her face in it in an effort to stifle her moans. In between thrusts, she quickly turned around so that the two of them were now facing one another, pulling Brennan's hips into her pelvis so that he was now on top of her. He seamlessly transitioned back into his backward and forward thrusts as he watched Sheila savor every subtle motion.

"Faster," she said. "Come on. Faster."

He quickened his pace even more and could now feel his heartbeat doing the same. Brennan was struggling to catch his breath, but he tried his best to maintain the pace of his thrusts. Then, just as he was about to finish, he slowed down and made a motion to withdraw himself from Sheila. Suddenly, he was shocked to find Sheila's hands grab his hips as if to force him to stay inside of her.

That's when it dawned on him. He suddenly thought of everything that the two of them had discussed since he got there. He thought of her telling him about how she had a timeline and she was far behind schedule with starting her family. Brennan realized that she was now trying to pressure him to help get her timeline in order, and he wasn't having any of it.

"This was a mistake," he said. "I've got to go." He left her bedroom without even waiting for a reply.

Brennan shuffled over to the couch and dressed as quickly as he could, feeling like he couldn't spend a second longer in that condo. Before heading for the door, he did a double-check just to make sure that he had all of his belongings on him. Car keys. Wallet. Cellphone. Everything seemed to be there. He thought about going back to Sheila and giving her a proper goodbye but decided against it. Brennan just made his way towards the door into the hallway and never looked back.

The next thing he knew he was already in the car park of her building. His felt dizzy. Hurrying to his car as if someone was chasing him, he struggled to catch his breath. As he got into his car, he had to focus to fit the keys into the ignition and get the engine running. He felt as if his entire body was shaking, and he had difficulty maneuvering the car out of the car park. Even as he was pulling onto the main road, all he could see was Abigail's face staring at him from the windshield.

Then he saw Abigail walking towards a faceless man

and kissing him. Brennan blinked and saw that the car was drifting towards the sidewalk, swerving towards the center of the lane just in time to avoid running into a lamp post. Once he was able to get the car back under control, he tried his best to not let his mind drift towards thoughts of Abigail being with other men. Instead, he focused his mind on Sheila and how good it had felt for him to be inside her just a few minutes before. Suddenly, he felt an immense weight of fear in his heart. He knew that if he could have nights like that with Sheila, then Abigail was capable of having nights like that with other men as well.

"She'll never find anyone interesting," he said to himself out loud. Brennan tried to convince himself to believe in what he was saying, but he found it difficult. It was Abigail who proposed this new arrangement in the first place, and he thought it foolish of himself to believe that she wouldn't want to sleep with other men. "Tonight with Sheila was just electric," he said. "But it was a mistake. It was a mistake."

Brennan continually tried to talk himself into believing the words that were coming out of his mouth.

What if I'm being selfish? he thought. Brennan couldn't ignore how good it had felt for him to be with Sheila. All of the intimacy that the two of them had shared in their fleeting moments felt so right to him, and so natural. The way that he flirted and seduced her seemed to be second nature to him. Yet, the idea of Abigail doing the same to another man felt so wrong. That's when he stopped to think about whether she was right about him being selfish. She had accused him of not wanting her to have freedom and individuality. She once accused him of feeling like he had a sense of ownership over her. His hands tightened around the steering wheel. Was she right? he wondered.

"Love is just so messed up!" yelled Brennan out of frustration. He thought about how little love and affection he had gotten from Abigail over the past few weeks. Somehow, he had gotten more out of Sheila in one night than he had from Abigail in months. What if I just find someone who loves me for real? he asked himself. Brennan thought that he had a good idea of what true love looked like, and it was nothing like what he and Abigail had at that time. "Maybe real love doesn't exist." He shook his head. Giving voice to his thoughts gave them more weight, more legitimacy. It didn't matter that no one was listening. "Most couples get divorced or separated anyway. Maybe Abigail is right, and we're all not meant to be with just one person for the rest of our lives."

Brennan continued to drive on in silence. He was tempted to turn the radio on, but he learned to embrace the silence. It allowed him to really think about the situation more. "I can't get a divorce," he told himself convincingly. "I need to fight for this family. I need to stay for the kids." As he drove home, he no longer thought about Sheila, Abigail, or the men that she could potentially be sleeping with. Instead, his mind was focused on Amber and Riley.

C h a p t e r   2 9

A b i g a i l

ABIGAIL FELT A rush of excitement every morning as she woke up to notifications on her Tinder and Bumble apps. However, it never took long for her excitement to dissipate once she actually read the messages. Practically every guy that she had grown mildly interested in would eventually just propose to have sex with her.

There was Jonathan, an engineer from Rochester. He was single and in his mid-thirties. Abigail reached out to him on Bumble, and the two of them hit it off right away. That day, Abigail just couldn't be separated from her phone. She loved the way that she and Jonathan connected, but by the end of the night, he asked her if they could meet that weekend to hookup. As interested as she was in getting to know him better, that proposition just turned her off to him entirely.

Then there was Daniel, a restaurant owner in St. Paul. He already had two kids of his own as well, but he was divorced from his wife. Abigail loved that he already had two kids because she felt like that was something that the two of them could bond over. She opened up the conversation by asking mostly about his parenting style and how the kids dealt with the divorce.

"It must have been tough on them to get caught up in the divorce," she messaged.

"It was," replied Daniel. "It took a while for them to really be okay with it. But even now, I think they're still hoping for me and their mother to get back together."

"And are you getting back together?"

"No chance," he said. "We just have too much baggage now.

"I'm sorry," apologized Abigail.

"Not too sorry, I hope," Daniel replied back. "I really like you, Abigail."

"I really like you too," she gushed.

"I was thinking that I would book a room at the Hilton in Minneapolis this weekend. And I was hoping that you would join me."

She rolled her eyes at this message, but continued to indulge him.

"And what would we do at the Hilton?"

"Well, we could try to have our bodies get to know one another better."

"Ew!" she thought. That was it. She stopped replying to him and blocked him off her app. There were a few other cases like this, and every single one just added another layer to her pile of discouragement. Still, she was relentless. She knew that if she kept on trying, she would eventually find a guy who was actually worth meeting up with. Most of the guys that she chatted with would always find a way to force the conversation to sex. But Abigail didn't feel like hooking up with anyone she didn't have a genuine emotional connection with. And it was difficult for her to build that emotional bond with them when they were just too eager to ask her what her favorite positions were in bed.

One morning, Abigail decided to try another approach. Instead of talking to guys her age, she thought that she would branch out to a younger demographic. She felt like she had nothing left to lose, figuring that she might have a little more luck with the younger boys.

That morning, she messaged four different guys spread across both Tinder and Bumble. At first, she was afraid that they would just ignore her because of her age. Yet, she was surprised to see that they were quite responsive to her. More than that, the younger men weren't as aggressive when it came to innuendo and sexual relations. One man in particular, named Joe, was a struggling entrepreneur who spent his days working on his start-up digital media agency. Most of their conversations revolved around him opening up to her about the challenges involved in keeping his business afloat while also finding alternative sources of income to support himself. Abigail found it charming that he was so willing to reveal this much about himself to her.

Another man, named Brian, was in his mid-twenties and was finishing up his residency at a hospital based in St. Paul. With Brian, Abigail felt like she could relate to him on a deeper level because of his medical background. The two of them really hit it off as they shared anecdotes and stories about their experiences while working at the hospital.

Abigail managed to maintain a lot of very wholesome relationships with these younger men. Of course, she encountered the occasional creep who would either ask her for nude photos or send her unsolicited photos of themselves. But for the most part, she felt like she was having a lot more fun messaging the younger guys.

When Brennan left for work one day, and the kids were already set up in their activity area, Abigail decided to spend some time taking a few new selfies of herself. She tried taking multiple shots from different angles, and she also changed her hair up a bit in between snaps.

Taking selfies had become a hobby that Abigail obsessed over. She didn't like doing it just out of vanity or self-obsession. Rather, she was interested in the nuance of being able to completely change the feel of a photo by making slight alterations to the lighting, poses, or facial expressions. She almost considered it an actual artform.

Once she had decided on her best shot of the day, she sent it out to Daniel who responded almost immediately.

"Wow, did you do something to your hair? You look very pretty," he wrote in the message.

"Oh, not really. Maybe it's the new conditioner I've been using," she suggested. She tried to play it cool in her messages, but she was gushing deep inside.

"Well, whatever it is, you look great. I'd love to talk more, but I'm still on duty. I'll message you later."

She texted him back with the emoji of a sad face, but she was very happy at how he had reacted to her photos. Abigail felt like a high-school girl with a crush staring down at her phone and smiling. She decided to try her luck with Joe and sent him the very same photo. She was smiling the whole time and was anxious for a reply. Sure enough, her phone lit up with a message from Joe.

"Well, good morning to you too," he texted her. "You look like you're having a great start to the day."

"What makes you say that?" she texted back, deciding to play it coy.

"Well, you can't look that good and not be having a good morning, right?"

"Oh, you're smooth. How's it going over there?"

"I'm actually about to head into a really big meeting with a potential client. Sorry. Maybe I'll talk to you later?"

"Oh boo," she said. "It's alright. I understand. Talk to you later."

While feigning disappointment, Abigail actually felt very good about herself. This was the feeling that she knew she was chasing for the longest time. She wanted to feel wanted, and that did wonders for her confidence.

For the rest of the day, Abigail went about her usual routine of looking after the kids and studying more about makeup and styling techniques. She also looked into buying a new phone with a better camera so that she could improve her selfies. In the afternoon, a close friend of hers from her days working at the hospital reached out to her. Abigail hadn't talked to her in years and decided that it was a good time to catch up.

"Hello?" said Abigail as she answered the phone.

"Hey there, girl!" responded the voice on the other line.

"Christine! Oh my god, it has been literal ages since I last heard from you!"

"I know, right?" replied Christine. "I'm sorry, darling. I know that I've been such a bad friend."

"Nonsense," insisted Abigail. "You've got so much going on for you now that you live in Europe."

"Oh, don't give me that. You know that I'm still the same old Minnesotan that you love!"

"Right," agreed Abigail. "So how are things going over there?" Christine had moved to Europe for a job opportunity she couldn't pass up.

"Ugh," replied Christine. "You first, please. I'll tell you about Europe later. Just fill me in on everything that's happening over there. I miss home so much."

"Well, if you visited more often, you wouldn't miss us so much."

"Flights are so costly, dear. I really would if I could. Now, go and spill the beans. What's happening over there?"

Abigail paused for a moment and thought about whether she should open up to her dear friend about what's been going on in her life. She was desperate to talk to someone about it because Brennan never wanted to talk about the details with her.

"Actually," she started. "I do have something to share about my life." It couldn't hurt, thought Abigail to herself. Christine hasn't been home in ages, and she rarely ever gets in touch with any of us.

"Why? What's happened? Are you pregnant again?"

"What?" laughed Abigail. "No! I'm happy with my two girls. It's not that."

"Then what is it?" cried a desperate Christine. "Please tell me already!"

"Well—" She paused again, trying to choose her words carefully. "Brennan and I have been going through a rough patch in our marriage."

"Oh no," said Christine apologetically. "I'm so sorry to hear that."

"Yeah. I just felt like he's been suffocating me in this marriage, you know?"

"Go on," prompted Christine.

"It's like I feel like I need to see what's out there and have more adventures. I need more spice in my life, and I know that I can't get it from him."

"Wait, Abigail," Christine interrupted. "You and Brennan aren't getting a divorce, are you?"

"No, we're not," replied Abigail. "We're just in the process of trying out… a new arrangement."

"What does that mean? Like living arrangements? Are you not living together anymore?"

"No, we still live together. I'm talking more about our marriage arrangements."

"What do you mean?" asked Christine. "You're killing me with the suspense here."

Abigail went quiet or a few seconds, then continued "We've been trying out an open marriage."

"What?" cried Christine. "Is that exactly what it sounds like?"

Abigail went on to explain how the experience has been for her so far. She vented out her frustrations over Brennan not wanting to fully participate in the process properly. She also told her about her challenges in meeting men and how she wanted someone she could connect with on an emotional level. Christine asked her about Brennan and whether he's been active with any other women, but Abigail just told her that Brennan never opened up about it. She had no idea what he was doing, but she knew that he was messaging other women.

"That's wild," said Christine. "So, how would you feel if you knew that Brennan had slept with another woman?"

"I don't know," confessed Abigail. "But I doubt that he has or that he ever will."

Christine continued to ask Abigail what it was like and what her experiences have been so far talking with other men. After that, the two of them got to talking about the life that Christine was building in Europe and the man that she was settling down with. Abigail was fully enthused to hear about how Christine's life had turned out after leaving the States.

"Oh, it's really been nice talking to you, dear. But I have to go and start getting dinner ready."

"Of course, darling. I look forward to talking to you again soon and hearing more about your adventures. You deserve this," she said.

"Thank you," replied Abigail. "I'll talk to you again soon. Goodbye!"

She hung up and placed her phone down on the couch beside her, breathing a sigh of relief. She felt so happy about being able to open up to someone about her feelings. Somehow, it helped her to know that someone else was made more aware of her emotional struggles in her marriage. It made her feel less alone. Thank goodness for Christine, she thought as she made her way towards the kitchen.

Brennan arrived home from work just as Abigail had finished setting up the dinner table. The kids were already situated in their high chairs together with their bowls of mashed potatoes and shredded chicken. Brennan had a very disheveled look about him. His tie was loose, and his shirt was unbuttoned in a couple of places. The circles under his eyes were more prominent, and it looked like there were sweat stains underneath his pits.

"Long day at the office?" asked Abigail.

"Yeah," replied Brennan. "I don't think I'm up for dinner tonight. I'm going to head upstairs and take a shower. I feel like I'm going to crash."

"Okay, well, I'll save some food for you in case you get hungry later tonight."

Brennan kissed Amber and Riley on their foreheads before going up the stairs and disappearing onto the second floor. Abigail cherished the alone time that she could spend with her two daughters over dinner. They spent the rest of the dinner talking about the recent *Trolls* movie that had just come out and how the two girls had memorized all of the songs in the film.

After dinner, Abigail went to help get the girls ready for bed. As they were in the shower, they continued to sing songs from the *Trolls* film to the point where Abigail started to memorize some of the words as well. By the time they had to change into their pajamas, the girls were so tired they were practically struggling to keep their eyes open as Abigail tucked them both into their beds. After the girls were sound asleep, Abigail walked over to their bedroom and saw that Brennan was just about to hop into bed himself.

"I'm sorry for skipping dinner, honey. Just so tired. It was meeting after meeting today. That was one of the more draining days of work that I've had in a long time," said Brennan.

"It's okay," she said. "There's a plate of pot roast for you in the fridge if you get hungry later. You'll just need to microwave it."

"I appreciate that, but I think I'm too tired to eat. How was your day?"

"Same old," replied Abigail. She paused for a bit. She was hesitant to bring up the phone call that she had with Christine. "Christine called today."

"Christine?" asked Brennan. "As in Christine Fulton? God, we haven't heard from her in years!"

"Yeah. She just wanted to catch up," confirmed

Abigail.

"So, how is she doing?"

"She's settled down over there, but she's not coming home any time soon. She met a guy that she's completely obsessed with. She claims that she won't come home because it's too expensive, but I know it's only because she doesn't want to be anywhere other than by her man's side."

"Sounds serious," said Brennan.

"Yeah," replied Abigail. "I also opened up to her about our open marriage."

"What?" demanded Brennan. His voice changed from being tired and groggy to one that was thunderous and upset. "What would you do that for?" Brennan's eyes were as round as the moon, and his eyebrows were so high that they were practically touching his hairline.

"Relax, Brennan. She's not coming back for a long time. No one else is going to know," said Abigail.

"She can still talk to other people on the phone! How could you be so careless?"

"I honestly don't see what you're getting all riled up about. It's not a big deal, okay?"

"Not a big deal? Aren't you the one who has been crying and obsessing over this for months?" Brennan was visibly upset, and his tone had grown more confrontational with every word.

"Whatever, Brennan. I just wanted someone to talk to about it because you never open up to me. I saw no harm in bringing it up with an old girlfriend of mine."

Brennan didn't say anything else. He stood up, grabbed his pillows, and stormed out of the room.

"What a child," muttered Abigail. She was also fuming at this point. She got up and walked to the bathroom. Her skin felt hot as she splashed cold water on her face to help calm herself down. She got ready for bed knowing that she wouldn't be sharing it with anyone else that night.

A few days passed by, and it was like Brennan had just

completely forgotten about the fight. Abigail wondered if he was just choosing to ignore it or if he had just truly gotten over the entire ordeal. Whatever the case, she didn't want to talk about it anymore either. Talking to Christine felt like no big deal to her, and she didn't understand why Brennan was so fussy about it. Maybe he realized that he was being a brat, she reasoned to herself.

Abigail also hadn't been in the best of moods because Brian had stopped replying to her. She racked her brain trying to come up with a probable reason for why he had just stopped messaging her all of a sudden. At first, she thought that he just got busy with his work at the hospital. Although, she also realized that even though he was busy in the past, he always found the time to reply to her messages here and there. Then she started thinking that perhaps it was because he had grown bored or tired of her. Abigail was worried that maybe Brian realized that he didn't want to get intimate with an older woman after all. It had been a somber Saturday for Abigail, and Brennan had taken notice of this.

"What's wrong?" he asked her as the two of them were sitting across one another in the living room. "You look like you've got a lot on your mind."

Abigail didn't answer right away. Instead, she shook her head and picked up her cell phone to browse through her social media feeds. She couldn't find anything that was interesting, and her mind didn't allow her to focus on what she was reading. She put the phone down and said to Brennan, "Do you remember that one time you went out drinking with Vince, Phillip, and the other guys?"

"What?" asked Brennan as he adjusted himself on the couch so he was facing her. "Which time are you talking about?"

"You know the one," replied Abigail. She gave him a stern look and there wasn't any hint of irony in her voice.

"Are you talking about that time we went drinking and played video games all night long?"

"Supposedly, that's what you were doing," said Abigail.

"Abigail, that was more than four years ago. And that was exactly what we were doing!" he defended.

"I remember that night well. You came home like, what? Five? Six in the morning?"

"Yeah, I was too drunk to drive and so I decided to stay over at Vince's place." He sighed as they had had this conversation before.

"This was before he and Megan were living together, so she wasn't there to witness you sleeping over."

"Do you still not believe me about that? It's been four years!"

"I was so mad at you that night. I was sick to my stomach, and I couldn't sleep," she confessed. "You didn't even think to call or message me to let me know that you were alright? You must have been hiding something."

"I was drunk. My better judgement was compromised. I'm sorry. I don't know what to tell you," he said.

"I still think that you cheated on me that night." She leaned forward. "You cheated on me, and all of you boys have been hiding the truth from me all of these years."

"You don't really believe that, do you?" Brennan shook his head.

"I do," replied Abigail.

Brennan rolled his eyes and went back to watching television. Abigail knew that that was his way of saying that he was done with the conversation.

"It was four years ago," he said before getting up and heading to the bedroom.

That night, Abigail was standing in front of her bathroom mirror with her phone in her hand. She was dressed in nothing but her underwear as she stared at the reflection of her body. On her phone an image of herself from before her pregnancy. The picture depicted Abigail and Brennan on vacation from five years prior where she was dressed in a two-piece bikini. She compared how her body looked back then to what it looked like in that moment and saw that it had become very different. I need to get that body back, Abigail thought.

She got dressed in her nightgown and headed to bed with her iPad. She opened up the internet browser and typed in "best diet for weight loss" into the search bar. Numerous articles from sites like Healthline, *Men's Health*, and WebMD popped up. She decided to open one of the articles with the headline "The Top 8 Diets for Losing Weight Fast." From there, Abigail began reading about the concepts of calorie restrictions and the role that nutrition plays in weight loss. She studied the different food and supplements that she should be eating in order to achieve her desired results. By the end of the night, Abigail had fallen asleep with the iPad on her chest while thinking about what diet plan would best suit her.

Abigail woke up the next morning and decided that it would be the first day of her new diet. Based on her research, she would need to cut back on her calories in order for her to lose a significant amount of weight. So, that Sunday morning, Abigail went down to the kitchen and prepared the usual breakfast for everyone in the family except for herself. She cooked up a batch of eggs, bacon, and waffles for everyone, and then went back upstairs and told Brennan that she would be heading to the grocery store.

"Breakfast is already on the stove. Can you take care of waking up the kids and getting them ready for breakfast?"

Brennan, who was still half asleep, grumbled "yes" and went to the bathroom to splash some water on his face. Abigail didn't want to waste too much time getting ready so she tied her hair up in a bun and threw on a white t-shirt to go along with a pair of blue jeans and sneakers.

"What do you need from the supermarket so badly?" asked Brennan, who was wide awake now.

"I'm just starting a new diet, and I need healthier food now," she explained. "None of the stuff in the pantry will do.

"Okay," said Brennan. "Bye"

Abigail headed out of the house and hopped into the car while taking mental notes of all the food that she needed to buy. In her mind, she was already plotting out what she needed to eat for the week. She had decided that she was going to restrict herself to just five hundred calories a day in order to really expedite her weight loss. Naturally, she understood that there weren't too many food items that would make her feel full without exceeding five hundred calories. That's why she had to make sure to purchase meal replacement diet shakes that would make her feel satiated.

When she got to the store, she found a few shakes that were lined up for her in the health aisle. A bunch of them were on the more calorically dense side and so she opted for the brand that only had two hundred calories per serving. This way, she had room for two shakes a day plus a light snack or so. Aside from buying the shakes, Abigail also purchased a few fruits, vegetables, teas, and healthy crackers. She was hell-bent on making this diet work and losing all of that excess fat.

By the time she lined up for the checkout counter, her cart was filled with low-calorie cereals, diet shakes, bananas, apples, celery sticks, and more. Abigail prepared her credit card as she was about to make her payment, and she smiled. She was proud of herself for having the willpower to make this drastic change in her life. It was rare for her to feel proud of herself.

When she got home, Brennan and the kids had just finished breakfast.

"Oh, you're home," said Brennan. "Let me help you unload the groceries."

"No, it's okay," replied Abigail. "I got it."

"Nonsense."

Brennan went up to Abigail and helped carry all of the grocery bags, setting them on the kitchen counter. He methodically unloaded each item together with Abigail and set them all aside.

"Abigail," he said, "these are just a bunch of fruits and diet shakes. What kind of diet are you going on?"

"I'm just trying to stay away from calories in general," she explained. "I need to lose weight."

"No, you don't. You look absolutely perfect. Doesn't Mommy look pretty, kids?"

"The prettiest!" replied Amber.

"Yeah. Momma pretty," chimed Riley.

"See? Even the kids think so," said Brennan.

"Don't make this hard for me. I want to lose weight right now, and I just want your support," replied Abigail as she loaded the groceries into the pantry.

"I'm not making it hard for you. I'm saying that you're fine just the way that you are."

"And I'm saying that I'm not happy with this body and that's why I'm going on a diet," said Abigail. "So, please. Just make me feel supported."

"Okay," said Brennan. "I support you."

Over the course of the week, Abigail stayed disciplined with her diet. On Monday, she took a diet shake first thing in the morning and was committed to not having anything else until dinner, which was another serving of the diet shake.

Tuesday came and she already felt sluggish around noon. The restricted calories had her feeling like she had no energy, and it was difficult for her to focus on her YouTube videos. That's when she decided to have a serving of grapes, but she was careful to not eat more than a hundred calories' worth. Whenever she was tempted to have a bite of bread or to fix herself up a bowl of cereal, she just thought about how she looked in that photo of herself in the bikini.

In particular, she fixated on her collarbones. She noticed in the photo that her collarbones were so pronounced and prominent. They had since begun to fade and lose their prominence underneath a layer of fa. Every single morning, she checked the mirror to see if there were any changes to how her collarbone looked.

This went on for days until Friday came along and she took a snapshot of herself. She compared the photo to one that she took before she started dieting and tried to see if there were any differences. In her mind, her collarbones had become a lot more visible now, but she was still skeptical. Maybe I'm just being biased, she thought.

That Friday night, before she and Brennan went to bed, she sat beside him and said, "Brennan, I need to ask you something, and you have to promise not to laugh."

"What is it, hun?"

"Are my collarbones more prominent now?"

"Your what?" He turned to look at her.

"My collarbones. Do they seem more visible to you?" asked Abigail as she slid the sleeves and collar of her gown further down so that Brennan could get a better look of her shoulders.

Brennan squinted his eyes as he examined his wife's clavicle. She looked at him and felt herself growing anxious over what he would say.

"You know what," said Brennan, "that crazy diet of yours must be working."

"Are you serious?" she asked.

"Yup. I never would have noticed if you didn't point them out, but your collarbones do indeed look a lot more visible now."

A huge smile swept across her face as Brennan had affirmed her success with her diet. She stood up and ran to the bathroom to look at herself once more before running back into the bedroom with Brennan.

"I'm thinking one more week of this diet and I'll be a lot closer to how I used to look before pregnancy."

Abigail went to sleep that night with a feeling of lightness and contentment in her heart. It had been a while since she last went to bed feeling fulfilled at something she had accomplished on her own.

Chapter 30

Brennan

SOMETHING IN HIM changed when Abigail told him that she had opened up to Christine about their open marriage. They had a short argument about it, but Brennan had had enough. He was tired of arguing. When he walked up to his bedroom and sat with his thoughts, he decided that Abigail was being selfish and that she no longer cared about his feelings. She violated the one rule of their agreement, and it greatly upset him. If this is really how things are going to be, then I'm going to make the most of it, Brennan told himself.

He doubled down on his efforts on the dating apps. Brennan couldn't be as aggressive on Bumble because girls had the advantage of messaging guys first. However, he compensated by putting a little more effort into his profile picture. He had taken pictures in different outfits until he had settled for one that he really liked.

Days had passed since Brennan and Abigail had the argument about Christine, but Brennan didn't bring it up anymore. Most of his days were consumed by him messaging different girls. Sure, there were some women who didn't find him interesting or who were turned off by his age. But Brennan also discovered that a lot of girls seemed to be interested in the fact that he was married.

"Hello," he wrote as he messaged one girl. "My name's Brennan."

"Hi," replied the girl. "I'm Cindy. Aren't you a little old to be on dating apps like these?"

"I'm not that old," defended Brennan. "But yeah. I'm actually unhappily married, and my wife and I have decided to see other people."

"Oh no," said Cindy. "Why? What happened?"

"You really want to talk about this here?" asked a surprised Brennan.

"I mean, yeah, it'll help me to know that you're not just some random creepy old dude who's looking for younger girls to hook up with."

"Point taken."

This was when he realized that he could use his situation with Abigail to his advantage. It seemed like a lot of the girls that he was chatting with were very sympathetic to his situation, and that made them more eager to converse with him. He also discovered that women were especially drawn to him whenever he would tell them about his best moments as a husband and a father.

"It's just really frustrating," Brennan wrote to Amanda, another girl he had been messaging with. "I tried to make her fall in love with me again by surprising her with flowers and a teddy bear one time. I wanted to show her that I could still be spontaneous."

"Awww, that's so sweet!" Amanda messaged back. "What did she do?"

"She told me to throw the teddy bear away and that it wasn't going to solve anything," he said.

"Oh my goodness, that's intense," empathized Amanda.

"Yeah. I don't know. I was really trying my hardest to

make this marriage work, for the kids most especially. I didn't want them to grow up in a broken home, you know?"

"It's so cute how great of a dad you are. You are so much about your little girls."

Brennan managed to get the sympathy and kindness of so many women because of conversations like these. He had found the formula to getting girls to become more comfortable and at ease with talking to an older male stranger like himself on an online dating app. Everything that he was ashamed of in the real world could be used to his advantage in the online dating space. Brennan also realized over the following days that most women in these dating apps were just like his wife. They craved emotional connections, and they weren't just looking to sleep around. This was one aspect of the online dating world that he wasn't all that uncomfortable with.

"I'm not really looking for anything serious," he told Jasmin. She was a pretty blonde who was around seven years younger than him. The two of them struck up a conversation because she found Brennan's profile picture cute.

"Oh," Jasmin texted back. "Well, I'm not really looking for any random hookups."

And that signaled the end of their conversations. So Brennan learned that he wouldn't be open about the fact that he wasn't interested in any emotional entanglements. I get so much emotional drama here at home as it is, he thought to himself. I just want to have fun . So he made it a point to always just play along with the girls he was talking to just so he could prolong the fun.

The next girl that Brennan actually ended up sleeping with was Claire. She was a barista who was also living in Minneapolis. Claire was a young fair-skinned brunette who was in her mid-twenties. She worked as a barista full-time as a way to help pay the bills while she pursued her passion of painting on the side. Brennan enjoyed talking to Claire because of her youth and energy.

"I would really love to see your paintings sometime," Brennan messaged her. "I'm sure you're very talented."

"Actually, I'm not that good yet. I'm still practicing," she replied. "But I could send you some pictures! I would love some feedback."

"Hmmmm," Brennan texted back. "I was thinking that I could see them in person. Paintings always look different in person than in pictures."

He felt himself grow nervous as he sent this text. He had never been so forward with any of the girls he was texting. It didn't help his nerves that Claire didn't message him back right away. Although, after what seemed like an eternity to Brennan, he got a notification for a message from Claire.

"I actually have the night off work tonight," she said. "Maybe you could come over to my apartment and take a look at my pieces."

"Pieces?" replied Brennan with a winking emoji.

"I mean art pieces haha," Claire texted back.

"Of course, of course. Text me the details."

Brennan visited Claire in her apartment after he was done with work. It was definitely not as fancy as Sheila's condo had been, but he didn't care much. He was mostly focused on the anxiety and nervousness that he was feeling. A bead of sweat streamed down his forehead and onto the side of his face as he rode the elevator up to Claire's apartment unit. It was the same kind of nervousness that he felt when he was with Sheila. Except this time, he felt like he had a better idea of what he was getting into.

Claire lived in a cramped studio apartment with a loft. There was barely any furniture, but there were stacks of unused canvases just lying around everywhere. By the window stood an easel with an unfinished painting. The apartment was also lined with bookshelves, and Claire seemed to have made use of whatever space she could find to mount her books on.

When Brennan went through the door, Claire took his coat and slung it over a lounge chair in her small living room space. "Are you hungry?" she asked Brennan.

"Not really," he replied.

"Good," she said. "Because I didn't prepare anything."

Claire went up to him and kissed him right on the lips, grabbing his face and pulling him to her. Brennan kissed her back and gently sucked on her lips as he gently tugged her hair from behind. He pulled away to catch his breath and said, "I thought I came here to look at your paintings."

"Among other things," Claire replied.

She grabbed his head again and plunged her lips straight into the side of his neck. Claire then took his hand and led him to the loft where her bed was located. She stripped herself down to her nude body and helped Brennan do the same. Before he knew it, he was already lying atop her and making love to her. As he pushed back and forth in slow methodical thrusts, she continued to nibble at his ears and whispered, "Slower, Brennan. Slower. Savor it." Brennan slowed his pace down and tried his best to focus on every sensation that was going through his body. Claire moaned slightly as he rocked her back and forth until her moans crescendoed to a volume loud enough for everyone on the apartment floor to hear.

After they had both climaxed, Brennan lay on his back beside her as the two of them tried to catch their breath. Staring up at the ceiling, Brennan said, "You're quite the artist."

"You're not too bad yourself," she replied. "I think it's time for a repeat performance."

Just when she said that, Brennan remembered the moment that Sheila had asked him to make love to her again. He had brought an extra condom this time with Claire, but he felt disgusted at the memory of Sheila trying to trick him into getting her pregnant. Brennan turned to

Claire and asked, "What's your take on kids, Claire?"

"Woah, Brennan," she said with an alarmed look on her face. "I'm just looking to have fun here. I don't want kids."

"That's good," he said. "That's exactly what I wanted to hear." He grabbed her head, pulling her closer to him, and kissed her. Brennan made slow and tender love to Claire once more before the two of them finally got around to looking at her paintings.

"Listen, Brennan," said Claire as they were going through her artwork. "I know that I said that I'm only looking to have fun."

"Yeah," said Brennan. "What about it?"

"Well," she replied. "It's true that I don't want to have kids… yet. But I'm also looking to settle down and get serious with my love life, you know?"

"Go on," he urged.

"I mean, eventually, I want the whole thing. The family. The house. Everything that you've got with your wife."

"I'm sure that you don't want what me and my wife have."

"You know what I mean," she said, slapping him on the arm. "I just mean like I'm not ready to get serious just yet. But I'm open to seeing where this goes. If you and your wife don't work things out, I'm open to…" she trailed off. "I'm saying that I like you, is all."

Brennan smiled and looked at her intently as if to see if she was being serious, but he couldn't tell if she was joking. "I like you too," he said. "But I can't do this to my wife, Claire."

"What do you mean?" she asked. "Doesn't she want the two of you to see other people?"

"She may say that she wants it, but I'm sure she doesn't mean it," said Brennan. "The truth is I feel really guilty about what you and I have just done. It felt good at the time, but I don't feel really good about it now."

"I'm sorry to hear that," said Claire.

"Yeah," he replied. "I'm sorry too. I think I better go."

Brennan left Claire's condo feeling relieved. He was stressed out to hear that she was interested in getting serious with him. He racked his brain trying to come up with an excuse to get out of there and guilt was what came to him first. Way to be quick on your feet there, Brennan, he thought to himself. The truth was that Brennan didn't want anything serious at all.

The next girl that Brennan slept with was Michelle. She worked as a baker and owned a pastry shop in Minneapolis. She was a short, cute girl who had long brown hair, brown almond eyes, thick lips, and a small thin nose that pointed upward. Brennan was immediately attracted to her profile photo on Tinder and messaged her right away.

Again, he used his usual technique of gaining her sympathy by explaining the situation that he had with his wife. He judged Michelle to be an inherently sympathetic individual, and he found it easy to reel her in. She was particularly fond of the fact that he was a dad of two little girls. According to her, she was a daddy's girl herself. She was thirty-one and had been running her bakeshop for around five years at that point. Brennan and Abigail had even been to the shop a couple of times to stock up on pastries before. They had been talking for a few days until Michelle finally invited Brennan to visit her at the store.

"Come by during closing time," she told him. "That way, you'll have my full attention."

Brennan decided to swing by a fast food joint to pick up a couple of burgers and fries for himself and Michelle before he headed over to the pastry shop. When he arrived, Michelle was already putting away what was leftover of their inventory. She had also saved a couple of chocolate croissants and muffins for Brennan.

"I didn't think that you would have had the chance to prepare dinner so I just decided to grab us something to eat," he said. "I hope you like cheeseburgers."

"Are you kidding me? I love cheeseburgers!" she replied with a smile. Michelle told her employees that they could leave early and that she could close up. She arranged a quaint little dinner setup with a small cafe table at the corner of her shop. Brennan and her had their first date in the corner over cheeseburgers, fries, and watered-down soda. Brennan asked Michelle a lot of questions about what it was like to run her own business and what got her into baking in the first place.

"It started when I was young," she explained. "My mother and her sisters were always baking around the house. Our house always smelled like butter and flour. I loved it so much, and they always let me hang around them. I guess I just wanted to carry that atmosphere into adulthood."

"Fascinating," said Brennan. "Well, it looks like you're doing pretty good for yourself. Your shop has managed to amass quite a following."

"Yeah," she replied with a smile. "I still pinch myself every day just to check if I'm dreaming."

"Oh," Brennan replied as he raised his hand to her cheeks. "Stop doing that. You would never want to harm these precious cheeks."

She smiled and gazed longingly into his eyes. Brennan leaned close and planted a kiss on her cheek, withdrew, and looked at her eyes once again. This time, it was Michelle who leaned in close and gave him a kiss right on the lips. Brennan opened his mouth and let her tongue inside. Michelle pulled back, stood up, and closed the blinds around the pastry shop's windows. Brennan sat on his chair and just admired how graceful she looked as she walked across the shop. She then turned the dimmer switch down so that both of them could only just make out each other's silhouettes in the faint light.

Michelle went back over to Brennan and pulled him to his feet. She led him all the way to the pastry counter and turned around. Brennan pressed himself into her back as he caressed her hips and thighs. Michelle leaned her head back and reached her hand up to caress Brennan's head. He kissed her on the side of the neck and slowly pulled her dress up as she removed her underwear. Brennan unbuttoned his pants and pulled them down to his ankles as he continued to caress Michelle's hips and bare butt.

Slowly, she bent over and supported herself by placing both her hands on the counter. Brennan gradually penetrated her and went deeper until his pelvis came into full contact with Michelle's butt. He withdrew and thrust himself into her again and again. Michelle let out a few stifled moans as her knees began to feel weak and buckle underneath her. She compensated by leaning forward onto the pastry counter more. Brennan leaned forward and grabbed a hold of her breast as he kissed her back.

Brennan and Michelle made intense love in the darkness of the pastry shop that night. They transitioned from the pastry counter to one of the dining tables and even made their way to the back of the kitchen. Michelle made a joke about how they were violating a number of health violations, and Brennan chuckled as he continued to make love to her. By the time they were finished, it was close to midnight, and there were barely any cars or pedestrians that could be heard from the outside.

"That was fun," said Brennan as he zipped his pants back up. "Do you know where I put my shirt?"

"It's right there by the table," Michelle replied while pointing at the table where they had dinner. "And yes, that was fun."

Brennan laughed as he walked over to the table to put his shirt back on.

"Was it fun enough for you to maybe want to do this again?" she asked.

"Maybe," he said while nodding his head. "If you continue to bribe me with pastries, it'll be hard for me to resist."

"You're going to end up putting me out of business,"

said Michelle as Brennan leaned in for a kiss.

"Listen," he said after kissing her. "I've got to go. It's getting late, and I haven't told my wife where I am. Despite our situation, she would still want to know that I'm safe."

"Oh, sure," she said. "I understand. Let's talk tomorrow?"

"Sure thing." He kissed her again before grabbing his bag and walking out the door. As he made his way to his car, Brennan was already thinking of some possible excuses he could make to not see Michelle again. He didn't want to just outright disappear from her life without any notice. He liked her too much for that. But he didn't like her enough to want to get serious with her or anything.

The next morning, while at work, Brennan received a text message from Michelle again. She wanted to know if he wanted to meet up that weekend for a real dinner.

"We can go to an actual restaurant this time," she proposed. "What do you think?"

"Michelle, that's sweet," he replied. "But my wife and I both promised that we would be discreet about this. We can't be going out on dates with other people in public."

"Oh, right," she said. "Silly me."

"Actually, Michelle," Brennan texted back, "there's something I want to talk to you about."

"What's that?" she asked. "Should I be scared?"

"No, not at all," he affirmed. "It's just that I don't think we should see each other anymore."

"What? Why? Was it something I said?"

"No. Not at all. I just went home late last night, and my wife was still awake when I arrived. She asked me about where I had been and who I was with."

"And?"

"Well, she's really uncomfortable with the fact that I was with you. She told me that she has a lot of friends that are regular customers of yours. And she feels like her friends would make fun of her if her husband kept on

179

sleeping with the pastry chef that they buy their bread from."

"I'm more than just a pastry chef, Brennan."

"I know you are," he said. "You're amazing. It's just that I need to respect my wife's wishes on this. For the sake of my family, I just have to do this. You can understand that, right?"

"I guess," replied Michelle. That was the last text that she would ever send him.

Brennan went through similar cycles with a handful of girls over the next couple of weeks. He would strike up conversations with them on the dating app and have them feel some kind of emotional attachment to him. Over time, he got even more proficient at arousing certain feelings out of the women he was conversing with.

Once they became more comfortable with him, he would find a way to go to bed with them just one time. After that, he would come up with some kind of excuse that would get him out of ever having to see them again. Some of the girls that he met were rather bland and forgettable. In Brennan's mind, all he wanted to do was get these girls in bed and be done with them. Although, there were certainly some experiences that stuck out in Brennan's memory.

There was this one girl, named Caitlyn, who Brennan thought was the prettiest girl he had ever found on the dating app. In her profile photo, she was dressed in a fitted white crop top along with black leggings that really showcased her slender build. She had bright blonde hair and striking blue eyes that contrasted well with the softer features of her face. Brennan didn't think that he would ever have a shot with a girl like that, but he still sent her a message. To his surprise, she replied to him, and they struck up a conversation. As they are talking, the girl revealed to him that she was a swinger.

"Does that mean you get around often?" asked Brennan.

"Fairly often, yeah," replied Caitlyn. "I get around. Is that a problem?"

"No," said Brennan after giving it some thought. "That's not a problem at all."

"So, are we hooking up tonight or what?"

"I get off work late tonight, but I can drop by your place right after."

She texted him the address, and Brennan was actually excited for it. All day long, he couldn't concentrate on work because he was excited about getting intimate with the prettiest girl that he had been with so far. It didn't help that Caitlyn sent him more photos of herself in different outfits. This only distracted him from work even more, and they added more fuel to his excitement.

Brennan didn't waste any time getting off from work once he had finished the final task of the day. He didn't even bother to pick up any food as he made his way to the address that Caitlyn gave him. She told him to meet her at the bar of this mid range hotel in downtown Minneapolis. He had mentioned that he wanted to avoid going out in public with her, but she assured him that he wouldn't be bumping into anyone in this hotel. To her credit, he had never heard of this hotel before, and he trusted her. Also, he considered her too hot to pass up on.

He made his way towards the hotel bar and saw no one that looked like Caitlyn. Brennan assumed that she was just running late. So he sat down at the bar and ordered a drink. Just as the bartender set a dry martini in front of him, a woman's voice from behind him said, "Can you make that two, please?"

Brennan turned around and saw a woman that looked like a far less attractive version of the Caitlyn he saw in the photos. In real life, her entire face was caked in thick layers of makeup. Her blonde hair was visibly fake, and she was immensely overweight. Brennan was in shock as he surveyed Caitlyn from head to foot.

"Caitlyn?" he asked.

"It's me, honey," she replied. "Do you like what you see?"

Brennan gulped and didn't answer. He took a sip of his drink and nodded his head begrudgingly. "So should we head upstairs or something?"

"Hold on there, bub," she said. "You've got to buy me a drink first."

The two of them sat at the bar and conversed as they slowly sipped on their martinis. Brennan kept on thinking about whether he should push through with it or not. He found the woman sitting across from him absolutely repulsive, but he never let her know that. He also felt deep inside of him that he wanted to have sex that night, but he wouldn't be getting any action at home. Caitlyn was the best shot he had at getting laid that night, and he didn't want to blow it. Eventually, the two of them finished their drinks and made their way up to the room that Caitlyn had already arranged for them.

"How much does this room cost?" asked Brennan.

"Don't worry about it," replied Caitlyn. "The owner owes me a favor. All you need to think about tonight is me and how much fun we're going to have."

The two of them made love twice that night. While Caitlyn was not what she had advertised on her dating profile, Brennan couldn't deny that she knew her way around bed. It was almost masterful the way that she had contorted her body in spite of her size. He had never had an experience quite like that with anyone. Brennan also noted that the best part about Caitlyn was that she knew that this was just a one-time thing. He liked that he didn't have to come up with an excuse to not see her again.

When the night was over, Brennan merely dressed in his clothes again before turning to Caitlyn to say goodbye. "It was an interesting night," he said.

"Interesting?" she asked. "You do me a disservice, Brennan. I blew your mind."

"That you certainly did."

"Let's not draw this goodbye out, Brennan. We're never going to hear from each other again. This was a one-time thing."

"You took the words right out of my mouth," he replied. He smiled at her and walked away from one of the most interesting nights that he had had in a long time.

Chapter 31

Abigail

ABIGAIL WAS SITTING in the cafe one afternoon as she fiddled with her empty cup of coffee. Her left leg was fidgeting uncontrollably as she felt her heart race with anticipation with every passing second. She was waiting for Stephen, a man who was ten full years younger than her. The two of them had developed quite a rapport through their texts, and she found him immensely cute from his pictures.

Abigail also loved the fact that he showered her with compliments whenever she sent him selfies of herself. In fact, she was so fond of Stephen that he was the first guy that she actually ended up wanting to meet in person. He owned a car detailing business in town, but it wasn't anything too big, so Abigail was confident that he wouldn't be someone that she or Brennan had any mutual friends with.

She put a lot of effort into how she looked that day. Abigail swapped out her usual yoga pants for a nicer flattering pair of dark wash jeans that went well with a loose-fitting white chambray button-up blouse. She was up late the night before trying to decide on how to wear her makeup and style her hair. She settled on a light curl so that her flowy hair would appear wavy and voluminous. As for her makeup, she decided that she would go for a light natural look. She didn't want to make it seem like she was trying too hard.

Abigail and Stephen arranged to meet at 3:00 p.m. in a cafe that was around a fifteen-minute drive from Abigail's house. Due to her excitement, she left the house extremely early to drop the kids off at her mom's place before arriving at the restaurant at 2:30 p.m. She didn't bring a book to read and help her pass the time, so she decided on ordering ahead and getting a cup of coffee.

At around five minutes past three, Stephen walked into the cafe. Abigail recognized him immediately. He had a clean military-style buzz cut that was faded to near perfection. He also sported a five o'clock shadow that still highlighted his chiseled chin and jawline. There were a few lines around his face that indicated his age, but he still exuded a youthful glow and energy about him. He was dressed in a simple white t-shirt underneath a brown suede bomber jacket to go along with a pair of light blue jeans and Chelsea boots. He cleans up pretty well for a mechanic, Abigail thought the moment she saw him.

Stephen saw her and walked over to her table where she stood and greeted him with a hug. "It's nice to finally be meeting in person," he said. "You're as pretty as you look in your pictures.

Abigail smiled and felt a warm rush of blood surge through her face. "Thank you," she replied. "I was also just thinking that you clean up pretty well for a car mechanic."

"Well, I'm not technically a mechanic," said Stephen. "I started out as one, but I don't do any of the mechanical work anymore. I just own the business now."

"Of course," she said. "I was just joking."

They both took their seats and Stephen noticed the

empty cup that already sat on the table.

"Oh, I'm sorry. Was I that late?"

"What?" replied Abigail. "Oh, no. I just got here super early and decided to order ahead. I hope that's okay. Can I get you anything?"

"Oh, no," said Stephen. "I hope you haven't paid for that yet. This one's on me. Let me go and place my order."

As Stephen walked over to the counter, Abigail eyed his body. He definitely had the build of a marine. His hulking shoulders were indicative of his active lifestyle. He had a svelte trim, and he looked like he spent considerable hours at the gym every day. This made Abigail nervous about how she looked even though she had lost a considerable amount of weight from her dieting. Stephen returned with a cup of coffee and a couple of slices of cake.

"I'm not sure if you're into sweets," he said as he sat down. "But I got us a little something either way. I hope you like cake."

"I'm actually on a strict diet," said Abigail. "But for you, I'll make this one exception."

"It shows," replied Stephen. "You look like you pay a lot of attention to your body."

"Well, thank you," she said with a smile. "You're one to talk. You look like you work at the gym."

He laughed and took a sip of his coffee. Abigail shifted in her seat as she eyed the people around the cafe. Stephen took note of this and asked her if something was wrong.

"Actually," she began. "There's no getting around our age difference, Stephen."

"Right," he said in reply.

"I don't want you to take this the wrong way or anything, but I'm completely new to this. I'm afraid that we might run into anyone I might now. Now, I'm not ashamed of being on a date with you, but my husband is surely not going to be comfortable about it. So, I'm just asking that if we ever run into someone I know, we just say that you're my nephew. Is that okay with you?"

She looked at him intently as she anticipated him to take offense to what she was asking. Instead, he smiled and held her hand. "Of course," he said. "I completely understand."

Abigail breathed a sigh of relief and thanked him. She told him that she was so appreciative of how receptive and accommodating he had been before changing the topic and asking Stephen more about his life. She learned about his childhood and how his parents had always provided him a life of comfort. He was born into money, and he acknowledged how this gave him the freedom to just pursue whatever he was passionate about.

"Not everyone has the opportunity to just take a risk on the things that they're most passionate about," he explained. "My parents were always my safety net, and they allowed me to pursue my passion for cars."

He explained how he got into the car detailing industry and talked about his struggles in learning how to run a business. Abigail tried her best to feign interest, but everything just felt so boring and uninteresting to her. The more that she and Stephen talked, the more disinterested she became. She found him to have a rather bland personality that seemed a lot more interesting through text exchanges than in real life. Abigail thought that she loved the fact that he continuously showered her with compliments. However, even that seemed to have lost its novelty over time.

Things only started to become interesting for Abigail when he asked her about her situation with Brennan and what that experience had been like for her so far. She opened up to him that this was the first time that she was meeting a guy in person.

"I'm flattered," said Stephen. "I hope I live up to your expectations."

Abigail almost rolled her eyes but decided to play along. "And what do you think those expectations might be?" she asked.

"Well," Stephen began. "It seems to me like the one thing you're really craving for is adventure and excitement. You want to… immerse yourself in new experiences."

"Fair assessment," she replied. "And you think you would be able to give me that?"

"If you let me," he said with a wink. He looked at her straight in the eyes to let her know that he was being serious.

"What did you have in mind?" she asked.

"What do you say we get out of here and I show you?" proposed Stephen.

Abigail felt like a bass drum had suddenly manifested itself in her chest. She developed a frog in her throat as she struggled to come up with any comprehensible response. She opened her mouth, but nothing came out. So she nodded her head instead and stood up from her chair. Stephen stood up as well and said, "Let's go back to my place. Just follow my car back to my apartment."

Abigail nodded without saying another word as she picked up her belongings and walked with Stephen towards the cafe's parking lot. She got into her car and waited for Stephen to drive onto the road before following him from behind. He led her all the way to his apartment, which was just a few blocks away.

She parked her car at a nearby parking lot and met up with Stephen at the lobby of his apartment. He grabbed her hand and led her to the elevator before making their way up to his unit. Stephen unlocked his apartment's door, and Abigail was immediately greeted with the strong smell of cedarwood with slight undertones of green herbs.

"Can I get you anything?" he asked her.

"I've had my fill at the cafe," she responded. Abigail decided that the time was now or never. She went up to Stephen and kissed him on the lips. As he locked lips with her, she slowly removed his bomber jacket and pulled his t-shirt off his back. They both removed their pants and went straight to Stephen's bedroom.

His apartment wasn't big, but it wasn't cramped either. Abigail noticed that he made good use of the limited space that he had. She saw that the kitchen was well-outfitted and that his living room was modestly decorated. Although she couldn't look around much as she was mostly interested in getting Stephen into the bedroom. His youth had been something that had energized her. It made her feel things that she hadn't felt in a long time.

As she embraced his chiseled frame, it made her feel sexier knowing that she was worthy of getting intimate with such a beautiful man. The two of them kissed their way through the apartment's hallway into the bedroom. They were now both completely naked at this point with each of their clothes scattered throughout various spots in the apartment.

Stephen lay her down on the bed and kissed her belly. Abigail was surprised to not feel any shame or insecurity in that moment. She loved the feeling of his lips pressing against her skin. "Kiss me all over," she told him. "Kiss me everywhere you want."

Stephen moved his lips towards the lower parts of Abigail's torso, gently kissing her along the way. He eventually made his way towards Abigail's hot zone, and she felt a great warmth all over her body as he inched closer towards her spot. Suddenly, she could feel his tongue moving in random circular patterns. "Yes," she whispered to him. "Taste me." Stephen made use of his tongue to play around with Abigail for a few minutes before she eventually grabbed his head and said, "I want you inside me now."

Stephen climbed on top of her and she helped guide him inside of her. Abigail felt a warmth in her groin as he penetrated her, and she let out a slight moan.

"Are you okay?" asked Stephen.

"Yes," she replied. "Keep going."

Stephen continuously thrusted his hips back and forth

at a slow rhythmic pace. He held himself steady as he stared straight into Abigail's eyes. She tried her best to look straight into his, but she couldn't help but close her eyes every time he moved inside her. It all felt so good as Abigail felt the blood rush to her face. She could feel her body was close to caving in on itself and was ready to let loose a big, loud moan until suddenly, the movement stopped. She felt Stephen's entire body stiffen as he lay on top of her. She opened her eyes and saw that he had his eyes closed with his mouth ajar.

"Did you finish?" she asked.

"Yeah," he replied. "Did you?"

"Oh—" She paused. "Yeah. I did."

"I'm glad," he said. "That was amazing.

Stephen crawled into bed and lay down with his blank face staring at the ceiling as he struggled to catch his breath. Abigail lay her head down beside his as she stared up at the ceiling herself. Well, that was unexpected, she thought. Now she was confused about what she had to do next. She needed to think of a way to get out of this situation.

"Listen, Stephen," she said. "I'm sorry to have to do this to you, but I need to go pick up my kids. My mother can only handle them for so long."

"You have to go already?" he asked, sitting up.

"Yeah, sorry," she replied as she got up from the bed. "Can you help me gather my clothes?"

Stephen got out of bed and helped Abigail track down her pants and blouse while she put her underwear back on. "Are you sure that you have to go so soon? Was it something I did?"

"No, Stephen," she lied. "It's just that I really need to pick up the girls or else I won't hear the end of it from my mother."

"Alright," he said as he got dressed as well. "I had a lot of fun. Did you have fun?"

Abigail looked at him and replied, "I had fun,

Stephen."

"Well, then maybe you would want to do this again sometime?"

"Oh, Stephen." She took his hand and led him to the couch where they both sat down. "I had fun, but this isn't something that I can do again."

"Why not?" he asked. "If you liked being with me, then why can't we do this again?"

"My life's just really complicated right now, Stephen. I'm still trying to figure things out myself. I don't want to drag you into any of my crazy," she told him.

"I would be okay with that," he said. "I could handle it."

"I think it's best if we just stay friends. If anything else happens along the line, then we deal with it when we get there. But for now, let's stay friends."

"Alright," he said with a look of utter dejection on his face.

Abigail kissed him on the forehead before gathering the rest of her belongings and walking out of his apartment.

Chapter 32

Brennan

BRENNAN DECIDED TO sign up for a less popular dating site that was more targeted towards married people who were interested in having affairs. This site suited Brennan perfectly because it had all of these different protocols that were designed to make dating more discreet and intimate. It took a full week for Brennan to really navigate his way around the site. He managed to get a few messages from married women, but he wasn't interested in any of them.

After fully building up his profile, he became more aggressive in his search for a woman that he could hook up with. I really need someone with more maturity right now, he told himself. He messaged a few women, but none of them had replied to him yet. I've just got to stay patient, he thought. Married women aren't as easy as younger women.

One day, while at work, Brennan received a notification on his phone. One of the girls he messaged on the new dating site actually responded to him. Her name was Charmaine Evans, and she was twenty-eight-years-old.

This meant that she was considerably younger than Brennan, but not young enough for him to think that she would be immature. She worked in the events planning industry, and that worried Brennan at first. He thought that anyone who worked in that field would be bound to know a few of his friends or acquaintances. However, he figured that she was too young to be in contact with anyone within his immediate circle.

"Hey," she messaged him. "I'm sorry it took so long for me to reply. I'm still trying to figure this app out. It's also been a struggle trying to hide this from the husband."

"Hi, no worries," he replied. "I take it that things aren't going so well in the marriage."

"I don't think anyone on this app has a marriage that's going well, do you?"

"No. Probably not… My name's Brennan."

"Hi, Brennan. I'm Charmaine. I see from your profile that you're just a couple of years older than me. Are you still with your wife or have you been separated?"

"We still live together," he responded. "We've got two kids as well. Both girls. Do you have any kids?"

"Yup," she answered. "Two boys. They're probably the only reason that I haven't left my husband yet."

"Oh, I'm sorry to hear that," he replied.

"Don't be," said Charmaine. "My husband is a dick. He's the one who's been wanting to sleep around with other women, so I've just decided to do the same. I wanted to make things work, but he chose to break my heart instead."

"That sucks," said Brennan. "I'd love to talk to you about it further, but I'm busy at work. My boss is going to ream me out if he sees me on my phone the whole afternoon. Maybe I can give you a call tonight after dinner?"

"Sure," she replied. Brennan breathed a sigh of relief before Charmaine sent him a follow-up message. "Make sure your wife won't be in the same room."

"Definitely," he said. "Talk to you later."

Instead of going back to work, Brennan wanted to find out everything that he could about Charmaine. He could only see her profile picture, and she was very pretty. Other than that and her first name, he had no idea who she was. It didn't help that looking for her name on Facebook produced lots of search results. He had no idea where she lived either. The dating app made sure to protect these kinds of details for its users. That was why Brennan signed up for the dating site in the first place. It had strict security and privacy protocols. Brennan found himself regretting all these strict security features as he obsessed over Charmaine all afternoon.

Later that night, after dinner, Brennan stayed behind in the living room when Abigail finished doing the dishes. "I think I'm going to watch a little TV before going to bed," he told Abigail. "I drank a cup of coffee this afternoon, and I don't think I'll be sleeping anytime soon."

"Okay," she replied. "Just try to moderate the volume a bit so you won't wake the kids up later on."

"Alright," he said. He sat on the couch and made himself comfortable as Abigail ushered the kids up the stairs to help them get ready for bed. Brennan texted Charmaine and told her, "My wife is getting the kids ready for bed. I'll call you once she's done and in our bedroom."

"Looking forward to it," she replied. "My husband's out of the house tonight. Big surprise there. You can call anytime."

Brennan decided to watch some TV for real while waiting for Abigail to finish bathing the kids and tucking them in. By his estimate, it wouldn't take her longer than thirty minutes. He settled on a sports documentary about the life of Muhammad Ali. Brennan wasn't much of a boxing fan, but he still found himself glued to the screen as he learned about Ali's struggle with the civil rights movement and life outside the boxing ring.

Suddenly, he heard footsteps coming from upstairs.

Abigail was walking through the hallway and into the bedroom, which he confirmed with the sound of a shutting door. After waiting a few seconds to see if Abigail would come out again, he picked his phone up and dialed Charmaine. He lowered the volume of the TV just so he could hear Charmaine properly, but not enough so that Abigail could hear him talking on the phone with someone.

After a couple of rings, Charmaine picked up the phone and said, "Hello? Took you long enough." She had a slight raspiness to the tone of her voice.

"I'm sorry," replied Brennan. "I had to wait for the coast to be clear, just as you instructed."

"I'm glad that you're a man who has no problem with taking orders and following instructions," she teased.

Brennan noticed that there was a certain distinction in the way she spoke. Charmaine had a way of overenunciating her consonants, as if she was very intentional in her manner of speaking.

"So, your husband is not around, is he?" he asked.

"Probably out making love to another woman right now is my guess," she suggested. "The kids have already gone to bed as well."

"How old are the kids?"

"Nine and ten," she replied. "My husband and I got married at a very young age. Well, I got knocked up, and he was forced into marrying me anyway. We were never really in love."

"Really? You've been married to a man you don't love for all these years?"

"Well, I didn't realize it at the time," she said. "I think I was young and naive enough to believe that I could learn to love him just because the two of us had kids together. But I'm slowly coming to realize that that's never going to happen. I tried my best, but he seems to not want to have anything to do with me."

"I hear you," he said. "I know the feeling."

"Oh?" she replied. "Do tell."

"Well, despite my best efforts, it seems like the wife isn't interested in spending the rest of her life with me anymore. Like you, I fought it for a little while, but I eventually gave in. You can only give so much without getting anything in return, you know?"

"Oh, I know," she said. "Trust me, I know."

"It seems like we have a lot in common, then," he told Charmaine.

"It seems like we do," she replied.

Both Brennan and Charmaine continued to vent about their frustrations in their individual marriages. But Brennan was careful to not reveal to Charmaine that he and Abigail were set up in their open marriage situation. He still wanted to respect their agreement that they wouldn't reveal these details to anyone. Instead, he told Charmaine that Abigail wasn't interested in getting intimate with him anymore and that his marriage felt like a sham. In turn, Charmaine complained to him about how much she and Robert were fighting in their relationship. She said that every discussion that the two of them had would eventually turn into an argument. She recounted to him one time about how a simple discussion about that particular day's weather had turned into a full-blown fight over Robert's infidelity.

"I'm just so tired of it, Brennan," she said. "I never used to be a confrontational person. I'm afraid that this marriage has turned me into a monster, and I hate it."

"I understand that," he told her. "It's sad when our supposedly loving relationships end up turning us into monsters."

"My goodness, look at the time," she said. "We've been talking for over an hour."

"Oh," said Brennan as he looked down at his watch. "We have."

"I better start getting ready for bed," she said. "You should too, before your wife starts getting suspicious."

"You're right," he replied. "But I'd love to talk to you again."

"I'll do you one better," she teased. "What if the two of us meet for lunch this Saturday so we can talk in person this time?"

"Oh," Brennan thought. "I don't think I have anything on my schedule for that day."

"Then it's a date," she said. "I'll send you my address and you can pick me up."

"Won't your husband be around when I pick you up?"

"He already said that he'll be out of town this weekend. He said that it's for business, but we both know what that really means," she replied. "But I'll let you know if there are any changes. If not, I'll be waiting for you to pick me up."

"You've got it," he said. "See you then. Good night!"

"Good night, Brennan," she said before hanging up.

Saturday came around and Brennan had already told Abigail that he would be heading out of town for work. His excuse was that he and his team needed to go visit a high-profile client in Wisconsin that was looking to upgrade their IT infrastructure.

"Normally I wouldn't have to go along on these trips, but it's a big account. The higher-ups are counting on me to close this deal," he told Abigail.

"Yeah, sure. Go ahead. I don't mind getting the kids to myself," she replied.

That was it. Brennan had his excuse. He could spend the entire weekend with Charmaine as he planned to. Brennan decided that he would take Charmaine to St. Paul for lunch just to make sure that they wouldn't run into anyone they knew. He drove over to the address that she sent him at just around a 11:15. Brennan was about to text her that he was outside, but she had already emerged from the front door of her house.

Charmaine was just as beautiful in person as she was in her picture. She was clearly of Asian descent and had long straight black hair. Her face was well-proportioned with very pronounced cheekbones and puffy lips that were painted a bright red. She wore her hair in a neat ponytail and had very light makeup on and was dressed in a brown turtleneck sweater and a pair of denim jeans with white sneakers.

"You look awfully pretty," he told her as she entered the passenger's seat.

"Thank you. You don't look too shabby yourself," she replied. Brennan did put an effort into his appearance that day. He wore a light-wash denim shirt that he tucked into a pair of white chinos that accentuated his legs well. He also made sure to shave and put some product in his hair to make it look like he made an effort.

"So what do you have planned?" asked Charmaine.

"We're going to St. Paul today."

"Why not stay within Minneapolis? Are you trying to hide me or something?" she asked with a slight hint of annoyance in her voice.

Brennan didn't answer right away. He opened his mouth as he scrambled for a reply before Charmaine interrupted him. "I'm kidding. Relax, would you? That's smart. We just have to make sure we're not going to run into anyone we know."

"You had me going there for a second," he said and smiled. "Don't worry. We're going to have a really good day today."

The drive to the restaurant took less than half an hour. There was relatively light traffic, and time just flew by for Brennan as they chatted away. They shared with one another what their alibis were to their respective spouses.

"I told my wife that we needed to see a client," he explained to Charmaine. "She doesn't know much about tech. If she did, she would have known that these guys take their weekend leisure time seriously. They wouldn't want to be meeting with tech guys during their weekends."

"I told my husband that a very old friend of mine from

China was flying in and that a bunch of us were gathering in St. Paul for the weekend," she said. "My husband hates my friends, and so I knew that he would never have offered to come along with me. Also, I knew that he had other plans already."

"With a girl?"

"You bet. It's nice to know that he's not the only one who's sneaking around today" She puts her hand on his leg.

"Who is watching over your kids?" inquired Brennan.

"Oh, I hire a sitter," she explained. "But they're getting much older already. I think they would prefer for me to leave them alone at the house all weekend so they can play their video games."

"I feel like it's the same with my girls and their toys, but they're far too young to be left alone. They also prefer to spend more time with their momma than with me."

"Oh, I'm sorry to hear that."

"Oh, don't be sorry. I don't feel bad about it," replied Brennan. "It's just that they're girls, you know. They can relate to their momma more than they would with me. I know they still love their dad, though."

"That's sweet. You really care about your girls, huh?" She smiled.

"It's why I'm still fighting things out in an unhappy marriage," he answered. "It's all for the little ones."

"The things we put up with for our children, huh?" retorted Charmaine.

They finally arrived at their destination. Brennan brought Charmaine to a fancy little restaurant called Oh My Steak. It was a prominent steak and seafood restaurant with a very luxurious and rustic interior. The floors were made up of a beautiful maple wood parquet, and its furniture looked like they were made up of dark cherry oak. On the far side of the restaurant stood a dazzling bar with an impressive collection of the world's finest single malt scotches. There was a big crowd when they entered, and Charmaine expressed her worries about being able to find a table.

"You didn't think that I wouldn't make a reservation, did you?" asked Brennan.

"Mr. Sutton?" inquired the maître d'. "Your table is ready. If you and your wife would just follow me."

Brennan took a quick glance at Charmaine and raised his eyebrows at her upon hearing the maître d' refer to her as his wife. She laughed and lightly nudged him in the ribs as they made their way towards the table. As they took their seats, Brennan asked her, "What do you want to drink? They've got the best selection of scotch whisky here."

"I'm honestly not much of a scotch girl," she replied. "I do love myself some champagne, though."

"Kindly get a bottle of champagne for the lady," said Brennan as he addressed the waiter. "And I'll have a shot of Macallan 18, neat."

"Right away, sir," replied the waiter.

Charmaine took a glance around and observed the other people who were dining at the restaurant. "Doesn't seem like we're going to run into anyone we know," she said.

"Not here," replied Brennan. "But I do love this place. It was recommended to me by an actual client a few years back. I'll come here for special occasions with the family or whenever I'm in town for business. They have really good steak here."

"Do they have anything else?" asked Charmaine. "I'm not too fond of red meat either."

"No worries," exclaimed Brennan. "More steak for me, then! They also serve up some great seafood. Do you like scallops?"

"Oh, I love scallops," she said.

"You'll have that, then," said Brennan. He motioned for the waiter to come over and said, "We're ready to take our food orders now."

"Very good, sir. What will you be having?" asked the waiter.

"Give me a medium-rare prime striploin and prepare a scallop risotto for the lady."

"Your food will be ready in around fifteen to twenty minutes," replied the waiter.

Just as he left, another server arrived with the champagne bottle and scotch. He opened the bottle and poured a glass for Charmaine, then placed the whisky glass on Brennan's side of the table.

"You won't have any champagne with me?" she asked.

"I already have my scotch!" he replied.

"I couldn't possibly finish this on my own," she said. "Can we have them cork this for when we come back?"

"So, we're coming back, are we?" asked Brennan with a smile on his face. Charmaine laughed and raised her glass in the air. The two of them clinked glasses and took a sip of their drinks.

"Not even on his best days would my husband ever have taken me out on a date like this," she said. "It's frustrating to realize just what I've been missing."

"Tell me about it," replied Brennan. "I can't even remember the last time I felt so excited about going out on a date."

"Marriage is such a weird construct, isn't it?" she asked.

"How do you mean?"

"Well," she cleared her throat before continuing. "In my case, I got married out of necessity. I didn't really want it. I was just made to believe that I did because I was pregnant with this man's child. I guess anyone could say that that was a bad start to the marriage, and that's why it has devolved to what it has become today."

"Okay. So what's so weird about that?"

"Now compare it to your case. You and your wife weren't forced into anything. You wanted to get married because the two of you loved one another. You really committed from the start to spending the rest of your lives with each other. You weren't young dumb kids like we were when we got married, were you? The two of you knew what you were getting yourselves into."

"Yes. What's your point?"

"My point is that you both had an ideal start to your marriage. It was a far cry from what me and Robert had when we got married. Yet, here the two of us are. We've come to a meeting point. A crossroads. You with the good start and me with the bad one. Both of our marriages have crumbled to bits."

"Wow." Brennan sighed. "I didn't know that you had such a bleak view on marriage."

"Bleak is too strong a word," she responded. "I think cynical would be a better way to describe my views."

"Well, either way, you're far from being an optimist." Brennan raised his scotch in the air and said, "To cynicism."

"To cynicism," responded Charmaine.

The two of them continued to talk about how they were coping with their marital situations. Brennan showed her everything he had learned so far about online dating and the steps he took to be as discreet as possible. Charmaine was more experienced than he was in this field and had even given him a few tips to get more girls to reply to his messages.

"Try uploading a picture of yourself with a dog," she said. "Do you have a dog?"

"No," he said. "We don't have a dog."

"Shame," she replied. "Girls love dogs. They'll see your profile photo of you with a dog, and their subconscious will automatically associate you with fatherhood. But it's different if you post a picture with a child because most girls don't want that baggage. A dog would essentially give you all of the benefits of looking paternal without all the drawbacks."

"Interesting. Do all girls look for men who could be fathers?"

"Yes. Whether they realize it or not, girls are attracted to paternal vibes. It's biological. It's just how we're wired."

"I never thought about it like that," Brennan responded.

"Stick around for a bit and maybe you can pick up a few other things from me," she said with a sly smile. "I'm full of little surprises."

Their food arrived, and Charmaine was excited to dig into her risotto. Brennan marveled at the uniformity of the charring that was done against the crust of his striploin. In spite of her earlier reluctance, Charmaine was eager to have a bite of Brennan's steak when he offered her a piece. She closed her eyes as she bit into the juicy slice of beef and said, "Amazing."

"I told you," he said. "Best restaurant in St. Paul."

"This risotto is amazing too. Would you like a bite?"

"Sure," he replied. She scooped a spoonful of risotto and a small slice of scallop onto her spoon and reached across the table. He leaned closer as Charmaine shoveled the spoon into his mouth.

"Wow," he exclaimed. "That is good."

"I wonder how my husband would feel about me feeding another man," she said.

"I can't even picture how my wife would react to me eating off another woman's plate," he replied.

"Alright, I'm sorry. That's enough about the spouses. I won't bring my husband up anymore. Let's get to know each other better. We're more than our marriage woes, right?"

"Right." He nodded.

The two of them finished up their meal and continued to talk about their interests. Charmaine was particularly amazed at the fact that Brennan didn't enjoy watching movies or television shows that weren't rooted in real life.

"So all you do is watch documentaries?" she asked.

"And the news… and sports," he defended.

"You're so weird!" she joked.

"It's not weird. I just don't find myself getting interested in fictional drama and stuff," he explained. "I find it hard to be entertained by something I know could never happen in real life."

"It's called escapism, Brennan. The whole point of watching those shows and movies is to escape reality. It's the same as reading novels. Don't tell me that you don't read books!"

"I read books. Biographies. History books. Motivational books."

"But no fiction…"

"No fiction."

"You are something else, Brennan Sutton," she said playfully. "So, what else do you have planned for the two of us today?"

"Well, I told my wife that I would be away all weekend. And I don't want to come off as being aggressive here, but I was thinking we could get a room for a little staycation somewhere," he proposed.

"Oh…" She sighed.

There was a sudden change in her expression and tone of voice. She broke her eye contact with him and began surveying the room again. Noticing that something was wrong, Brennan said, "We don't have to if you don't want to. I don't want to pressure you or anything. I don't want you to think that I'm just after… well, you know."

"No, I know," she said. "I know that you're not that type of guy. Well, at least with me. I can tell that you're not just about wanting to get me in bed. Am I right, Brennan?"

"Yeah," he said. "Of course."

"Okay. The truth is that I really like you. Under normal circumstances, I would say yes to spending the night with you without even thinking about it. But I like you too much. I kind of want to see where this goes. I don't want to have sex just yet. Are you okay with taking it slow?"

Brennan was surprised at what she asked him. He never thought that he would meet a girl on an online dating site and have her ask him to take things slow. "Oh," he said. "Sure. Not a problem at all. I really like you too."

"Okay," she replied. "I'm glad. But I'd still love to spend the rest of the day with you if you're still up for it."

"Of course I am," he shrugged. "Let me ask for the check so we can get out of here."

"Okay, I'm paying for lunch," she said as she opened her purse and reached for her wallet.

"Nonsense," he replied. He put his hand on the table. "Your money's no good here." He called the waiter over.

"Brennan, please," she insisted. "It's the least I could do. You're the one who had to drive me all the way out here."

"It was my pleasure," he said. "Please don't deprive me of the opportunity to pay for a wonderful lunch with a beautiful girl."

"Fine," she said. "But only because you've been so sweet. Next time, I'm paying, okay?"

"Deal."

After picking up the check, Brennan led Charmaine out of the restaurant and back to his car. "So where are we headed now?" she asked.

"How does a trip to the beach sound?"

"I love the beach!" she replied while clapping her hands together.

"Have you been to Phalen? They've got a gorgeous lake there, and we can walk and talk along the sand."

"That sounds like a lovely idea."

Brennan drove the two of them over to Phalen Regional Park over at the northeastern side of the city. It was a relatively short drive, and the two of them listened to music along the way.

"So what kind of music do you like to listen to?" she asked Brennan.

"Anything, really," he replied. "I'm a huge blues guy myself, but I can appreciate different forms of music. How about you?"

"I can't say that I'm familiar with the blues. Maybe you can introduce me to it sometime. I'm more of a showtunes kind of gal," she answered. "I'm a sucker for musicals. Broadway. West End. I love theatre and movie musicals."

"Okay, now that's an area of music that I'm not too familiar with," confessed Brennan.

"Let me hijack your car stereo," she said. "I'll let you listen."

Abigail played a song from the Broadway musical Hamilton and told Brennan about the story.

"I've heard about how big that musical is," he said. "But I can't wrap my head around how a musical about Alexander Hamilton could ever be interesting."

"Just give it a chance," she said. After playing him a couple of songs, Brennan found himself bobbing his head to the beat of the music.

"Okay," he confessed. "You're right. It's really good."

"Right? We'll listen to more on the way home," suggested Charmaine.

Once they arrived at the park, Brennan parked the car and led Charmaine towards the beach. It was one of the largest lakes in the city, and it served as the centerpiece for the regional park, which was also outfitted with a golf course, beach, and trekking trails.

"It's beautiful here," said Charmaine.

"We're pretty lucky that it's not crowded," replied Brennan. "The last time I was here, the park was swarming with people."

"Seems like the universe is on our side today," she commented.

The two of them said nothing for a while as they walked and gazed over towards the lake. They were walking alongside one another as Charmaine slowly reached out and wrapped her arm around Brennan's elbow.

"Are you cold?" he asked.

"No," she said. "But this feels nice."

The two of them smiled at one another and continued to walk along the lakeshore.

"You might think that I'm crazy for saying this, Brennan. Considering how little time we've spent talking and getting to know one another, I already feel really comfortable with you. Is that strange?"

He looked at her intently and could see that there was no hint of irony in her voice or facial expression.

"It's not strange at all," he replied. "In fact, I feel the same way."

She looked at him and smiled before saying, "I really appreciate that you respect my decision to wait before… well, you know."

"No problem at all," he replied. "Maybe it's the age or everything that I've been through lately. I don't know. But that's not what I'm about anymore."

Charmaine stopped walking and turned to face him. She looked at him straight in the eyes before closing hers and leaning in for a kiss. Brennan kissed her right back as he grazed her cheek with the palm of his hand. They both gently pulled away at the same time, and Brennan felt as if they were the only two people in the world. Charmaine looked around and walked towards a rocky patch on the sand. Brennan observed her as she seemed to have been looking for something within the patch. After a couple of seconds, she picked something up and returned to Brennan with a couple of pebbles in her hand. She reached out and gave him one of the pebbles.

"What's this for?" he asked.

"Are you familiar with penguins?" replied Charmaine.

"Yes. They're cute, but what do they have to do with these pebbles?"

"Well," Charmaine explained. "It's a common mating ritual for male penguins to venture out and find these really fancy and rare pebbles to give to the female penguins they want to mate with. If the female is impressed, then she accepts the pebble, and they become mates for life."

"Are you looking for me to be your mate for life?" he asked her with a chuckle.

"I don't know yet," she replied. "But I do like your companionship, and I want for us to keep spending more time together."

"I would like that too," Brennan said in return as he accepted one of the pebbles.

"Let these pebbles serve as our own little mementos for this first date and for this feeling," she said.

"And what feeling is that?" asked Brennan.

"The feeling you get when you know that something special is about to take place," replied Charmaine.

They both smiled at one another as Brennan leaned in to give Charmaine another kiss.

Chapter 33

Brennan

"LET'S GO OUT to the club tonight," Charmaine texted Brennan while he was at work. "I heard the bar there makes a really good Old Fashioned. I figured that a whiskey lover like you could appreciate that."

"Sounds tempting," he replied. "But I honestly haven't been to a club in years. Where is it?"

"It's pretty near my place. We could actually just walk it," she texted back.

"I guess a dark club is as good a place as any to help us be discreet," he said. "I figure none of my friends go to clubs these days either. So we won't run into anyone I know. I don't have my car with me, though. It's currently being worked on at the shop. I'll have to pick you up in an Uber, if that's okay."

"That's perfectly fine with me."

"I take it that your husband won't be home?"

"Away on a golf tournament… supposedly," answered Charmaine. "Enough about him. Pick me up at around nine. And wear that new suit of yours."

"Will do," Brennan texted back.

After he set the phone down, Brennan felt a surge of excitement course through his body. The idea of going to a nightclub on a weekday made him feel like he was back in college again, before he met Abigail. Abigail, he thought. What's my excuse going to be?

Brennan went home from work that night fully prepared. "Hey, honey," he told Abigail over dinner. "I have to head out over dinner. One of my boss's old clients is in town, and he wants us all to go out for drinks."

"Drinks, huh?" asked Abigail without even taking her eyes off her food. "Alright, then. I assume you'll be home late."

"Yeah," he said. "Don't wai—"

"Don't wait up," she interrupted. "I know."

After finishing his dinner, Brennan went up to the bedroom to change into the new suit that he bought with Charmaine when they went shopping together. It was a tailored Italian cotton suit, and he paired it with a crisp white shirt underneath. He also sprayed on a couple of splashes of the new Tom Ford perfume that he bought with Charmaine as well. I smell like a hundred bucks, he thought to himself. He took one good look at the mirror, and for the first time in a long time, he felt like he was attractive. "I look damn good," Brennan said to himself aloud.

"You do," said Abigail who was halfway through the bedroom door. "Have fun tonight."

"I'll try," he replied. "You know how boring my boss and his friends can be."

"I sure do," she answered.

Brennan grabbed his phone and booked an Uber. The driver was only a few minutes away and so he decided to just wait downstairs.

"I'm gonna go now," he told Abigail. Without waiting for her to reply, he was already out of the bedroom door and descending the staircase. He quickly went to the kitchen and poured himself a glass of water. He hadn't been to a club in years, and he felt nervous about it. His phone buzzed and a notification popped up informing him that his Uber driver was nearby. Brennan went out onto the lawn and saw the car coming.

"Brennan?" asked the Uber driver as he hopped into the backseat.

"Yup," replied Brennan.

"Alright, let me just check where we're headed here," said the driver. "We're going to The Exchange Lounge. Is that correct, sir?"

"Yeah," answered Brennan. "But we've got to pick someone up along the way first. Do you mind? It's not too far out of the way, and I'll make sure to tip you."

"Sure, sir," he replied. "Not a problem. Where to?"

Brennan gave the driver Charmaine's address, and off they went. As they were nearing her house, he texted her to let her know to meet him.

"I'll be right down," she answered him. "See you."

The Uber pulled up to the house, and Charmaine was already standing on the porch dressed in a silky black dress and stilettos. Her hair was curled to a light wave, and she had smokey eye makeup on.

"You look absolutely stunning," Brennan said to her.

"And you look really good in that suit," she replied.

They continued on towards The Exchange. Charmaine told Brennan that it was one of the more exclusive clubs in the city.

"Will we be able to get in?" asked Brennan.

"You let me worry about that," she answered.

As they approached the club, Brennan could see that Charmaine wasn't kidding. There was a long line of people stretching out through the entire block just waiting to get into the lounge. "Damn," he said. "How are we going to get in?"

"Don't stress," she replied. "We're good."

"Do you have a reservation?" he asked.

"Something like that."

The Uber driver dropped them off right at the front of the lounge's entrance. As promised, Brennan tipped the grateful driver who thanked him and bowed his head as he accepted the money.

"So, do we go to the back of the line?" Brennan wondered aloud.

"Nope," she replied as she grabbed his hand. "Follow me."

Charmaine led Brennan all the way to the front of the line where the bouncers stood. Brennan could already feel his palms getting sweaty, but he trusted Charmaine would be able to get them inside.

"Back of the line, miss," said the bouncer.

"I'm on the list," she said.

The bouncer eyed her from head to foot and looked Brennan straight in the eye before saying, "Come with me." He took Brennan and Charmaine to the entrance of the bar where a lady with a clipboard was standing. "She says she's on the list," the bouncer told the lady.

"What's your name, m'am?" she asked Charmaine.

"Charmaine Evans," she replied. "I'm friends with Mr. Drake, the owner."

"Oh," said the lady with the clipboard. "Yeah, I see your name on the list. It says here you can get in for free."

"It should," replied Charmaine with a smile. "Oh, and he's with me," she said gesturing towards Brennan.

"Sure," said the lady. "You can go right inside. Have a good night."

"Thank you," replied Charmaine.

As they walked through the club's doors, Brennan whispered into her ear, "You're friends with the owner? Would he be friends with your husband too?"

"Don't worry about it," she said. "The owner never comes here. I met him a long while back because of work, and I told him to always keep my name on the guest list."

"So that's why you were so confident," said Brennan.

The Exchange Lounge had a very industrial

contemporary style to it. The walls were lined with unfinished concrete and the floors were made of dirty white marble. There were brown leather couches and lounge chairs that were sporadically scattered all throughout the space with a modest dance floor right in the center of the club. It was rather crowded, and every single table was taken. Brennan looked around and saw a bunch of people who looked like they were his age. He saw that they were all dressed in expensive-looking suits and that the men always had women draped around their arms.

"It's kinda loud here, don't you think?" he asked Charmaine.

"That's part of the fun," she said. "Sensory overload."

She led him towards the bar where she ordered a dry martini for herself and an Old Fashioned for Brennan.

"Coming right up," replied the bartender.

"Whenever you're in clubs," she told Brennan. "Always let the girls order. Bartenders pay more attention to girls."

"I'll take note of that," he replied.

When the bartender placed their drinks on the bar, Brennan was surprised to see a couple of shot glasses filled with a clear liquid alongside the Old Fashioned and the martini.

"Who ordered these?" he asked as he gestured towards the shot glasses.

"I did," she answered him. "I'm going to assume that you're not much of a dancer?"

"I'm not, but what does that have to do with anything?"

"Well, you will be by the end of the night. You're just going to need a little liquid courage first.

"So," she asked as she handed him the shot of vodka. "What are we toasting to this time?"

Brennan thought about it for a second and replied, "To being outside of your comfort zone."

"I like that," she said as she raised her glass. "Cheers!"

The two of them downed the vodka in one gulp and immediately chased it with their cocktails.

"I think mixing drinks is a bad idea," said Brennan.

"Get used to it," she replied. "The whole night is going to be filled with bad ideas."

"I don't think a shot of vodka and an Old Fashioned will be enough to make me a good dancer," he told her.

"You don't have to be a good dancer," she said. "The place is packed! No one here is a good dancer. You just have to go with the flow and move along with the music."

He didn't talk for a bit, and he looked at her through half-lidded eyes before saying, "Maybe you could show me how."

She looked right back at him and smiled. With her drink in one hand, she used her free arm to lead him towards the center of the dance floor. As she was dragging him along, he could feel the warmth of the vodka settling into his stomach. He took another sip of his Old Fashioned to help get rid of the strong taste of liquor from his mouth.

Before he knew it, the two of them were in the middle of a crowded dance floor. Charmaine turned to face him and placed her arm on top of his shoulder. She pushed her pelvis up into his and started swaying from left to right.

"Move to the beat of the music," she told him. "Move along with me."

Brennan closed his eyes and tried to move his hips in unison with Charmaine's as he concentrated on the rhythm of the music. In that moment, he felt as if it was just the two of them in the middle of that dance floor. It was like they were transported back to that beach in St. Paul when they each held a pebble in their hands.

He opened his eyes and saw Charmaine masterfully swaying in front of him without spilling her drink. She looked so comfortable and at ease with everything while Brennan felt as stiff as a board. Charmaine leaned in closer to his ear and whispered, "You've just got to relax."

Then, she twirled around and now had hers back turned to him. She pressed her butt up against his crotch and started grinding. Brennan felt himself grow hotter, but he couldn't tell if it was because of the alcohol or the dancing. She pushed her butt against him in slow circular motions as he tried to sway along with the music himself. He tried to take another sip of his drink, but realized that it was completely empty. Brennan looked around him for a waiter and saw that a bunch of guys were looking his way. That's when he realized that they weren't looking at him. They were looking at Charmaine and were trying to figure out how Brennan could land a girl like her. He smiled and nodded in the direction of a group of guys who were looking at him. They nodded back and raised their drinks at him as if to congratulate him for having such a hot girl with him that night.

"Hey," Brennan whispered into Charmaine's ear. "Let's go get more of that vodka."

Chapter 34

Abigail

IT WAS A Thursday night, and Abigail was at a sushi restaurant waiting for Kevin to arrive. She started messaging Kevin around a couple of weeks prior and didn't really take him seriously at first. To Abigail, he wasn't the most interesting guy in the world. However, over time, she had grown fond of the attention that he was giving her. He was always one of the quickest guys to reply whenever she was in the mood to talk. Kevin also never pulled back any of his compliments for her whenever she sent selfies. He made her feel good about being herself, and she decided that she was ready to meet him. He was all too eager to have dinner with her and agreed to go wherever she wanted.

She decided on a small sushi place in the downtown Minneapolis area. Abigail told Brennan that she was going out on a date, but she assured him that it would be in a part of town that none of their friends ever visited. It was a lowbrow sushi restaurant in a relatively quiet part of town. She wasn't expecting much from the restaurant in terms of its food, but she was eager to meet Kevin. Abigail had gotten there early because she wanted to scout the place first and make sure that no one she knew was there. Once she was sure that the coast was clear, she texted Kevin to let him know that she was waiting for him.

Kevin was thirty-seven and single. He had never gotten married because he centered his whole life around building his event-catering business. He used to work as a chef back in his early twenties for low to mid-scale restaurants. Eventually, he decided that he was done with being an employee and that he wanted to run his own business.

While they were still getting to know one another through texts, Abigail was fascinated with Kevin's ambitiousness. She marveled at how he was able to build his catering company from scratch with no help from outside investors or any contacts. He bootstrapped the money he needed for the capital investment from his own savings and took a risk with it.

He shared with Abigail that it was a struggle for him early on. Eventually, with effort and commitment, he managed to build a successful catering company that could function on its own. He explained that he had been so busy managing the business that dating women always proved fruitless in the past. Now, he had more free time and was willing to dive back into the dating pool again. Abigail empathized with him on this as she also shared how she needed to give up her career to become a full-time mom and housewife. Over time, Abigail found that she could really relate to him on a more emotional level. That's why she gave in to the idea of going out on a date with him.

They agreed to meet at the restaurant at 8:00 p.m. sharp, but Kevin showed up a few minutes before that. When he walked through the door, he saw Abigail seated at the table, and he had a surprised look on his face.

"Hi," said Kevin. "I'm surprised you're already here. So nice to finally see you in person." He approached Abigail and gave her a hug.

"Oh, I'm always on time," she said. "Punctuality is kind of my thing."

"I like that," he replied. "I like girls who value their time."

Abigail took note of how he dressed and was impressed with the outfit that he had on. He was wearing a crisp light blue shirt underneath a navy sports jacket. She also noticed the two-tone Rolex that he had on.

"I'm sorry about the venue," she said. "I must imagine that you don't dine at places like these often, especially given the fact that you work in the food industry."

"Oh, it's no trouble," said Kevin. "It's true. I don't dine much at places like this, but it's only because I rarely ever eat out. I mostly just cook for myself at home or I order takeout."

"But you must be curious why I asked for us to meet here, right?"

"It's because you don't want to run into anyone you know."

She nodded her head and asked, "Is that okay with you?"

"It's fine," he responded. "I perfectly understand. The situation you're in with your husband… it's strange."

"You don't even know half of it."

"We don't have to talk about him if you don't want to. Tonight, we can just make it about us. Would you like that?"

"I'd love that," answered Abigail and smiled.

Now that she was able to get a good look of him, Abigail realized just how much he looked better in person compared to his online photos. He was clearly of Middle Eastern descent as evidenced by his brown skin, round eyes, and strong facial features. He had a well-trimmed beard and a muscular build. Abigail also found herself enamored by his soft and gentle eyes, which offered a great contrast to his striking masculine features. There was also a subtle gentleness in the way that he talked and conducted himself around her. It somewhat reminded her of Brennan.

"You're a lot prettier in person," he told her. "I must say that if I were just meeting you for the first time, I would never believe that you're a mother of two."

"You're just saying that, but I'm flattered," she gushed. "Random question. Correct me if I'm wrong, but I recall you saying that your business practically runs itself now?"

"Yes," he said. "I'm fortunate enough to have built the catering company to a point where it can function without me. It's almost like passive income for me now."

"Fascinating," she replied. "I only ask because I wonder how you spend your days. I mean, I'm without a job, but I have my kids to look after and a home to maintain. I still consider myself relatively busy."

"That's a perfectly reasonable question," he said. "Honestly, my days are pretty boring. I spend a lot of time working out. I try to make it a point to take care of my body."

"It shows," she interrupted. "I'm sorry. Go on."

"Thank you," he laughed. "Aside from that, I'll go to the office every once in a while just to check on everyone. But again, they don't really need me. I'm fortunate enough to have assembled a great team. The truth is I struggle to find activities to fill my days with."

"And that's why you've decided to start dating."

"Exactly right."

"Well, I'm not sure if I can help you with finding things to fill your days with, but I'm glad that I could be with you tonight."

"I'm glad as well," he replied. "I'm very lucky to be having dinner with a beautiful, classy lady like you."

The two of them continued to talk and bond over dinner. Kevin ordered a couple of beers for the two of them to go along with a few selections of sushi. As their food was served, Abigail observed Kevin's face as he glanced at the pale-looking fish that was placed before him. She laughed at the horror that was on his face.

"Hey," she said. "It's okay. You don't have to eat that."

"It honestly looks like it's turned," he replied. "What do you say we just go back to my place and I cook you something instead?"

"That sounds good," she replied. "That sounds great, actually."

"Great," he said. "Did you bring a car?"

"No," she answered. "I took an Uber coming here."

"Hitch a ride with me, then," he said. "Let me take care of this." Kevin reached into his wallet, grabbed a hundred-dollar bill, and left it on the table.

"Kevin," she said. "That was way too much."

"Nah," he replied. "I've been blessed with a lot. I have a soft spot for struggling restaurants like this. I always try my best to help these businesses and their workers."

"That's really noble," she replied.

"Thank you," he said. "I try."

The two of them walked out of the restaurant and to a nearby parking lot where Kevin's car was parked. Abigail had seen luxurious cars before, but she didn't expect to be riding in a Porsche that night.

"That's a really nice car," she mentioned. "I don't think I've ever been in a Porsche before."

"Do you want to give it a drive?" he asked.

"Oh, I'd be too nervous," she replied. "The passenger seat is fine by me."

"Suit yourself," said Kevin. "But the offer still stands if ever you change your mind."

The two of them got into the car and were off to Kevin's place. Neither of them said anything for a while as music from the car's stereo was the only thing filling the silence.

"So," said Kevin as he broke the silence. "What do you feel like eating?"

"I don't know," replied Abigail. "Surprise me."

"Well, we were already having Japanese earlier. How

about I fix you up some proper sushi?"

"That sounds good to me," she said.

"I've also got a really good bottle of sake that a friend from Japan gifted to me a while back. It's the good stuff."

"Oh, seems like you've got a plan brewing for tonight." said Abigail.

"Maybe," he replied with a grin.

He pulled into the lobby of his condo and Abigail caught a glimpse of how luxurious his lifestyle was. The doorman opened the front door of the car for her while a valet attendant took Kevin's keys from him as he exited the car.

"Good evening, Mr. Dalton," said the doorman. "And good evening to you, miss..."

"Sutton," she replied.

"Good evening, Ms. Sutton," he greeted again.

"Good evening to you too," she told him.

Kevin smiled at the doorman and escorted Abigail towards the elevator shafts. Abigail wrapped her arm around his as they walked together and waited for the elevator doors to open. Once they were inside and on the way up, she felt herself getting nervous. They alighted the elevator once they reached Kevin's floor and made their way towards his condo unit. He reached his hand for the door, but before he could even open it, Abigail grabbed his face and kissed him hard on the lips. He kissed her in return as he blindly fumbled his way towards swiping his keycard through the door's scanner.

Once the door was opened, the two of them found their way inside his condo's foyer while kissing. Abigail didn't notice much of his apartment as Kevin barely had the chance to turn on the lights. He pushed her up against the door and put his hands underneath her butt as he lifted her up in the air. Kevin thrust his pelvis in between her legs and pressed himself up against her as he continued to kiss her face and neck.

"Kevin," she whispered. "I think I've suddenly lost my

appetite."

"So have I," he replied. "Bedroom?"

"Let's go."

Kevin carried Abigail all the way to the bedroom with the two of them locking lips the whole time. Abigail felt Kevin shoved his tongue deep into her mouth and she returned the favor. The room was dark when they entered, and he didn't bother to turn on the lights either. He laid Abigail down on his bed and reached for the night lamp on his bedside table. The room was faintly lit now, and Abigail had a better look at Kevin's face. She held his face in her hands and stared into his eyes without saying anything, then unzipped his pants. She took out his erection and tugged it in repetitive motions. Kevin removed the rest of his clothes as Abigail felt him growing stiffer and stiffer with every stroke.

He was now situated on top of her on the bed as he methodically removed her blouse and unhooked her bra. In a matter of seconds, they were both completely naked. Kevin spun them around and lay flat on the bed so that Abigail was now in the top position. She felt the intensity of his eyes as he looked up at her and gazed at her chest. She took both of his hands and laid them on her breasts, beginning to slowly position her pelvis on top of his. She grabbed his shaft and gradually inserted it inside her as she dipped her hips downwards. Once she felt Kevin inside of her, she slowly rotated her hips without breaking eye contact with him, feeling herself get warmer and wetter with each passing second.

Somehow, Abigail could feel Kevin's erection grow larger and harder after every thrust. She gradually picked up the pace of her hip's gyrations, and Kevin let out a loud moan. Abigail felt herself burning hot at this point. Every time she moved, she felt like an itch was being scratched inside of her. She released a modest moan and was surprised to see how much pleasure that brought her. She moaned again and again with each one becoming louder than the last. She didn't realize that she and Kevin had reached a point where they were both practically screaming out loud until she felt his legs stiffen for a brief moment and then eventually go limp. At that moment, she also felt an immense warmth course through her body, and she gave in to the wave of relief that swept over her. She collapsed right into his arms as they locked each other in a tight embrace while they tried to catch their breath.

"That was magnificent," said Kevin in hushed tones.

"The night isn't over, Kevin," replied Abigail. "We're just getting started."

Chapter 35

Brennan

BRENNAN AND ABIGAIL were sleeping in separate bedrooms now. Abigail stayed in the master bedroom while Brennan moved to the guest bedroom. It wasn't because they were fighting but because Abigail was no longer able to fall back asleep when the girls were paying them some late night visits after they both had fallen asleep. This wasn't an issue for Brennan because he could just go back to sleep after allowing the kids to curl up beside them in bed. However, this had started to be a real problem for Abigail who struggled with going back to sleep whenever she was awoken in the middle of the night.

So a decision was made for Brennan to move to another room so that Abigail wouldn't be interrupted anymore. They had both trained the girls to visit Brennan's room whenever they woke up in the middle of the night. Since then, at least one of the girls spent their nights in Brennan's bed, slipping in some time just after midnight, like clockwork.

This was perfect for Brennan because he had been struggling with looking for private opportunities to have conversations with Charmaine on the phone. He used to always wait for everyone in the house to be asleep before he could call, and he was losing a lot of valuable sleep because of it. Now that he had his own room, he had a brief window of opportunity to talk to Charmaine between getting ready for bed and before one of the girls would visit late at night.

For the most part, the conversations between Brennan and Charmaine were wholesome. They spent a lot of time talking about the feelings they had for one another and daydreaming about the kinds of trips and vacations that they could take together. Occasionally, their conversations could also get really hot and heavy. Brennan never made it a point to lock his bedroom door in order to avoid suspicion, but he was always wary of having one of the girls walk in on him while he was talking with Charmaine, especially when they were having sexual talks.

"Oh, Brennan," Charmaine told him one night while they were on a video call. "I feel so hot right now. I want to feel your body against mine."

She then directed the camera towards her chest which was flushed red. Charmaine then slowly pulled down one strap of her night gown to show off more of her cleavage.

"What are you doing?" asked Brennan. "You're being very naughty."

"I can't help it," she replied. "I'm so wet."

She then positioned her angle to show her hand rubbing against the outside of her exposed panties.

"Brennan," she said. "I want you inside of me."

Brennan then pulled his t-shirt up to his chin and pulled his pajamas down to reveal his package. He pointed his camera towards his groin and told Charmaine, "Look what you've done. He's completely awake now."

"Brennan," she replied. "Rub him for me, please." She then let out a soft moan as she continued to finger herself.

Brennan did as he was told and stroked his phallus with his fingers as he began to stiffen.

"Faster," Charmaine demanded. "Let me hear how much you like it."

Suddenly, Brennan could hear footsteps from outside his door. He quickly pulled his pants up and shirt down.

"Someone's coming," he told Charmaine. "I'll talk to you later. Miss you. Goodbye."

He ended the call before she could even get the chance to reply to him. Just as he put the phone down, his door slowly swung open, and the two little girls came barging in. Riley was crying, and Amber was holding her by the hand.

"Riley," said Brennan. "What's wrong?"

"She had a bad dream, Daddy," replied Amber. "Can we sleep here tonight?"

"Of course, girls," answered Brennan. He scooped both of them up in his arms and laid them on the bed, tucking them in before he turned out the lights.

"I'll leave Daddy's bedside light on so that you won't be scared, okay?" said Brennan as he switched his lamp on.

He grabbed his phone and texted Charmaine, "Hey. Sorry. It was the girls. Bad dream. I'll talk to you again soon. We need to finish what we started."

"Oh. I already finished," replied Charmaine. "Think about that while you sleep. Good night."

After a couple weeks of secret meetups and late-night video calls, Charmaine and Brennan decided to spend a weekend out of town at a luxurious spa resort. "You've been working so hard at the office," Charmaine told him. "You deserve a little self-love and pampering." It was hard for Brennan to pass up.

After doing their research together, the two of them settled on Smith's Resort in Brainerd. The resort was situated along Gull Lake and was known for offering a variety of upscale dining options and a high-end spa.

The two of them also liked the fact that it was a long way from Minneapolis. "I just want to go somewhere where we can be ourselves without having to look over our shoulder every five minutes," said Brennan.

Charmaine handled all of the arrangements and booked a private car with a chauffeur to take them there as well. "At least we can relax on the drive there."

The day of the trip came. Brennan had already told Abigail previously that he would have to go on a weekend golf trip with some of his big clients and bosses. This was the perfect alibi for him because Smith's Resort actually had a golf course as well.

"But you don't even have your own golf clubs," said Abigail.

"Yeah," replied Brennan. "My boss has an extra set that he's going to lend me. I'm not really going to be playing seriously. I just have to be there and make conversation."

"Whatever you say," answered Abigail. "Have fun."

Brennan went out on the curb waiting for the private car that Charmaine had booked for them. He gripped his weekend bag tightly and readjusted his scarf to cover more of his neck as it was a particularly cold morning in Minneapolis. The car arrived at his house, and Brennan was surprised to see that Charmaine was already sitting in the backseat when he opened the door.

"You're here!" he said. "I thought I was going to pick you up along the way!"

"Surprise," she replied with a faint smile. "I just thought that I'd pick you up myself." Although, Brennan noticed that there was a lack of enthusiasm in her voice.

"Everything okay?" he asked her as he took a seat beside her in the car.

"Yeah," she replied. "It's just been a really tiring week, and I didn't get enough sleep last night. I really needed to finalize a lot of work stuff before going away for the weekend. And it's a really long drive going over there."

"How long?"

"Around two and a half hours, according to Google."

"That's alright. You can sleep on the way. Use my shoulder as a pillow if you want."

"Are you sure? I don't want you to just be sitting here with no one to talk to along the way."

"It's really no problem. I like the quiet. It'll give me some time to think."

"What do you have to think about?" she asked him.

"A lot of things," he replied with a smirk. "Now go ahead and take a nap. I want you to have enough energy to enjoy the weekend once we get there."

"You're the sweetest, do you know that?" she said. Charmaine proceeded to close her eyes as she lay her head on Brennan's shoulder. "I just need a few minutes. I promise I won't be asleep the whole way."

"Don't worry about that," replied Brennan. "Go ahead and rest."

Charmaine slept through the whole way to the resort. All throughout the drive, Brennan made sure that her head never fell off his shoulder. He really did want her to rest and regain her energy. In all that effort to keep Charmaine comfortable, Brennan had to put himself in all kinds of uncomfortable positions. For the most part, he had to contort his body in such a way that one of his hands was supporting part of Charmaine's head so that it wouldn't fall or jiggle too much during the rough parts of the drive.

When they were pulling into the reception area of the resort, Brennan gently tapped her on her arm to wake her up. They got to the resort at noon just as the sun was directly beaming down at them from overhead. As Charmaine came to, it took a few seconds for her to realize that she slept for the entire drive over there.

"Oh my goodness," she told him. "I'm so sorry." Brennan noticed that she had the most concerned and apologetic look on her face. "Brennan, your shirt!"

Brennan looked down at his right shoulder and saw that Charmaine's makeup had smeared the white shirt he was wearing.

"I'm really sorry," she said. "Let me arrange to have that laundered."

"Don't worry about it so much," he told her. "It's just a shirt."

"I can't believe I left you alone for the whole drive."

"You didn't leave me alone."

"Oh, you know what I mean." Charmaine had a very disgruntled look on her face.

"Hey, it's alright. I managed to get some much-needed sleep too," he lied.

"Really? Okay. I'm sorry. I'll make it up to you," she told him.

"I can't wait to see how you'll do that," he answered.

Once the car pulled into the front of the reception, the resort's staff were quick to help unload Charmaine's and Brennan's bags. Brennan tipped the chauffeur and reminded him of when to pick them up for the return trip home. "Hello, Mr. and Mrs. Evans," said one of the staffers who were unloading their bags. "If you would please follow us to the reception, so we can check you in."

Brennan and Charmaine laughed at one another upon hearing themselves being referred to as a married couple. Brennan enjoyed the idea so much that he didn't even bother to correct the staff anymore.

"Come on, Mrs. Evans," he told Charmaine. "Let's get checked in."

The Smith resort was an objectively beautiful place. It had a very quaint and rustic aesthetic that didn't skimp on the finest and most lavish details. The impressive picturesque backdrop of Gull Lake only added to the charm. The moment that they both walked through the lobby, Brennan knew that they made the right choice in going there. While walking towards the reception, they saw that a bridal entourage was having a photoshoot out on the patio overlooking the lake. The resort was known to be a popular venue for weddings and other special events as well.

"Look at that," said Charmaine as she gestured towards the women in fancy gowns. "I didn't look that happy during my wedding day."

"Well, at least you're happy now, right?" Brennan said with a grin.

"Right." She smiled back.

After checking in, they were led to their room. They had booked a lower-level suite with a large patio and a beautiful view of the lake. The room itself was a sight for sore eyes and was the most elegant resort suite that Brennan had ever stayed in. It had very high ceilings and was rustically decorated. However, it was also fitted with high-end electronics like smart surround sound systems and a large plasma TV. The outdoor patio was built like the deck of a ship. It was also equipped with a full lounge and dining set where they could eat and drink all day under the sun as they overlooked the lake.

"This place is gorgeous," said Charmaine.

"Magnificent," agreed Brennan as he took in the view of the lake.

"Let's hang out here and sit in the sun for a bit," proposed Charmaine.

"I'd like that. Get settled down. I'll just go unpack for a bit, and I'll join you after."

"Don't take too long."

Brennan went back inside their suite and rang up room service to order a bottle of champagne.

"We'll have one sent up right away, sir," the voice on the other line told him.

Brennan unzipped his bags and unloaded his toiletries before placing them on the bathroom counter. After doing that, he hung all of his shirts up in the suite's closet. Just as he finished hanging up his last shirt, the suite's doorbell rang.

"Who's that?" asked Charmaine from the patio. "And what's taking you so long?"

"Let me go check," he answered back. "I'll be right there!"

Brennan opened the door and saw the bellboy with a

cart housing a bucket of ice, a bottle of champagne, and a couple of champagne glasses. "Where do you want this, sir?" he asked.

Brennan gave him a sign to wait as he quickly changed shirts.

"Can you wheel this out to the patio for me?" Brennan asked him as he handed him a ten-dollar bill.

"Gladly, sir," replied the bellboy.

As Brennan escorted the champagne out to the patio, he saw the look of surprise sweep over Charmaine's face.

"No wonder you took so long!" she told him.

The bellboy popped the bottle of champagne open and poured them both a glass.

"Thank you," Brennan told the bellboy. "That'll be all."

"Finally," said Charmaine. "Our weekend getaway can start."

Brennan handed her a glass of champagne and bent to kiss her as she lay back in the lounge chair. He raised his glass and said, "To our weekend getaway." They clinked glasses and sipped the champagne. The cold liquid felt bubbly and refreshing as it flowed through Brennan's mouth and throat. "That's some of the good stuff," he told Charmaine. Brennan took a seat beside her on the lounge chair where the two of them would spend the rest of the afternoon.

The two of them went over how they would spend the rest of the weekend. Brennan conveyed that he was mostly interested in trying out the food at the restaurant and having drinks at the bar with Charmaine. She agreed and told him that she wanted to avail a couple's spa package for the two of them as well.

They looked over the resort pamphlet to try to see what else they could do over the weekend while they were there, and they were fully engrossed in the pamphlet when Brennan heard a soft buzzing sound. Charmaine must have heard it too because they both looked up at the same time and saw an insect resembling a hornet zipping along the patio. Brennan felt Charmaine's grip on his arm stiffen as she caught sight of the bug.

As if the insect almost sensed her fear, it began to make its way towards her and caused her to scream and jump from her seat. Brennan saw this as an opportunity to portray his bravery and rolled up the resort pamphlet in his hand. Just as the hornet was within range, he swung at it with the pamphlet and managed to knock it off its intended trajectory. The blow was not strong enough to kill the hornet, but it looked disoriented as it flew in erratic circles before finally zipping away from the patio.

As the two of them watched the insect fly away, Brennan could feel his heart thumping. He was also afraid of bugs, but he didn't want to reveal this fact about himself to Charmaine.

"My hero," she said as she leaned her head against his chest. "I have a fear of flying insects."

"Don't worry," he assured her. "That bug won't be bothering you anymore, not while I have this trusty weapon." He gestured towards the rolled up pamphlet and made Charmaine laugh. As the sun was about to set, they decided to put some music on and order food to be brought to them.

"Let's just have dinner here while watching the sunset, please?" she asked Brennan. "Then we can get dressed up and head to the bar after."

"Sounds like a plan."

After browsing through the menu, Brennan called room service and placed their orders for dinner. He also ordered an additional bottle of champagne as the initial batch they ordered was already running out. It only took around half an hour for the resort to prepare their scrumptious dinner of buttered mussels, baked lobster, and grilled striploin with mashed potatoes and boiled vegetables. Brennan uncorked the second bottle of champagne himself as he and Charmaine sat down to enjoy their splendid dinner while watching the sun set.

"It's so romantic here," said Charmaine. "I love that I get to spend this moment with you. Look at this amazing view."

"It really is amazing," he replied, looking straight at her. She laughed as the two of them toasted to an incredible weekend again. They enjoyed their dinner while having light conversations about their favorite books and television shows. Brennan noticed that Charmaine was becoming a lot more talkative, and her skin had taken on a prominent shade of light red. The champagne was obviously starting to have its effect on her.

"I couldn't possibly eat another bite," said Charmaine as she set her utensils down on her plate.

"I'm pretty stuffed too," replied Brennan. "But I could use another drink, though."

"Are you trying to get me drunk, Brennan?" Charmaine asked him with a coy smile on her face. "Because it's working."

"Maybe." He smirked. "We've practically had a bottle of champagne each since checking in. Maybe we should call it a night. Wouldn't want you to think that I'm taking advantage of you."

"Excuse me," she replied. "I may be Asian, but I can still drink you under the table, mister."

"Okay, then. Shall we head to the bar?"

"Not looking like this. Give me a few minutes to freshen up and change into something a little more appropriate."

She smiled at him and walked back into the suite as Brennan stayed outside to enjoy the cooling breeze of the night. He could also feel the alcohol slowly creeping up and taking over his system, but he knew that he could still handle a few more drinks at the bar with Charmaine. Just as he was about to head inside to change his clothes himself, Charmaine emerged onto the patio in a beautiful fitted cocktail dress.

"When did you have the time to do your hair?"

Brennan asked her as he took notice of her curls.

"A girl has her secrets," she replied. "Are you ready to head up to the bar?"

"Yup. Let me go put on a blazer. I need to at least try to look like I'm worthy of escorting you."

"Very funny."

Brennan threw a navy blazer on top of his white linen shirt that paired well with his slim khaki pants. They were out of the suite and making their way to the bar when they noticed that a bunch of other people were headed in the same direction

"Looks like the bar is the place to be tonight," said Brennan.

"Oh," Charmaine chimed. "We can't go overboard with the alcohol tonight, okay? I booked our spa appointment for 9 a.m. tomorrow morning."

"Ambitious of you to think that we'll wake up that early."

"They didn't have any other open slots for the rest of the day. I had no choice."

"Don't worry. I'll make sure to get us to our appointment on time."

She smiled at him and planted a kiss on his cheek as she hooked her arm in his. They arrived at the bar and quickly occupied two vacant stools before anyone else could grab them. Brennan looked around and saw that the bar was almost full that night. They seated themselves beside a couple of girls who were locked in an animated conversation while sipping their cocktails. Brennan ordered an Old Fashioned for himself and a dry martini with extra olives for Charmaine.

"Okay," said Charmaine. "Two-drink limit for tonight, okay? I'm serious about that spa appointment."

"Don't worry about it," he told her. "I'm also serious about getting us there on time."

The two of them clinked glasses for the nth time that day and took a sip of their drinks.

"I'm really glad to be here with you," she told him. They looked deep into each other's eyes.

Brennan didn't say anything and then leaned in for a kiss.

"Aw," said one of the girls seated beside them. "Sorry to intrude, but the two of you look absolutely adorable."

"Thank you," replied a gushing Charmaine. "I'm Charmaine, and this is my boyfriend, Brennan."

"I'm Mary," the girl said. "This is my friend, Cleo. Nice to meet you guys."

Brennan smiled at the girls and nodded his head in acknowledgement. They were both blonde and dressed in casual cocktail dresses themselves. Cleo was slightly taller than Mary, and they looked nothing alike aside from their hair color. Mary was a little stockier in build with a round face while Cleo had more bony facial features.

"What brings the two of you to the resort?" he asked them.

"Oh, we're business partners, and we're celebrating a big deal we've just closed," replied Cleo.

"In that case, allow me to pay for your next round of drinks so we can join in your celebration," Brennan offered."

"Thank you!" said Mary. "That's awfully kind of you. What brings the two of you here?"

"We're just looking for a romantic getaway from the stress of everyday life," replied Charmaine. "This place seems like it's perfect for that, don't you think?"

"You can say that again," replied Mary. "It's so beautiful here!"

"I mean, it's a little pricey, but it's definitely worth it," added Cleo. "How long have the two of you been together?"

"Oh, we've been dating for just a few months," answered Charmaine. "But it feels like it's been so much longer than that. Right, Brennan?" She looked at him and smiled.

Brennan nodded his head and added, "Much longer."

Charmaine laughed and turned her attention back to the two girls. "So what line of work are you in?"

"We run an events agency together," replied Cleo. "We met when we were working in corporate, but we decided to pivot into events."

"Yeah," added Mary. "A desk job just isn't for us."

"Oh my goodness," retorted Charmaine. "I work in events too!"

"That's amazing!" said Cleo. "What are the chances?"

"I understand just how stressful this line of work can be," said Charmaine. "My week's been pretty rough. No wonder the two of you are looking to get away."

"You can say that again," said Cleo. "Actually, we learned about this place because we had to organize a wedding for a client here."

"Yup," chimed Mary. "We just found the place so beautiful and so we decided to come here for a weekend vacation."

"Where are you guys from?" asked Charmaine.

"Chicago," replied Cleo.

"Well, then let me get the next round of drinks to welcome you into Minnesota. I hope you drink tequila."

Charmaine motioned to the bartender to pour out some shots for everyone. That's when Brennan interjected, "Are you sure that's a good idea, honey? We have to be up early tomorrow, remember?"

"Just one shot wouldn't hurt," she said. "Come to think about it, maybe you shouldn't have one just in case."

Brennan laughed and said, "Yeah. I'm fine with my Old Fashioned."

The bartender served up three shots for the girls. Charmaine handed them out to her new friends and raised a glass before saying, "To friendship!"

That first shot signaled a downward spiral for Charmaine. She practically ignored Brennan for the next couple of hours as she and the other girls chatted away about what it was like working in the events industry. Brennan had no idea what it was like to work in events and didn't really get the chance to add to the conversation. Still, he was having a good time just listening to the girls.

Charmaine and the girls ordered one shot after another until they had practically consumed two tequila bottles' worth of shots. By the eighth shot, Charmaine was barely comprehensible. She was slurring her words and struggling to keep herself upright at the bar. The other girls weren't in much better shape either.

"Hey, man," Brennan said to the bartender. "Can you call someone from the hotel staff to help these girls back to their room?"

"Yes, sir," replied the bartender.

Brennan waited until a male staffer had arrived to escort Cleo and Mary back to their respective suites. Brennan gave him a tip and told him to take care of them. "Listen, ladies," Brennan addressed the girls. "This is my friend here, and he's going to help you get back to your rooms. We better call it a night."

The girls were much too drunk to protest, and Charmaine was practically half asleep at that point. "Hey, Charm," said Brennan. "What do you say we head back to the suite?"

Charmaine muttered something that Brennan couldn't understand. He hoisted her light and delicate frame up into his arms as she wrapped her hands around his neck and rested her head on his chest.

"Thank you," she whispered under her breath. He carried Charmaine all the way to their suite and laid her down on their bed. She was practically passed out at that point, and Brennan had to undress her. He got the trash can and placed it on the floor beside her just in case she needed to throw up in the middle of the night, then went to the bathroom to wash up.

Before going to bed, he set the alarm of his phone to 8:00 a.m. to make sure that they had enough time in the morning to get ready for their spa appointment. After he set up the alarm, he gave a sleeping Charmaine a kiss on the forehead before passing out on the bed himself.

The next morning, Brennan woke up as soon as the alarm sounded. He turned to his side and saw Charmaine was still sleeping. He stood up to check on the trash can beside the bed and found it empty. "Wow," he thought. "That girl knows how to handle her alcohol." He decided to give her a few more minutes of extra sleep as he stepped into the bathroom to wash his face and brush his teeth. After he was done, he walked towards Charmaine and gently nudged her arm to rouse her. She didn't respond right away, and it took a few gentle nudges from Brennan before she finally began to stir.

"What happened last night?" she mumbled with her eyes still closed. "My head really hurts."

"You might have had a little too much to drink," Brennan replied. "The tequila shots? Remember?"

"Oh, yeah," she replied. "That wasn't a good idea."

"Yup. But you have to get up now. We have a spa appointment in a few minutes."

"Okay. I need coffee first."

"I'll call room service. You just start getting ready."

He helped pull Charmaine up from bed and ushered her into the bathroom. After he was able to get her to start washing her face, he went back out to order some coffee from room service. Within the next half-hour, both Charmaine and Brennan were fully awake and ready for their spa appointment.

"You were a complete mess last night," Brennan told her while they were walking.

"I know," she said. "I'm so sorry. I totally ruined our night together."

"It's okay," Brennan told her. "I know how stressed you've been with your work. It was nice seeing you finally be able to unwind."

"Thank you for being so understanding," she replied as

she pecked him on the cheek. "I promise that the rest of the weekend will be all about us."

As they walked through the spa doors, they were greeted by the strong scents of eucalyptus and the soothing sounds of nature coming through the spa's stereo system. "Hi," said the woman standing behind reception. "Welcome to the spa. How can we help you today?"

"Hi," replied Charmaine. "We have a reservation for a couple's package at 9:00 a.m.? It should be under Charmaine Evans."

"Ah, yes, Ms. Evans. We've been expecting you. Please take a seat, and your massage therapists will be with you shortly."

After a couple of minutes, two female therapists emerged. The receptionist got up from her desk and introduced the two therapists to Charmaine and Brennan.

"This is Ashley and Mandy. They'll be taking care of you today. Our couples' massages are actually conducted within the spa cottage for extra privacy and intimacy. Ashley and Mandy will escort the two of you there, and they'll make sure to address any need you might have. Please don't be afraid to ask them for anything," the receptionist explained. "We hope you enjoy your spa experience with us."

The therapists escorted Brennan and Charmaine to the spa cottage where they were assigned a private room for just the two of them.

"You're actually the only ones here right now," said Ashley. "It's like you get the whole spa to yourselves."

"That's nice," replied Charmaine. "That's exactly what we were going for."

"We're going to leave you alone so that you can undress and settle yourselves down on the massage tables," explained Mandy. "Whenever you're ready, just ring the bell here on the side table, and we'll come back to get started."

Charmaine and Brennan both undressed and laid

themselves down beneath the sheets.

"This is exactly what I need after last night," grumbled Charmaine as she reached for the bell. Within a few seconds of ringing the bell, the massage therapists came back in and went straight to work on the couple.

"Take it easy on me," said Charmaine. "I had a rough night."

"And don't hold back on me," added Brennan. "I've got a lot of kinks that need to be straightened out."

"Yes, sir," replied Brennan's therapist. He wasn't sure whether it was Ashley or Mandy who was assigned to him, but he didn't care. The moment he felt his therapist rub her soft hands against his firm back muscles, he automatically felt more relaxed. The soft and subtle pain of her palms sent signals to his muscles, telling them to ease up. The soothing scent of eucalyptus and the warming sensation of the oil helped Brennan acquire a deeper sense of calm. Within minutes, he was practically knocked out.

Brennan woke up to Charmaine gently nudging him on the face and wearing a soft white robe. It was just the two of them in the private space.

"Oh, man," said Brennan. "I must have dozed off."

"Yeah," replied Charmaine. "You were practically snoring five minutes into it."

"That's so embarrassing."

"No. It was cute. Anyway, it's my fault that you were up so late last night."

"So what do we do now?"

"They left a robe for you and took our stuff to put it in some lockers. They said that they're taking us to the relaxation room as part of the couple's package."

"Relaxation room? What's that?"

"Beats me. We'll find out when we get there."

After Brennan put on his robe, he peeled back the curtains of their massage space. Ashley and Mandy were just a few yards away waiting for them.

"We hope you enjoyed yourselves," said Ashley as they

emerged from the private room. "If you'll just follow us, we can make our way to the relaxation room."

Charmaine and Brennan followed Ashley and Mandy towards another part of the cottage that was separated by a huge glass door. They entered a huge hallway that was lined with oriental drapes. Ashley motioned for them to walk through the drapes and into a small dimly lit room with a large bed with clean white sheets right in the middle. There were candles situated all throughout the corners of the room. Brennan and Charmaine stood as they watched Ashley and Mandy slowly light all of the candles. Instead of the overwhelming aroma of eucalyptus that enveloped the massage parlor, the relaxation room had a lighter lavender scent that coated it. Brennan still had no idea what they were supposed to do in that room and was too afraid to ask out of fear of sounding ignorant. Once Mandy and Ashley were finished lighting the candles, they bowed their heads towards Brennan and Charmaine.

"This is the relaxation room," said Ashley. "Take some time to sit in silence and meditate on your thoughts to expel any negative feelings or emotions that you might be holding in. Once you're ready, you can go back to the reception where you will be given your complimentary tea."

"Alright," said Charmaine. "Thanks, Ashley."

The two therapists left Charmaine and Brennan alone in the room with nothing but the scented candles and low-level bed. Brennan took a good look around and said, "Well, maybe we should start meditating now."

"I don't feel like meditating," replied Charmaine.

"Oh?" said Brennan. "What do you feel like doing?"

Charmaine turned to look towards the beaded drapes that separated the room from the hallway and looked back at Brennan before licking her lips. He stared straight into her eyes and knew what she wanted to do.

"Here?" asked a shocked Brennan. "Now?"

Charmaine didn't even wait for a reply. She was already

removing her robe. Within a few seconds, she was already completely nude and rubbing her fingers against the outer walls of her vagina.

"Charmaine," said Brennan suddenly very nervous. "Anyone can walk in at any time."

"That's what makes this fun," replied Charmaine as she untied Brennan's robe. They were now both completely naked, and she proceeded to tug against his erection. "Let's get a little dangerous, shall we?"

She pushed him back onto the bed so that he was now lying face up towards the ceiling. Charmaine straddled him and didn't waste any time lowering herself on top of his shaft. Once he was completely inside of her, she leaned forward and nibbled on Brennan's neck. She moved her hips up and down as she tried to hit various spots inside of her. Brennan grabbed a hold of her hips, but Charmaine pulled his arms back and pinned them down on the bed.

"You just relax and meditate," she said. "Let me do all of the work"

Brennan closed his eyes and let Charmaine take full control. He couldn't see what she was doing, but he could feel every single sensation. It was as if all of the goodness from the sex was only heightened by the vulnerability of his surroundings. He felt her quicken the pace. Brennan sensed that she was working hard on top of him, but he resisted the urge to open his eyes and see what she was doing. He grabbed onto the sheets of the bed and tightened his grip until he eventually reached a climax that was signaled by a loud moan.

Charmaine collapsed right on top of him and laughed. "Well," she said as she tried to catch her breath. "Feeling relaxed now?"

"Very," he replied. "You bring me a lot of peace, Charmaine."

She stared into his eyes and said nothing for a few seconds. She merely smiled and put her hand against his cheek. Finally, she opened her mouth and said, "I'm in love with you, Brennan."

Brennan looked back at her and felt his heart skip a literal beat. His lips gradually curved upward before replying, "I love you too."

Chapter 36

Abigail

ABIGAIL NOTICED THAT Brennan was going out a lot more often, and she knew that it wasn't always for work anymore. She had tried before to get him to open up to her about his dating life, but he never did. This wasn't a big problem for her back when he was rarely ever out. But it was becoming a lot more stressful now that he was out multiple times a week.

One night, after putting the kids to bed, Abigail decided to go to the guest room where Brennan was staying to have a chat with him. She went up to the door and opened it without knocking. She saw Brennan hurriedly put his phone down as if he were looking at something that he shouldn't have been looking at.

"Hey," he said with a surprised look on his face. "What's up?"

"I'm sorry," replied Abigail. "I should have knocked. Did I interrupt anything?"

"No, not at all. What's on your mind?"

"I think we need to talk."

"Sure. What about?"

"I know that you've been going on a lot of dates. I'm not dumb."

Brennan didn't reply. He sat there with a dumbfounded look on his face as he struggled to find the right words to say.

"You don't have to defend yourself," Abigail continued. "I understand. I want this for you. This is what I wanted for us. And I'm not asking you to open up to me about the details. I know that it makes you uncomfortable."

"Okay," said Brennan. "What exactly is this about?"

"I just need for us to fix our scheduling," she said. "I can't go on dates if you're the one who keeps going out. We need to have a better system. You've been out a lot, and I've been stuck at home with the kids all the time."

"I never thought about that," admitted Brennan. "I'm sorry."

"It's okay. Water under the bridge. We just need to work out a way that we both get equal opportunities to go out."

"You're right. What did you have in mind?"

"Well, I was thinking that I could have Mondays and Wednesdays. You could have Tuesdays and Thursdays. Then for the weekends, we could alternate. I take the first and third weekends of the month while you take the second and the fourth," she replied.

"Sounds fair," said Brennan. "That sounds more than fair."

"Alright, then. I guess that's it." She turned to leave and just as she was about to exit the room, she turned back to Brennan and said, "Brennan, I'm really happy that you've started to embrace this."

Brennan opened his mouth to reply, but Abigail had already shut the door behind her.

C h a p t e r 3 7

B r e n n a n

"I'VE JUST FINISHED reading your latest assignment," said Brennan. "It's good work. Your professor is going to be impressed."

"You really think so?" asked Charmaine. "I hope so. I put a lot of work into this."

"It really shows," he replied.

Charmaine had decided to enroll in a specialty course for event management. It was an online course that didn't demand too much of her time, but it was rather expensive, and she didn't want to take it for granted. "I could really use this as a steppingstone for my career," she explained to Brennan. "A lot of the big companies are really looking for certifications and stuff when hiring event managers."

"Perfectly understandable. You should definitely pursue it if you think it's going to help you gain an advantage."

"I love that you're always supporting me, babe."

"It's all because I love you, babe."

It had been a few weeks since the resort trip, and they were growing more fond of one another every day.

Brennan always let Charmaine know that he was supportive of her, and he spent as much time with her as he could get. She made sure to tell him that she was deeply appreciative of his efforts to be with her, but one night, she decided to bring up a sensitive issue during one of their conversations.

"Brennan," she told him while they were talking over the phone. "Do you really love me?"

"Of course I do, Charmaine," he replied. "Why would you ever doubt that?"

"I don't know," she said. "It's just that we've never really talked about... us. We've never talked about where we're going or what we're doing."

"You're right." He sighed. "What's on your mind?"

"Well..." Charmaine paused. "You know that I've been ready to leave my husband for the longest time now. I just want to know where your head is at."

Brennan didn't answer right away. He felt pressured to give Charmaine an answer because he didn't want her to think that he was hesitating.

"I've thought about it," said Brennan. "But it's just really complicated because of the kids. If we divorce, Abigail is going to try to gain custody of them, and I wouldn't be able to handle that. In your case, you would get custody of your sons for sure. You're the one they like more. In my case, it's not that simple."

"You're right," she replied. Brennan breathed a sigh of relief that he had said the right thing. "But at the end of the day," Charmaine continued, "you have to be more selfish, Brennan. You have to look out for yourself."

"What do you mean?"

"I mean you deserve so much better than what you're going through with your wife," she explained. "She's so mean and unreasonable with you. You shouldn't have to put up with that."

"Honestly, that's not the first time I've heard someone tell me that."

"Obviously. Anyone can see that you're too good to be with her."

"A lot of the girls that I've talked to or dated before you have told me the same thing. But I had always just assumed that they were saying so to try to get me to be more vulnerable with them or something. With you, I'm starting to actually believe it, though," he explained.

"Well, you should," she said.

"It's just that I haven't felt this way about my wife and my marriage for a long time, you know? I know a lot of people go through separations and divorces when things get tough in a marriage. But call me old fashioned. I still think there's a part in me that believes in trying to make things work."

"Does this mean you're staying with her?"

"It means that I don't know what I should do, Charmaine. I'm just trying to be honest here. I love you, and I want to be with you. But things are a lot more complicated than that. Like, if we get together and things get hard, I wouldn't just want to throw it away, right? I don't know. There's just a lot to think about."

"It's okay," she whispered over the phone. "I understand. I just need to know that we're going somewhere, you know? I need that security."

"I understand that too," he said. "Please know that I'm not ruling anything out. Otherwise, I wouldn't be spending all my time with you."

"Alright," she answered. "I can accept that."

Chapter 38

Abigail

"BRENNAN," ABIGAIL SAID as she knocked on Brennan's door. "Can I come in?"

"Sure," he replied.

"I need to ask you something."

"What's that?"

"I was thinking about enrolling the kids in daycare. I mean, I think they're already old enough, and I think it would do them some good to be exposed to other people," she said.

"Oh," replied Brennan and paused. "That sounds fine. Where is this coming from?"

"I don't know," she answered. "I guess I just want more time during the day to do more things for myself. At least I won't have to worry about keeping the kids entertained all the time."

Brennan didn't answer her right away. She looked at him and saw that he was seriously thinking about what she had asked him.

"Sounds like a good idea," he replied. "Go for it."

"Alright," she said with a smile on her face. "Thank

you."

She turned towards the door to leave and just before she shut it closed, she said, "You know, I'm really enjoying this new dynamic between us."

Brennan looked up at her with a puzzled look on his face. "What do you mean?"

"I mean, we haven't had a fight in ages. I can't even remember the last time. And it's like we're always in a good mood. Haven't you noticed?"

"Well, now that you mention it," he answered. "Things have been really good between us."

"Right?" she said with enthusiasm. "I've also noticed that you're a lot happier."

"And you're a lot happier," he replied back.

She smiled at him but didn't say anything else. Abigail closed the door and went back to her room where her cellphone filled with unanswered messages was waiting for her. This was how it had been in the Sutton household for quite some time. Abigail was spending more time on her phone throughout the day just messaging different guys. But when Brennan came home at night, they would have a couple of hours with the kids to just be a family. They would have dinner together or even play games whenever the kids were feeling energetic late at night. After the kids went to sleep, Abigail and Brennan would retreat into their own little cyber worlds. Even though Brennan didn't talk about it much, Abigail knew that he was getting serious with the people he was chatting with. She had no idea how many girls Brennan was talking to, but she knew that he was really getting into it.

Over the course of the next few days, Abigail sought to find the perfect daycare center for her kids. It didn't take her very long to find one that was relatively close to home. It was perfect for her because it meant she wouldn't have to waste too much time or gasoline on driving the kids to and from daycare.

The moment that she had enrolled the girls for daycare,

she started telling the guys she was chatting with that she had a lot more free time now. Abigail wasn't very keen on seeing just one guy over and over again. She wasn't ready for that kind of commitment. She always wanted her men to feel like they needed to compete for her time. More than that, she didn't want to tie herself down to one man. "I don't want to feel suffocated," she always told the men that she was messaging with.

Her first lunch date was spent getting coffee with a man named Oscar. The two of them had been messaging for a while, and Abigail found him very good looking in his profile picture. She agreed to meet him that afternoon over coffee for a chance to get to know one another better. Unfortunately, when she got there, she saw that he looked like a shadow of the man that was in the profile picture. In real life, his sunken eyes and disheveled hair was a far cry from the clean-cut youthful man that was on his social media profile.

From the moment she saw him, she knew that it wasn't going to be a good date. She stayed for a while and made casual conversation with him just to be respectful. To make matters worse, he wasn't very interesting to talk to either.

"So, I'm building this incredible computer at home, and I'm really excited about sourcing all the pieces for the motherboard," he told her. "I'm also debating whether I really need a full 8K screen or if I should just settle for a 4K monitor."

Abigail didn't understand what he was saying and didn't much care. She merely nodded her head for most of the conversation and excused herself by saying that she needed to get the kids. "That was a disaster," she muttered under her breath as she walked away from him.

Later that day she was on the way home with the kids in the backseat. They were telling her about everything that had happened in daycare that day. Abigail tried to reciprocate the enthusiasm that they were showing her, but she just couldn't get over the disappointment of her date.

Once they got home, she was surprised to see Brennan's car already parked in the driveway.

"Daddy's home!" yelled Amber from the backseat.

The three girls walked through the door and found Brennan in the living room watching TV. He stood up to give the two girls a hug and gave them both a kiss on the cheek. He turned to look at Abigail and paused for a moment before saying, "You look like you've had a bad day."

"What?" replied a surprised Abigail. "Oh, yeah. No biggie."

"Seems like you could use a hug," said Brennan.

To Abigail's surprise, he leaned in close to her and gave her a warm and intimate hug. Abigail hugged him back, and they stood there for a couple of seconds embracing each other's warmth. After pulling away, Abigail smiled at Brennan and said, "That was nice. I needed that. Thanks."

Chapter 39

Brennan

"WHERE ARE YOU?" texted Charmaine. "Are you on your way?"

Brennan was already in an Uber and making his way to Charmaine's place after work. It was a Thursday, and that meant that it was his turn to go out for the night. Charmaine's husband was out of town, and the kids were away on a school field trip. Charmaine still felt paranoid about having Brennan's car parked in her driveway for an extended period. She knew that her neighbors still maintained friendly relations with her husband, so he left his car behind at the office and took an Uber instead.

The last time that Brennan had visited Charmaine's house, it was when he picked her up for their date at St. Paul. He didn't have a good opportunity to really examine the house's exteriors, and he couldn't even remember what it looked like. Just as he was pulling into Charmaine's home, he texted her to tell her that he was nearby. She appeared on the front porch with a huge smile on her face once she saw the Uber pulling in. She walked down her lawn to greet Brennan and give him a big hug.

"Come on," she said. "Let's get inside before anyone sees us."

It was already getting dark, but Brennan could see that a lot of money and effort went into the construction of their house. It was painted an eggshell white and had an impressive teakwood porch on the front exterior of the structure. It was also fitted with classical Victorian windows that gave the house a vintage aesthetic. The large front door was painted a deep green and was artfully decorated with intricate engravings.

Charmaine ushered Brennan into her home, and he was surprised to see that the house was fully lit. The large chandelier in the center of the living room immediately caught his eye. Just below it was a elegant Mediterranean-style coffee table and a white throw rug that looked like it had been made out of the fur of a polar bear. Brennan noticed that the house was relatively clean, but it was also evident that it was lived in. There was evidence of young boys living in the home from the video game consoles under the television. There was also a modest trophy case that was filled with various medals and awards from sporting events. Everywhere he turned, Brennan saw paintings lining the walls. He didn't know much about art, but he knew enough to know that those paintings amounted to a small fortune.

"Beautiful home," he told her.

"Thank you," she said. "We've made gradual improvements to build it up to what it is today."

"You've outdone yourself," he replied.

"Sorry about the clutter," she apologized as she gestured toward the mound of sneakers that were piled up along the walls of the foyer. "Sometimes the boys just leave their stuff around, and I make it a point to have them clean after themselves. I'm leaving that there for when they come back."

"That's a good lesson to teach them," he said. "My

wife wouldn't be able to take that, though. She has this OCD about her. If she sees something out of place, her mind would compel her to put things in order."

"Oh, well, I don't have OCD. But I always want to be clean. It's a trait I want to instill in the boys too."

"Of course. That's good."

"Shall we see the rest of the house?"

"As long as I'm guaranteed a chance to see the bedroom,"

"You're funny."

The two of them made their way through the first floor, and Charmaine gave him a quick tour of the living room and the kitchen. Brennan rarely spent much time in the kitchen, but he saw that Charmaine's was outfitted with some of the best equipment that money could buy. She also had a small wine cellar that housed an impressive collection of reds and whites. Charmaine offered for the two of them to see the second floor of the house, to which Brennan politely obliged.

As they ascended the staircase, Brennan couldn't help but notice the portraits of the Evans family that lined the walls. It was his first time seeing pictures of the kids, and they had strong hints of their mom's genes in them. He also saw a picture of Charmaine's husband. Robert Evans didn't look as evil or as abhorrent as Brennan had envisioned him to be. In his mind, Robert had always been this unseen villainous character who looked like the stereotypical antagonist from any movie. Yet, looking at his portrait, Brennan realized that he was completely wrong. Robert looked like a plain old regular guy. This made him feel very uncomfortable. It made him feel guilty to entertain the idea that Robert was just an average guy like he was. In that scenario, he felt like he was the villain.

He tried to shake the thought away from his mind as they continued up the stairs. However, just as they turned into the hallway on the second floor, Brennan was greeted with even more family portraits. There was even one photo with just Robert and Charmaine in it. They looked so happy as they were locked in a tight embrace on a beach while staring into each other's eyes and laughing. It reminded Brennan of the time that he took Charmaine to the beach on their first date. That's when he realized that all of the great moments he had shared with Charmaine haven't been entirely original. He knew that Charmaine and Robert had their own history as well. As much as he wanted to deny it, he knew that Robert had a special place in Charmaine's heart, and it made him sad. The more that he stared at pictures of Robert and Charmaine being happy together, the more uncomfortable he became.

"Are you okay?" asked Charmaine. "You look really interested in these photos."

"Oh," replied Brennan. "Yeah. I was just curious about your family life."

"You were wondering how the two people who looked so happy together in those photos could grow to resent one another so badly?" she asked.

"It's like you read my mind."

"Life happens, Brennan. Life happens. Anyway, this is the bedroom."

Charmaine opened the door to their bedroom, and it was just as beautifully decorated as the rest of the house was. On the far end of the room, there was a large four-poster bed that was draped with a clean white linen cloth, and Brennan became entranced by it. He didn't take the time to notice the rest of the room because all he could focus on was the bed. Charmaine stood right in the middle of the room before turning to Brennan and asking, "Well, what do you think?"

Brennan didn't say anything. He just continued to stare at the bed before focusing his eyes back on Charmaine. He walked towards her in the middle of the room and held her tightly in his arms.

"Brennan?" she asked. "What's gotten into you?"

Brennan quietly looked over at the bed and pictured

Charmaine lying down on it. He also saw Robert lying down beside her and both of them were naked. He closed his eyes and tightened his grasp on Charmaine. "I just like this feeling," he told her. "I like being in your arms."

"I like being in your arms too," she replied. She closed her eyes and leaned her head against his chest.

The two of them just stood there in the middle of the room for a few minutes without saying anything. Brennan was hooked on the conflict that was brewing inside of him. He knew how wrong it was of him to be locked in an embrace with another man's woman inside the bedroom that they shared together. Yet, being in Charmaine's arms also felt so right to him. "I feel like whenever I'm in your arms, there's a big bubble that forms around us," whispered Brennan.

Suddenly, he felt a fire burning inside of him. He pulled away from Charmaine and looked straight into her eyes. He could sense that she was feeling that same fire. Brennan leaned in and kissed her tenderly on the lips as he caressed her face with his fingers. He ruffled through her hair as he continued to kiss Charmaine in the bedroom that she shared with her husband. Suddenly, he felt her stiffen and freeze.

"Ssshhh," she said. "Stop. Quiet."

"Why?" asked Brennan. "What's wrong?"

"Just keep quiet for a second," she replied.

That's when he heard it too. There was a sound of a car's motor that was echoing from the street outside. It seemed to be lingering right outside the house.

"I think my husband's home," she said.

The two of them stayed quiet and continued to listen. The car engine suddenly turned off, and they heard the subsequent slamming of the door and jingling of car keys.

"He's here," said Charmaine. "He's here. You better hide."

"What? No. I need to get out of here," replied Brennan. "Is there a backdoor that I could go through?"

"We can't risk it," replied Charmaine. "I don't want neighbors to see you."

"So what do we do?" asked a panicking Brennan. "Where do I go?"

"Stay here. Get under the bed. I'll go outside and drive him away," she replied. "He shouldn't be here anyway."

With that, she walked out of the door and Brennan was left on his own. He did as he was told and knelt down to crawl under the bed. But as he tried to fit himself underneath the bed, he found that there were a bunch of boxes piled under it , and he didn't have time to move them out of the way and squeeze himself in.

By then Brennan was hyperventilating. He looked around the room to survey his options and saw the large wooden cabinet situated at the corner of the bedroom. At first glance, Brennan figured that it was big enough for him to hide inside. He walked over to the cabinet and opened it to find an array of coats and shirts that he needed to shove aside in order for him to fit. Just as he was about to enter, he heard the angry muffled voices of Charmaine and Robert. Their voices were getting louder and clearer with each passing second. Brennan took this to mean that the two of them were making their way to the bedroom.

"You're a slut and a terrible wife!" Brennan heard from the hallway.

"And you're a selfish pig," replied Charmaine at the top of her lungs.

Brennan shuffled into the cabinet, and after some struggle, managed to wedge himself between the large collection of coats and shirts. Now he had to find a way to close the cabinet door from the inside. He grabbed one side of the cabinet door and closed it all the way. Then, he grabbed the other half of the door and moved to close it. Just as the door was about to close completely and pinch his fingers, he let it go with just enough momentum to have the closet close all the way. Brennan realized that the enclosed space made it difficult for him to breathe. The fact that his heart was thumping rather quickly was not helping the situation. He thought about whether he should leave a slight gap in between the two closet doors to help him breathe but decided against it.

Charmaine's voice was getting louder now. Brennan took this as her way of trying to warn him that they were getting closer to the room.

"Fuck you!" screamed the booming voice of a man as the bedroom doors swung open. Brennan was tempted to peek at what was taking place outside the closet but resisted the urge. He knew he needed to stay as still and silent as possible. "You're such a fucking whore!" Robert screamed again. That's when Brennan felt his heart sink. He realized that he hadn't put his phone into vibrate mode and that it could ring any minute. He knew that a lot of the girls on the dating sites mostly messaged him around that time too.

As slowly as he could, he reached his hand into his pocket and flicked the phone's ringer off. Brennan could hear Robert pacing about in the room and pulling drawers as if he were looking for something. He could hear the footsteps getting louder as Robert neared the cabinet when Charmaine started screaming from the hallway.

"Oh, I'm a fucking whore?" yelled Charmaine. Suddenly there was a loud crash.

"You idiot," yelled Robert as he stomped back out of the room and into the hallway. The door slammed shut behind him, and Brennan could no longer make out what they were yelling to one another. Brennan realized that Charmaine was leading him away from the bedroom. Then Brennan heard another loud slam of the door succeeded by the roar of the engine. Robert was pulling out of the driveway and driving away from the house. Brennan breathed a sigh of relief and creaked open the cabinet doors.

Chapter 40

Abigail

"HEY," ABIGAIL SAID to him on Saturday morning while the family was enjoying their breakfast. "I was thinking that we could take the kids to the park today. It's been a while since the girls have had the chance to go out with us. What do you think?"

"What?" asked Brennan who had just looked up from his phone. "I'm sorry. I didn't catch that."

"I said I think we should go to the park with the girls," repeated Abigail.

"Yes, Daddy," added Amber. "Can we go to the park today, please?"

Riley couldn't be bothered as she continued to watch her videos on the iPad.

Brennan looked like he hesitated for a moment, and Abigail understood that he already had plans. She had no way of confirming that it would be with a girl that he was dating, but she was almost certain of it. Abigail raised her eyebrows at him as if to guilt him into agreeing.

"Daddy already has something to attend to, dear," he

told Amber with an apologetic voice. "But Mommy can take you to the park today, and Daddy will promise to be there next time, okay?"

"Okay." Amber sighed. "Fine."

Abigail shook her head as she continued to eat her food. "Alright," she said. "It seems like we're going to have a girls' day out today. Amber and Riley, I want you to finish all of the fruit that are on your plate. You'll need that energy at the park."

"Alright, Mommy," replied Amber. "Riley, put the iPad down. Finish your vegetables so we can go to the park!"

Brennan shot an apologetic glance towards Abigail and mouthed the words "I'm sorry." Abigail merely nodded her head in acknowledgement but kept a straight face.

After they finished their breakfast, Abigail ushered the girls back to their room and changed their clothes for a day at the park. She decided that it would be cute to dress them in matching dresses that their grandmother had gotten for them while they went shopping one day. Abigail always loved it when the girls wore those dresses together.

It was a sunny day that was accompanied by a slight chilly breeze in Minneapolis. Abigail decided to have the girls bring their coats as well, just in case it got too cold for them. Right before they left the house, Amber saw Brennan sitting in the living room and asked, "Are you sure you don't want to come along, Daddy?"

"Daddy has a lot of stuff to do today," replied Abigail before Brennan could even open his mouth. "Let Daddy have his time for himself, okay, sweetie?"

"Okay, but Daddy always takes us for ice cream after the park. Will you take us for ice cream, Mommy?"

"Yes, I will," she answered. "Let's get to the car now before I change my mind."

The girls burst through the front door and ran to the car. Abigail saw that Brennan was about to say something to her, but she closed the door before he could get a word out. She decided to not think about whoever Brennan may be hooking up with and enjoy spending time with her kids.

It was a fun drive over to the park with the girls. Abigail taught them how to play I Spy and that kept them preoccupied during the drive. Once they got to the park, Amber darted towards the monkey bars while Riley asked Abigail if she could go on the swings.

"Sure, honey," she answered. "Do you want Mommy to push you?"

"No, thank you," she replied. "I can do it."

She watched her little girl struggle to climb herself onto the swing as her tiny feet dangled in the air. Riley reached down with one leg in an attempt to push off. After a short struggle, she was eventually able to find a way to kick off the ground consistently enough for her swing to develop some momentum. Abigail felt her eyes well up as she proudly watched her little girl conquer the swings on her own.

She looked towards the monkey bars and saw that Amber had struck up a conversation with a little boy who looked like he was just about her age. Abigail wondered what the two of them were talking about and laughed at how innocent and cute they looked. The boy had denim overalls on which draped over a gingham shirt. Abigail chuckled at how dapperly he was dressed, and the sight of him and Amber talking warmed her heart.

She found a bench towards the side of the park that she could sit on while still being able to see the girls. Abigail sat down and grabbed her phone to take pictures of Riley on the swing. She was also able to take a shot of Amber talking to the dapper little boy in overalls.

Abigail looked around the park to see if she could spot the boy's parents. There was a couple who was sitting on a bench towards the other side of the play area, and they caught Abigail's attention. They were also looking directly at Amber and the boy with huge smiles on their faces. Abigail assumed that they were the boy's parents with how eagerly they were watching the scene before them unfold.

After snapping a few pictures, she decided to send them out to a few guys that she was messaging on her dating apps. "Look at my kids," she wrote. "Aren't they the cutest?"

Kenny was the first man to text her back. She was surprised by this because Kenny was significantly younger and didn't even have any kids himself. He had just graduated from university and was trying to make it as an investment specialist in a big bank. She didn't know much about him, but she knew that he was an ambitious guy who had big dreams for himself. Abigail didn't expect him to share her enthusiasm about her kids, but she always deemed him to be a nice person whenever they talked.

"They look adorable," he said. "They look just like you too!"

"Thank you," replied Abigail. "That means a lot."

"Who's that little boy?" he asked. "I thought you only had two girls."

"Oh, yeah," she said. "Amber seems to have made a friend here at the park."

"So nice of you to take your kids out to the park on the weekend," he mentioned. "Is your husband around too?"

"No," she answered. "He has other plans. Apparently, whatever they are, they're more interesting than spending time with his kids."

Chapter 41

Brennan

BRENNAN WAS UP late that night with Amber and Riley because they couldn't sleep. It seemed like the energy that they had earlier had carried over well into the night. They were both enthusiastic about telling their dad everything that they had done at the park. The girls had somehow also convinced both Brennan and Abigail to join them in the living room for a late-night viewing of Finding Nemo. The girls had always adored Disney movies, and they begged both of their parents to watch it with them. Abigail was in jovial spirits and said yes immediately. Brennan felt like he didn't want to be the bad guy and agreed to watch the movie with the family as well.

This was the first time since Abigail and Brennan got into an open marriage that the whole family gathered around the living room to watch something together. Before they started the movie, Brennan thought it best to leave his phone in his bedroom in case Charmaine called. He didn't want her to disrupt their family time, and he didn't want Abigail to see her calling him so late at night.

Brennan also mistakenly thought that the girls would

fall asleep halfway through the movie and that would get him off the book. But the girls had real energy and were even asking Brennan and Abigail if they could put on Frozen immediately after Finding Nemo was finished. Abigail put her foot down and told the girls that it was too late, and that it absolutely, positively, for sure, no buts was time for bed. The girls put up a little fight at first, but eventually agreed, and Abigail and Brennan carried them back to their bedroom.

"I'll tuck them in," said Abigail. "You can go ahead."

"Are you sure?" he asked.

"Yeah," she replied. "Girls, say good night to Daddy."

"Good night, Daddy!" said Amber as she ran over to Brennan to give him a kiss.

Riley was already lying down in bed and halfway through falling asleep as she mumbled, "Goodni.. Dee."

"Good night, sweetheart," replied a laughing Brennan.

He went back into his bedroom and immediately saw that the notification light on his phone was blinking. "I knew she would call," he muttered under his breath. He went to his phone and there was an unopened voice mail from Charmaine and a text message as well. He suddenly felt butterflies fluttering in his stomach. "What are you, thirteen?" he laughed to himself.

He decided to open the voice message first and put the phone to his ear but was surprised to hear a man's voice instead of Charmaine's. It was a deep baritone with a prominent rasp, and it reminded Brennan of his high school gym teacher. Right away, he realized that he had already heard this voice before when he was hiding behind the closed doors of a bedroom closet.

"I don't know who you are," said the voice. "And you don't know who I am. But I know that you've been fucking my wife. Do you know that the two of us have been married for a decade?"

There was a pause, but the message wasn't over yet. Brennan felt the butterflies in his stomach disappear instantly, transformed into nervous anxiety as he felt his heart rate quicken. The voice went on.

"This is Robert Evans, and I am Charmaine's husband. I don't know what kind of sick game you're playing at, but I suggest that you get over whatever midlife crisis you're going through. I know that you have a family of your own, and I would be more than willing to destroy you if you aren't careful. Stay away from my wife."

The message ended and Brennan felt himself going numb. He glanced back down at his phone and opened the text message that Charmaine had sent him. This time, it really was Charmaine.

"Hey, OMG, I'm so sorry. My husband got a hold of my phone, and he read my text messages. I don't know how much he was able to read before I got it back from him. I think he sent you a voicemail too. I'm so sorry about this," she texted.

"Honestly," replied Brennan. "I'm a little shaken up. But don't worry. He doesn't scare me. We just have to be extra careful next time."

"What did he say? Did he threaten you? Brennan, I'm so sorry," she wrote back.

"It doesn't matter what he said," he texted. "All that matters is that I love you and that I'm willing to fight for you."

"Oh, Brennan," she replied. "It's so nice to hear you say that. I love you, and I'm ready to fight for you too."

C h a p t e r   4 2

A b i g a i l

"OH NO," SHE muttered under her breath after scouring her bedroom. "I think I've lost my cellphone charger."

Abigail thought for a while about when she had last used it. That's when she realized that it was probably at the Loews Minneapolis Hotel. She remembered bringing her charger along with her a couple of nights prior when she met up with Christian, a guy that worked in finance. Abigail found him cute and charming, but he was too young for her. She felt like she couldn't take him seriously because of his youth, but she did indulge in a one-night stand with him. Unfortunately, in her haste to leave early, she must have forgotten her cellphone charger in the process.

Abigail figured that she could drive all the way to the hotel herself and pick it up, but then she realized it'd be more convenient to ask Brennan to do it since it was on his way to work. She walked over to his bedroom and knocked on his door before going in. "Hey," she said as she entered. "Can I ask you for a favor?"

Brennan was on his cellphone when she came in, but

he had put it down once she was inside the room. "What's up?"

"I left my cell phone charger at the Loews Hotel. I know that it's on your way to work. Would you mind picking it up for me tomorrow morning on your commute?"

Brennan stared at her for a while and didn't answer. Even though she didn't say anything about it, Abigail knew that Brennan understood what she was in the hotel for. She also knew that he was becoming uncomfortable because of it. Brennan reached into his bedside drawer and pulled out a phone charger.

"Here," he said. "Use this instead."

"Oh," replied Abigail. "I don't want to take that from you. The one I left behind was still working really well."

"Just use that," replied Brennan. "That's an extra one I have. Just use that."

"But what about…"

"Forget about it," he interrupted. "Just consider that charger lost and use my spare one instead. I'm not going to that hotel."

"Okay," said Abigail. "Thanks."

She walked out of the room, understanding why Brennan didn't want to pick her charger up for her. He would never have wanted to visit a hotel where his wife had intimate relations with another man. Things had been going so well that she expected he had gotten used to the idea of her sleeping with other men, but she reminded herself to not mention anything about her affairs to Brennan. He has to get used to the idea soon, she thought. This is how it's going to be from now on.

Chapter 43

Brennan

IT WAS LATE one night, and Brennan was wondering why Charmaine hadn't messaged him yet. Usually, he would send her a message right after dinner, and she would reply almost immediately. Yet, she hadn't responded to him all night, and he was already preparing to go to bed. "Maybe she's busy with a work thing," he told himself. Just as he was about to doze off, his phone began ringing. Brennan grabbed it and answered the call.

"Hello?" said Charmaine's voice on the other line. "Sorry, I didn't reply earlier. Something happened."

"Why?" asked Brennan. "What happened to you?"

"I'm actually at the police station now," she explained to him.

"What? Why? What happened? Do you need me to come over there?" Brennan was almost yelling, but he tried to keep his voice down when he realized that everyone else in the house was probably sleeping already.

"No, it's okay," she said. "I'm safe. It's just that Robert and I got into a really big fight. A HUGE one. He got so mad that he ended up throwing a candelabra at my face, and now I've got a huge cut on my cheek."

"That asshole," said Brennan.

"The neighbors were getting worried because they somehow sensed that this was a different kind of fight we were having and one of them called the cops. I'm kind of lucky. I think that Robert would have killed me if the cops didn't arrive."

"I'm so sorry that you had to go through that. Is there anything I can do?"

"No," she replied. "I just wanted to hear your voice. I'm safe. They have him in custody. I just have to finish up the police report, and I'll be heading back home. The cops were nice enough to offer to escort me back home too. You should probably get some sleep now. I'll talk to you tomorrow."

"Okay, but you call me if you need me for anything," he told her.

"I will. I love you."

"I love you too."

Over the course of the next few weeks, Brennan spent more time with Charmaine. She was going through a lot of emotional and physical turmoil as the result of that night when her husband struck her. Over time, Brennan became more convinced of how real his feelings for Charmaine were. He wanted nothing more than to take care of this woman and protect her. He hated that she was going through such a tough time, but he knew that this meant that she and her husband were finally going to break up.

"So I've been doing a lot of thinking," said Brennan to her while they were on a coffee date one weekend. "I've been thinking a lot about what we talked about before — about our future."

"Oh?" replied Charmaine. She didn't say anything else and waited for Brennan to keep on going.

"Yeah, well I think it looks like things are pretty much over between you and your husband. I mean, I know that your attorneys have told you that you can't talk to each other throughout this whole ordeal. But it seems like this is the end of the line for the two of you, right?" he asked as he mumbled through his words.

"What are you saying, Brennan?" she asked.

"Well, the more I've thought about it," he continued, "the more I've realized that I really want to be with you. It's you who I want to spend all of my time with."

"Right," she said. "Brennan, about that..."

Brennan was taken aback. He sat his coffee down. "What's on your mind?" he asked.

"Well, I've talked to my lawyers, and I've been broaching the idea of dropping the charges."

"What? Why? After what he did to you?"

"I know. What he did was horrible, and things have been really bad between us lately," she explained. "But he's still the father of my children. I have to think about them too. It's the same thing as what you said to me about your kids."

"Oh," he said. "I understand. It's just that…" he trailed off.

"What?" she asked.

"Nothing," he lied. "You're right. You have your kids to think about."

The days after that conversation, Brennan found himself in a daze. He wasn't sure where he stood with Abigail. He was also unsure where he stood with Charmaine. It was like he was stuck in a weird relationship limbo, failing at two relationships, and it ate away at his insides.

Sometimes, throughout the day, Brennan envisioned himself being back in Charmaine's bedroom. He imagined being in their closet and hearing Robert's scary footsteps make their way around the room. Sometimes he would even get nightmares about Charmaine opening the closet doors and telling Robert to beat Brennan up. Brennan felt like he was virtually functioning on autopilot until he got a call during his lunch break at the office one day.

"Hello?" he said as he answered the phone.

"Brennan," replied Charmaine. "It's good to hear your voice."

"It's good to hear yours too," he told her.

"Listen, I know that our last conversation didn't exactly make you feel good, and I'm sorry about that," she paused as she waited for Brennan to say something. He didn't reply, and she took that as a signal to keep on talking. "Anyway, I was wondering if you wanted to have dinner with me tonight after work."

"Alright," he said. "What's the plan?"

"Actually, my mother is in town for a surprise visit. When she heard what had happened between me and Robert, she decided to fly out. I was thinking that she could tag along so that the two of you could meet."

What? Brennan thought to himself. Why would she want to introduce me to her mother?

"It's not weird or anything," she went on as if she were able to read his mind. "I've actually been really open to her about what you and I have been doing. She perfectly understands the situation, and she's dying to meet you."

"Oh, alright," he said. "No problem. Text me where you'll be, and I'll come right after work."

Brennan was himself again for the rest of the afternoon. He found that Charmaine had that mystifying effect on him. He had never felt that way about a girl since he first met Abigail. That's how he knew that this was serious business.

After work, he made his way to the restaurant that Charmaine told him she and her mother were. When he got there, they were both laughing hysterically, and he also noticed that there was an almost-empty bottle of wine on the table.

Brennan made his way towards them as they let out another loud laugh that reverberated around the restaurant. Charmaine's mother noticed Brennan first, and she nodded towards Charmaine, gesturing for her to look towards the walkway. As if she were embarrassed about laughing so boisterously, Charmaine quickly stood up and smoothed out her dress with her hands.

"Hi," she said to Brennan, kissing him on the cheek. "So glad that you could make it."

"It seems like I'm late to the party," replied Brennan with a smile. "How are we doing over here, ladies?"

"It's my mom's fault," defended Charmaine. "She's always the instigator when it comes to these things."

"Guilty as charged," added Charmaine's mom with both of her hands up. "Hi, I'm Rose. It's nice to finally meet you, Brennan." She held out her hand towards him, and Brennan shook it before leaning down to give her a kiss on the cheek.

"The pleasure is all mine, Rose," he said. "Now I know where Charmaine gets her charming looks from." He wasn't lying. Brennan had seen mothers and daughters who looked alike before, but the resemblance between Charmaine and Rose was uncanny to him. The two of them could have been sisters. When he told them about it, Charmaine was quick to reply, "We get that a lot. It's the Asian gene. My mom looks like she never ages, doesn't she?"

"I think any woman your mom's age would be lucky to look even just half as good as she does right now," he said.

"Now, Brennan. There's no need for flattery," said Rose. "I already like you. There's no need to win me over with your smooth charm."

"I think we need another bottle of wine over here. I want to join the party," he said.

Brennan ordered a bottle of red wine together with everyone's food and assured everyone that dinner was on him. After a slight back and forth, the two ladies eventually gave up and graciously accepted a free dinner at Brennan's expense. "Rose, you're my guest. It's the least I could do," he defended. Brennan had never had a problem with interacting with people who were older than him.

However, it was a lot easier with Rose because she wasn't that much older than him to begin with. He asked her a lot of questions about what Charmaine was like when she was younger and what their family life had been like. Rose didn't disappoint him with the number of stories that she told about Charmaine's hijinks in her youth. Apparently, Charmaine had been quite a rebel as a child.

"I think her rebellious phase is still ongoing, Rose," joked Brennan.

"Ha. Ha. Very funny," replied Charmaine.

"Oh, she's definitely a fighter," said Rose. "That's why I got a bit concerned when she got married to Robert. Sure, he was a fine man, but he was a fighter too. And it rarely ever works when two fighters get into a relationship. At the end of the day, someone's going to have to give in."

"Let's not talk about Robert, Mom," said Charmaine and took another sip of her champagne.

"Right. Sorry. That's the last time we'll bring him up. Anyway, the point that I was trying to make was that Charmaine always needed someone to look out for her blind spots when she was younger. I used to be that person, but I can't be that person anymore," she explained. "I'm just saying she needs a stable guy who can help bring her down a couple of notches, and I've noticed that she's been a lot calmer since the two of you started dating."

"Well," said Brennan, "that's nice of you to say, but I think Charmaine is taking good care of herself. Of course, I still care about her a great deal as well."

"I know you do," said Rose. "It shows in the way that you look at her."

Neither Brennan or Charmaine said anything after that. He could feel his skin getting hot, and he knew that he was about to blush. Judging by how Charmaine was keeping quiet, he knew that she was experiencing the same. The rest of the night went rather smoothly for the three of them. They talked mostly about what Charmaine and her siblings were like growing up in an Asian family within

America.

After dinner was over and they were saying their goodbyes, Brennan made sure to call them an Uber as neither of the two girls seemed fit enough to drive. "I can drive," contested Charmaine.

"No, you can't," replied Brennan.

"See?" said Rose. "She really needs someone to take care of her the way that you do, Brennan."

He smiled and said that it was his pleasure. Once Rose and Charmaine were safely inside their Uber, Brennan waved goodbye to both of them and smiled. He told Rose that it was nice to meet her and that he was looking forward to seeing her again.

"Soon. Hopefully," she replied.

Brennan watched them drive away and wondered what the whole night had been about. It was clear to him from their previous conversation that Charmaine was still thinking about staying with Robert. Yet, there she was, inviting him to dinners with her mother. Still, it made him feel good inside to know that her mother liked him. He also couldn't help but smile at knowing that they both trusted him to take care of her.

Chapter 44

Abigail

AFTER DROPPING THE kids off at daycare, Abigail was off to meet Kevin again for lunch. This time, Abigail let him be the one to choose a place for them to meet. He settled on a Moroccan restaurant that Abigail had never eaten at before. She had never even tried Moroccan food in her life.

"It's really good," Kevin told her. "I can't believe you've never tried it."

"I trust you. I'll see you there," she replied.

The moment that Abigail entered the restaurant, she was overwhelmed by the colors of the decorations and the smells emanating from the kitchen. The walls were painted a bright orange while all of the furniture were either purple, yellow, red, or sky blue. There was so much vibrancy in the aesthetic of the restaurant that Abigail didn't know what to fixate on. She saw Kevin sitting towards the side on top of a large Moroccan carpet in front of a low table. She took a seat across from him on the carpet after giving him a quick peck on the cheek.

"Interesting place that you've chosen," she said. "I love

it."

"I knew you would."

"How would you have known?"

"Well," he explained. "From our conversations, you're always talking a lot about how you like to explore with your palate. I know that you've had the usual cuisines like Thai, Chinese, and Indian. But I was fairly certain that you'd never had Moroccan food before."

"In fairness, not many people I know have had Moroccan food before," she defended. "I'm not an uncultured swine." She pouted with her lips.

Kevin shook his head. "I know you aren't. Not many people know about the wonders of Moroccan cuisine. That's why I brought you here," he said with a smile. "I've also taken the liberty of ordering for us. I trust that you don't have any allergies?"

"None," she replied. "Thanks for this. You're awfully sweet."

"Sweet?" he asked. "How?"

"I don't know," she said. "Maybe it's just because this is exactly the kind of date that my husband would never take me on."

"You ain't seen nothing yet," he exclaimed. "In Moroccan culture, it's actually very common for their people to eat with their hands. So, that's what we're going to be doing here."

"What?" she said with a surprised laugh. "No utensils?"

"No utensils," he answered. "As a general rule, Moroccans only eat with one hand — the right hand. The left hand is typically only used to pick up bread or to give food to other people. This is because the left hand never touches the mouth, so you're okay to hand food to others with it."

"Interesting," she said.

Just as she said that, a waiter came by and handed them each a bowl of water with lemon and orange wedges floating on the surface.

"What's this? Some kind of soup?"

"No," answered a laughing Kevin. "Since we eat with our hands, it's important that you wash them first. Dip your fingers into the bowl and use the lemon and orange wedges to sanitize them."

"Oh," she said. "I've never done this before!"

After they finished washing their hands, the waiter removed the bowls from their table and put down a small clay bowl that held a variety of different thinly sliced vegetables with olives and a light red sauce.

"This is called a tagine," explained Kevin. "There's some meat underneath all of those vegetables, and they pair great with some Moroccan bread."

The waiter then laid down a plate of what looked like a pie, although Abigail couldn't tell what was inside of it. As if he were reading her mind, Kevin said, "This is a Moroccan savory pie. It's called a chicken bastilla. Traditionally, they make this with pigeon meat, but they don't serve it at this restaurant."

Finally, the waiter also served a bowl of what looked like yellow colored grains that had a very fine texture. Abigail's eyes lit up immediately and she said, "I recognize that! That's couscous!"

"Good eye," said Kevin. "Yup. It's a traditional Moroccan dish as well."

"I didn't know that! I just know it to be a health food," she explained.

"Well," said Kevin, "let's dig in."

As Kevin had explained, they weren't using utensils for this meal. Abigail still felt hesitant about digging in first and she chose to observe how Kevin ate before she did anything. Everything that he did with his food, she did the same. Kevin noticed this and called her out on it. They both laughed, and Abigail admitted that she was feeling both excited and anxious. She loved the food and complemented Kevin for his choice of restaurant.

"Maybe you would want some wine?" he asked. "Let's

order by the glass. It's early, after all."

"That sounds great," she said. "A glass of wine would be lovely with this delicious meal."

After ordering a glass of wine for each of them, Kevin said, "You know, there's another aspect of Moroccan culture I haven't told you about. Usually, when two intimate people are sharing a meal together, it's not uncommon for them to feed each other with their hands."

"Really?" she said with a suspicious grin.

"Really. It's their way of showing affection and letting the other know that they would take care of them," explained Kevin.

Without skipping a beat, he scooped up some vegetables from the tagine and placed it on top of a ball of couscous. He rolled them up in his fingers and offered them to Abigail. She felt awkward about allowing him to feed her with his hand, but she did it anyway. In the end, she was surprised at how natural that felt and how endearing Kevin was to her.

"This is a really nice date, Kevin," she said. "Thank you."

"Any time," he replied.

The two of them enjoyed their lunch together and shared a bunch of laughs. Kevin recounted to Abigail a few of his disastrous stories while working for crazy clients during the earlier years of his business. He talked to her about how one client had insisted on overhauling the entire menu for a wedding reception on the day of the event itself. Kevin's staff had already prepared all of the food, and the client insisted that they change everything up. It was an absolute disaster for him as he tried to negotiate that the request wasn't feasible, and there was no way for him to come up with a whole new menu from scratch on short notice. He said that the client eventually agreed but also asked for a discount because they didn't get what they really wanted.

"So what did you do?" asked Abigail.

"Well, honestly, I was just so tired of dealing with her that I just ended up giving her the discount," admitted Kevin.

"That's crazy."

"That's not the crazy part. What is crazy is that she contacted me a couple of months later because she wanted to hire me for another event."

"And what did you say?"

"I told her that our company had closed down. here was no way that I was working for her again."

The rest of the conversation went on like this. Abigail had found that she really enjoyed Kevin's company. But the more they talked, the more she questioned whether the two of them were romantically compatible at all. She liked spending time with him, but she also knew that there was something missing. He wasn't the person that she was looking for.

After lunch was over, Abigail expressed her regrets for having to leave for her hair appointment.

"It's just that I haven't had my hair done in a long time, and I'm always putting it off," she reasoned.

"No need to explain," replied Kevin. "For what it's worth, I think you're really pretty as you are."

"You're sweet, Kevin," she answered. Abigail gave him a kiss on the cheek. "Until next time! I had a lot of fun."

"Ditto," he said.

When they parted ways, Abigail rushed over to the salon as she was running late for her appointment. She got there just in time, and her stylist was already waiting for her.

"Hey, Angel," said Abigail as she laid her belongings down on the table next to the chair. "Just a little trim, please. You already know what I like."

"How about we add a little bit of color?" suggested Angel.

"Do you think so?" asked Abigail as she eyed herself in the mirror. She found that she was already fond of the way that she looked. She was also more confident than she'd been in years. Abigail wondered if Kevin had anything to do with that. "Actually," said Abigail. "I think I'll keep the color the same. I just need you to tidy it up a little."

"Sure thing," replied Angel.

As Abigail settled into her chair, she opened her phone and saw that there was a new message waiting for her. She thought that it would be from Kevin, but instead, it was from Kenny, the young aspiring investment banker that she was messaging with. Abigail was surprised because it had been a while since the two of them had talked, but she always enjoyed conversing with him. The two of them had never even met in person, but Abigail considered him one of her favorite people to talk to because of his youth and optimism.

"Hey, Abigail," the message read. "Do you mind if we talk for a bit? I need some advice."

"Sure," she texted back. "What's up?"

"It's kind of weird," he said. "But I need dating advice. I know that's weird of me to be asking of someone I met on a dating app."

"Not at all," replied Abigail. "I don't know if I have any good advice to give you, but it's worth a try."

"Okay, well," he went on, "I've been dating this girl. She's amazing. I really like her, and the two of us have great chemistry. She's also really understanding of the fact that I work long hours at the office."

"That's great, Kenny!" she responded. "I'm really happy for you! But what do you need advice with?"

"Yeah, this is the thing," he said. "I have really judgmental friends. Like, they're really hard to impress. That's why I haven't introduced them to her yet. Her name is Leanne."

"Aw," she said. "That's a cute name."

"Well, Leanne is asking me why I won't let her meet my friends," he explained. "She thinks that I'm ashamed of her. But I'm really not!"

"What's the problem, then?" asked Abigail.

"Well, Leanne is kind of overweight. That isn't a problem to me at all. I don't care that she's a little curvy. In fact, I really like it. It's just that I know that my friends will give me shit for it," he said. "And I'm scared that they'll make fun of her."

"Hey, Kenny," said Abigail. "Do you really like Leanne? Do you think that you have a chance at a future with this woman?"

"Honestly," he answered. "I really do."

"There you have it," she said. "Just go and let her meet your friends. Let them know how serious you are about dating her and that she means a lot to you. The way they react will tell you a lot about the nature of your friendship. You just need to remind yourself of what's most important to you."

"You're right," he said. "Thanks for the great advice. I really appreciate you helping me out. There's no one else I could turn to for this problem of mine."

"No worries at all," replied Abigail. "Keep me posted. Let me know how it goes, okay?"

"Will do," texted Kenny. "Thanks again."

Chapter 45

Brennan

"LISTEN," CHARMAINE TOLD Brennan while they were talking late one night. "I've been holding off on bringing this up, but I just have to say it. My son Brian has a classmate who's throwing a birthday party this Saturday, and he's been invited."

"Alright," he replied. "What's up? What's so weird about that?"

"Well, the parents are invited as well, and I'm letting Matthew tag along since he's also friends with Brian's friends," she explained. "I was kind of hoping that you would go too."

"What?" said Brennan. "Really?"

"Yeah," she answered. "It's just that I don't want the other parents to see me with the kids alone and in a vulnerable state, you know? I'd feel a lot better and more comfortable if you were there with me."

"And the kids would be okay with that?" he asked.

"Yeah," she said. "We can just tell everyone that you're a friend of mine. No biggie."

"Alright, then," he answered. "It's not how I imagined

spending my weekend, but I'll be there."

The day of the birthday party came, and Brennan went to pick Charmaine up with her kids. When he arrived, he met Brian and Matthew in person for the first time. He had seen their pictures and Charmaine had talked about them a lot, but he had never actually encountered them in real life. It was uncanny how much the two of them looked alike. Brennan thought that if he were meeting them without any prior knowledge, he would have assumed them to be twins. They were fair-skinned and they had awkward lanky bodies that were common for boys their age. The only real difference between them was that Brian was around a couple of inches taller than Matthew.

"Hey, guys," said Brennan as they entered his car.

"Boys," said Charmaine. "This is my friend that I was telling you about. Say hi to Brennan."

"Hey, Brennan," said Brian.

"Hey," added Matthew.

"Are you boys excited for this party?" asked Brennan.

They didn't answer. Brennan turned to look and they were both glued on their cellphones.

"Sure they are," answered Charmaine on their behalf. She looked at Brennan and shrugged her shoulders as if to say "what can I do?"

When they arrived at the venue for the party, Brennan dropped Charmaine and the kids right off at the front of the house before he drove further down the block to find a parking slot. When Brennan rejoined Charmaine and the boys, she automatically got to introducing him to the rest of the parents of the other children. The boys didn't even waste another second before they set off on their own to hang out with the other kids. The party was held in the backyard of the home where there was a pool. The parents of the celebrant had also arranged for buffet tables and a bouncy castle to be set up. An animal wildlife expert was also set to come in later in the day for a showcase of some exotic creatures for the kids to interact with.

It was clear to Brennan from the start that Charmaine didn't really have any close relationships with the other parents. He understood why she had wanted him to be there with her. She didn't relate well with the other parents because they were older than she was. A bunch of them were even older than Brennan.

As planned, she introduced him as her friend to the rest of the people at the party. None of them really paid him any attention, and that suited both of them fine. Both Brennan and Charmaine spent the majority of the party by themselves. For the most part, Brennan didn't mind. When it was time to take photos, he even got to pose for a photo together with Charmaine and the kids. He anticipated that it would feel awkward posing with some other man's family for a photo, but it felt right with him. Eventually, Brennan was able to strike up a conversation with a few of the other parents. After introducing himself as Charmaine's friend, none of them really asked him anything more about the nature of the relationship. They seemed to respect that he was older than Charmaine. He found himself having a good time, and when the party was over, the two boys went over to him.

"Hey, Brennan," said Brian. "Do you want to watch a movie tonight with us?"

"I don't know," he replied. "What's showing?"

"They've got the new Spider-Man movie out!" answered Matthew. "Can you take us?"

"Yeah," added Brian. "Can you take us?"

"Oh, I don't know," answered Brennan. "We're going to have to ask your mother." She was within earshot, and she heard the whole conversation. Charmaine looked at Brennan and mouthed the words, "if you want to." Brennan nodded his head and told the boys, "It looks like we're going to the movies!"

Charmaine came over as Brian and Matthew cheered and gave each other a high five. They raced each other to the front of the house and back to where the car was parked. On the drive over to the movie theater, Brennan asked the boys who their favorite superheroes were. The three boys got into a lighthearted debate over who the strongest characters were in comic book lore. Charmaine didn't know much about what they were talking about, but Brennan could tell that she was enjoying listening to them talk to one another.

When they got to the movie theatre, the boys asked their mom if they could get money to buy popcorn and candy. Upon hearing this, Brennan whipped out his wallet and gave them both ten dollars each. "Go ahead, boys," he said. "It's on me."

"Alright!" cheered Matthew. "Thanks, Uncle Brennan!"

"You're bribing them, I see," teased Charmaine. "I think it's working."

"That's the plan," replied Brennan.

She looked at him intently for a few seconds before saying, "I can tell that you're a good dad."

"I try to be," he said with an air of melancholy.

Chapter 46

Abigail

KEVIN AND ABIGAIL went out a few more times. The foodie in him really excited her, and she found that she had a lot of fun on their dates. Over time, the novelty of dating Kevin wore off for Abigail. She found that she was becoming less and less excited about going out on dates with him. She didn't want to tell him that her feelings for him were wearing off, but she was slowly weaning herself out of that situation as well. Also, she made it clear to him that she was still open to dating other guys and talking to men on the dating sites.

Another thing that made matters worse for her with her relationship to Kevin was that he wasn't fulfilling her sexual needs. The two of them had a fairly active sex life, but she never really looked forward to these sexual encounters the same way that she looked forward to the food that they were going to eat. She noted that Kevin had not once been able to really please her in the bedroom. Once Kevin fell asleep after making love, she would secretly try to finish herself off. She knew that she couldn't keep this up for much longer, but she also knew that she wasn't really as happy as she should have been in this new setup.

One day, Abigail was writing in her journal about her feelings, and she decided that she could use writing as an outlet for her to talk about her emotions without being judged or scolded by Brennan.

"I don't know," she wrote. "I feel as if I expected so much from all of the other men. I felt like they could provide me with everything that Brennan couldn't. And yet, it turns out that they've all just been disappointments. It's gotten to a point where I'm seriously reconsidering what we're doing. Kevin's great, but he's not much better than the rest of them. I can't even say that he's better than Brennan."

The kids burst through the door of her bedroom one night while she was writing, and both of them were crying. Abigail stood up from her chair and immediately approached the two of them.

"Girls?" she asked. "What's wrong? Why are you crying?"

"We miss Daddy," said Amber while Riley continued to cry hysterically. "Daddy doesn't play with us anymore. He's always out and we never see him."

"I miss Daddy," echoed Riley as she cried even more.

"But Daddy will be home tomorrow, girls," said Abigail. "Don't worry."

"Whenever he's home, he's always on his phone. He always says that he's working. That's why he can't play with us or read us to sleep anymore," said Amber.

"I'll talk to Daddy, okay?" said Abigail. "How about the two of you go back to your room, and Mommy will follow right after to read you a bedtime story?"

"Okay," said Amber as she tried to stifle her tears. She took her little sister's hand and led her out of the room.

Abigail went back to her desk and continued writing in her journal.

"It seems like Brennan is enjoying this setup a lot more

than I am. He was the one who didn't want to go through with this at first," she wrote. "Yet, he's the one who's always out with his women. He's the one who's always on his phone messaging them. I think it's because he's always been the more emotional one of the two of us."

She paused and caught her breath for a second. She realized that she was on the verge of tears and that there was a heavy weight on her chest. Abigail couldn't shake the crying faces of her two daughters from her mind.

"That's the difference between Brennan and me," she continued to write. "He's totally lost himself in this open marriage. He's lost control of his feelings. It's not good for the family. It's not good for the kids. Maybe it's time for me to reel him back in."

Chapter 47

Brennan

"IT'S BRIAN'S BIRTHDAY next week," Charmaine told Brian when they were talking over the phone. "He says that he wants you to attend his party."

"Really?" he replied. "Why?"

"It seems like you made quite an impression on him the last time," she answered. "So, will you go?"

"Won't his dad be there?" he asked.

"Nope," she said. "Their dad already took them out for a day at the arcade because he won't be around for the actual birthday. He claims it's another business trip that he can't get out of."

"Have you really just stopped giving him the benefit of the doubt?"

"I stopped doing that a long time ago."

"Okay, then. If he specifically asked for me to be there, then I'll be there."

"Great," she replied. "He'll be so happy when I tell him. The kids really like you, you know?"

"Why wouldn't they?" he joked.

"Okay, don't let it go to your head."

"So, when is the party exactly? I need time to buy his gift."

"Oh, you don't have to. He's getting a lot of gifts from his dad, uncles, and aunts already. He's good."

"One more can't hurt, right?" he insisted. "When it comes to kids, no amount of birthday gifts are ever enough."

"If you say so," she conceded.

The next day, Brennan excused himself from the office during his lunch break. He decided to take a walk to the nearby mall and browse for potential gifts that she could give to Brian. Brennan struggled with finding a gift because he knew that Brian was at that awkward age where he wasn't really interested in toys anymore, but he was also too young to appreciate things a teenager would like. He thought about getting Brian some clothes, but he knew that these weren't things that a young boy like him would be interested in.

As he was about to call it quits, Brennan's eyes lit up the moment he saw the video game store. He recalled seeing the console that was in their living room that night when he first visited them. He also remembered Charmaine telling him on their first date that the boys would have been happy to just stay at home alone with their video games. It was a real eureka moment for Brennan when he saw the store. When he took the boys out to the movies that one time, he also remembered both of them talking about a Spider-Man video game that they really wanted.

He walked over towards the counter and asked someone to help him find the new Spider-Man game for PlayStation. Brennan discovered that it was an immensely popular game and that the store was always having trouble keeping it in stock. Fortunately for him, they still had a couple copies of the game in the store. However, they were the premium version of the game that came with extra merchandise and online credits. They also demanded a hefty price tag. Brennan took one look at the price and was immediately shocked.

"This is how much video games cost now?" he asked as he glanced down at the one hundred fifty dollar price tag. "This is insane!"

"That's a special edition, sir," replied the store attendant. "But, yeah, console games are really getting up there in price."

"It's fine," he said. "I'll take it."

"Is this for your son, sir?" asked the attendant.

Brennan didn't want to have to explain the situation and just replied yes.

"Well," continued the attendant. "You may not know much about video games, but I'm certain that he's going to love you for this."

"I hope so," muttered Brennan in reply.

C h a p t e r   4 8

A b i g a i l

ABIGAIL WAS IN her room doing her daily rounds of browsing through her messages. At that point, it almost felt like a chore for her to go through their messages and propositions. She no longer had the giddiness and excitement that she once had when they first started the open marriage. She never found herself experimenting with her makeup or her selfies. In fact, she had made it a point not to send selfies out to guys. Occasionally, she would stumble upon a man who was great at making conversation, and she would indulge him for a bit. However, she wasn't really interested in meeting anyone in person anymore. Once she had called it quits on Kevin, she was done with everything.

"Listen, Kevin," she told him the last night they went out on a date at an Ethiopian restaurant. "I really like you. I really like us. It's been a great time."

"It sure has," Kevin replied. "I really like you too."

"Yeah, I know," she answered. "You've been really sweet, and I'm so thankful for it. This is why this is going to be really difficult."

"What?" he asked. "What's going to be difficult?"

"This. This date. It's going to be our last," she told him. "I don't think we can see each other anymore after this."

"Why?" he said. "Is it me? Did I do something?"

"No," she answered. "It's not your fault at all. Don't blame yourself."

"Is it someone else? Have you met a better guy?" he asked.

"It's not that either, Kevin," she replied. "It's me. I'm the one who has changed."

"I don't understand, Abigail," he said. "You said that you liked me."

"I do," she affirmed. "I really do. It's just that I've come to a realization about certain aspects of my life that won't allow me to keep this up any further. I don't expect you to understand my decision. But all I'm asking from you now is to respect it."

"Okay," he said. "I honestly wouldn't be able to understand it even if I tried, Abigail."

"I know," she answered. "I'm difficult. It's true that I really do like you. That's why I'm hoping that the two of us can remain friends." She reached out for his hand.

"I don't know, Abigail. I have a lot of friends. Like I said, I'm feeling the pressure to settle down with someone at this point in my life. Can you understand that?" he asked. He looked away.

"Yes, I do," she replied. "I think I should go."

She reached into her wallet and was about to pull out some cash to pay for her share of the bill.

"Don't bother," he interrupted. "Just go. This is on me. Consider it a parting gift."

"I'm so sorry that I hurt you, Kevin," she said.

"You didn't hurt me," he answered. "I'm just disappointed."

Abigail didn't want to find herself in another one of those kinds of situations. This is why she made it a point to keep things casual with the guys that she was dating. She was no longer interested in getting serious with any of them anyway. The emptiness and suffocation that she was feeling a few months prior had completely dissipated. She had gotten her taste of freedom, and that was enough for her. At that moment, Abigail was perfectly fine with the nature of her marriage to Brennan. She appreciated the history they had together and she was proud of how the two of them were able to make an open marriage work.

"I'm really happy with where we're at," she wrote in her journal. "I love that I have a whole new group of friends that I can just talk to whenever I'm bored. I also love that there's no pressure from them for me to act a certain way. More importantly, I love how I've stopped putting so much pressure on myself to succeed at this. The whole idea of an open marriage sounded so fun and exciting at first. And it was. But over time, it lost its luster. I think I'm ready to put that phase of my life behind me. Although, ironically enough, I don't think Brennan is ready to do so himself. We'll have to wait to see how things play out. For now, I'm okay. I'm content."

One Monday, while Brennan was at work, Abigail was driving back home after having dropped the kids off at daycare. She parked her car and walked up to the door where she noticed there was a sealed envelope stuck to the door. It was a peculiar scenario because the mailman typically left letters in their mailbox at the curb. She peered closer to take a look at what was written across the envelope in bold handwritten print:

"For Abigail Sutton's Eyes Only"

Abigail was intrigued. She turned behind her to look down the street in case she could catch the person who left the letter there. However, she found the neighborhood to be completely deserted. She took the letter from the door and brought it with her as she entered her home. With her hands shaking, Abigail walked over to the living room coffee table and laid the letter on top of it, then grabbed a letter opener and sliced the envelope open. As she did so, she tried to analyze the handwriting on the envelope, but she couldn't recognize whose it was. She unfurled the folded letter and read:

Dear Mrs. Sutton,

You don't know me, and I don't know you. Although, I do know of you. My name is Robert Evans. The two of us have never met. However, I can't say the same for our spouses. I currently find myself in a collapsing marriage that is nearing its end. A while back, I suspected my wife of engaging in extramarital relations with other men. As such, I decided to hire a private investigator to look into the matter. I am now going to share with you the findings of the case.

Your husband, one Brennan Sutton, has had sustained romantic relations with my wife, Charmaine Evans. My private investigator trailed them going to a posh night club together. My wife has also brought your husband along with her to school functions together with our children. Brennan has even reportedly been buying and giving gifts to them I also have it on good authority that Brennan and Charmaine have had sexual relations in my own home. Maybe even in yours too. I can't be sure. I just want you to know that you are married to a man who has broken my family apart. I also want you to know that I believe he has plans to do the same to your family. My private investigator has told me that Brennan and Charmaine have been talking about planning a life together as they plot to leave the both of us.

I don't know what kind of marriage you have with your husband, Mrs. Sutton. I wouldn't want to make any assumptions on your home life. I understand that we are all human and that we all have our own individual quirks and philosophies. But I advise that you err on the side of caution if everything that I'm telling you now is new information to you. If Brennan hasn't been totally honest with you, maybe shedding some more light on the truth can give you a certain advantage. Maybe you don't have to end up with a broken family the way that he broke mine.

Sincerely,
Robert Evans

Chapter 49

Brennan

BRENNAN RETURNED HOME from a tiring Monday at the office. In his mind, all he wanted to do was see his kids and spend the night talking to Charmaine. He opened the door expecting to see the kids in the living room ready to greet him. Instead, he saw Abigail sitting at the dining room table. This was unusual to him as Abigail was usually preparing dinner around this time. Brennan approached her slowly and noticed that she had a gloomy expression on her face and her eyes were extremely puffy.

"Hey," he said. "What's wrong? Where are the kids?"

Brennan noticed that there was an unfurled piece of paper on the table in front of Abigail.

"What's that?" he asked.

"The kids are with my mom. They'll be staying over there tonight," she answered.

"Oh? What's happening right now? Are you okay? Have you been crying? What's wrong?" he asked.

"I got a letter today," she said still staring at the piece of paper on the table. "It was an interesting read. I think you better read it yourself."

Brennan set his things down on the floor and took his usual seat at the table across from Abigail. He took the letter and stared at it for a while. "Who is this from?" he asked.

Abigail didn't answer. She just kept staring at the letter. Then she looked him straight in the eye and said, "Just read it."

Brennan read the letter, and he panicked as soon as he saw who it was from. He looked at Abigail and saw a fire of fury in her eyes. He was about to ask her how she had gotten the letter, but decided against it. He sat and read the letter while he felt the heat of Abigail's stare burning a hole right through the paper. Once he was done reading, he put the letter back on the table.

"Abigail," he whispered.

"Shut up," she interrupted. "What the hell were you thinking?"

"What are you talking about?" Brennan replied. "I did exactly what you wanted! I dated other people! Why are you so upset?" Both of their voices were raised now, and there was palpable tension in the air.

"Don't you dare!" she said. "You know full well that this wasn't the point of our arrangement, Brennan! We were supposed to go out and explore our sexuality. We weren't supposed to be breaking families apart!"

"That's the thing, Abigail," he said. "You and I have very different understandings of things. You don't even fully understand the situation between me and Charmaine."

"Is it not true that you started attending social functions with this woman, Brennan?" she asked. Brennan didn't answer. "See? You're speechless. Even you're too blind to see how fucked up all of this is."

"Don't put that on me. You were the one who wanted this for us. You were the one who wanted to start seeing other people."

"Shut up, Brennan! You know that we were only

supposed to date people on the side. Maybe even go to bed with them. Sure. But we were never supposed to fall in love with them, Brennan. We were never supposed to break marriages and families apart! Why do I have to keep repeating that?"

"Can you just stop yelling at me so that we can have a civil and rational conversation about this?"

"Oh, the time for civility and rationality is long gone, Brennan. All of that got tossed out the window the moment you fell in love with this woman. Tell me. Do you not understand how lucky you are?"

"Lucky? How am I lucky?"

"Ask any guy on the street if they would be happy to have a wife who gave them a free pass to sleep with anyone they wanted to. Ask them if they wouldn't want a wife who genuinely welcomed the idea of their husband engaging in sexual relations with another woman. That's precisely the dream scenario that I gave you, Brennan. And you screwed it all up!" Abigail stood up and began pacing around the kitchen while Brennan remained seated. A vein had emerged on her temple that was the size of a caterpillar, and it looked to Brennan like it was about to pop. "Do you know what your problem is, Brennan? You get too emotional. Who would've known that you would be the woman in this relationship."

"Hold on for just a minute."

"No," she demanded as she pointed a finger at him. "Don't interrupt me. You really fucked this up, Brennan. For everyone. For me and you. For that woman's family. You're just one really big fuck-up!"

"What do you want me to do?" he demanded. He was also standing at this point, and Brennan could feel his skin growing warmer. "The way I see it, we're only in this mess because it's what you wanted for the both of us. So, please, tell me what you think I should do."

"Obviously, you've got to break things off with this whore before things get too complicated. I know that you're already in too deep, but you don't want to make things worse, Brennan. She has kids. YOU have kids."

"It's not that simple."

"Then make it simple! Think about your kids, Brennan. You better not dare break this family up. Even if you just think about abandoning me and the girls, I swear on our children that I will make your life a living hell!"

"Do you know what?" Brennan raised his voice even louder this time. "I am sick and tired of you thinking that you can just keep on controlling me. The way I see it, everything that has happened so far is your fault. You're the reason that we got into this open marriage bullshit in the first place."

"Fuck off!"

"I'm not done." He got up in her face. "At this point, you can threaten me all you want. I don't care. This is what you wanted in the first place, and you don't get to turn back now just because it's inconvenient for you. You made your bed. Now lie in it. You can't stop me from seeing Charmaine." Brennan's face was red by now.

"Okay, then. If you keep saying that this is all my fault, then I'm calling it off. We're done with the open marriage. We can't see other people anymore," she threw her arms up in the air.

"How convenient. Again, you're not going to be able to control me anymore. Curse me all you want. But I'm a grown man who will do as I please."

Before Abigail could mount a reply, Brennan grabbed his keys and was already making his way towards the door.

"Hey," said Abigail. "Where are you going? We're not done yet!"

"Yes, we are," replied Brennan before slamming the door behind him.

He walked to the car and put it in reverse before peeling out of the driveway and onto the open road. Brennan was hyperventilating, and he could feel himself getting angrier with every breath. He couldn't shake

Abigail's hypocrisy from his mind.

He was driving fast now, but he wasn't sure about where he wanted to go. Brennan thought about driving straight to Charmaine's house, but he figured that she was having her own problems now. Judging from the letter, Robert was serious about his threats to leave her. Instead, he continued to drive without a destination as he tried to calm himself down. He switched the radio on and turned the stereo up to full volume, hoping the music would drown out the intensity of his feelings.

Without even realizing it, he began to cry, tears rolling down his cheeks uncontrollably. He didn't understand why he was so sad. All he knew was that he was so overwhelmed by everything. As he drove, his mind jumped from thoughts of Charmaine to his kids and Abigail. He realized that these were all the people he loved most in the world, and he knew that choosing one would mean having to let go of the other. He found himself driving along a lake and decided to park his car towards the side of the road. Brennan tilted his head back onto the headrest and closed his eyes as he continued to weep.

Chapter 50

Abigail

"WHAT A FUCKING idiot!" she shouted right after Brennan slammed the front door in her face. "Yeah, just run away, you coward! Run away from your problems like a sissy!"

She stormed towards the couch and sat down, her breathing short and rapid. She could almost feel her face getting warmer with every breath. She cried as she grabbed the TV remote and hurled it towards the wall causing a small hole in the wall. Her crying went on for a good five minutes. She didn't realize that she was holding in so much frustration in her heart and was surprised to see it all coming out like that. When she was able to calm down for a bit, she looked up and stared towards the staircase that led to their bedrooms. "Maybe I'm to blame," she whispered to herself. "Maybe Brennan's right. This is partly my fault."

Abigail turned to her right and looked at the coffee table that stood beside the couch. There was a picture of her whole family while they were on vacation at Disneyland in Anaheim. The two girls and Brennan were wearing Mickey Mouse ears, and they had the biggest smiles on their faces. She ran her finger along the frame as a pang of nostalgia swept across her body. It was at that moment that Abigail realized what she wanted. She stared at Brennan's smiling face, as happy as can be with his family. Abigail knew that this was the man she loved and that she never wanted to let her family go. "I need to save my family," she said. "I need to save us."

Chapter 51

Brennan

BRENNAN CAME HOME to find Abigail still sitting in the living room. Her eyes were just as puffy as when he'd left. He expected her to scream at him and ream him out again. Instead, she motioned for him to approach her and take a seat beside her on the couch. He reluctantly walked over to her without knowing what to expect. "I don't want to fight," he said as he took his seat.

"Me too," she said. "I'm tired of fighting."

"What's on your mind?" he asked.

She took a deep breath and stared into her lap. Abigail gathered herself and looked into Brennan's eyes as she asked, "Do you love her?"

Brennan was taken aback by the question. He hesitated, and with a cracking voice, said, "I… think so."

"I can't blame you," she said. "I know that this isn't what I wanted to happen, but I shouldn't have forced this on you. I should have understood what a struggle it was for you to do this for me." She began crying again but quickly wiped her tears away as soon as they fell.

"It was really hard," he confessed. "I was perfectly

happy in our marriage. It killed me every day to see you so unhappy when you were with me. I didn't know what to do, but I knew that I needed to act. That's why it killed me even more when you asked me for an open marriage."

"I know," she sympathized. "That must have been really hard for you. I made it hard on you."

"You can understand, right?" Brennan was also crying now. "I felt so much animosity and hatred from you. I felt like you were disgusted by me. So, even though I didn't want to, I managed to find love from another woman. She cared for me and was respectful of me. She didn't pick fights with me, and she wore me down. I was helpless. I was desperate to get from her what I didn't get from you."

Abigail began to cry even harder as Brennan said those words. She knew that her efforts to wipe her tears away were futile at that point and so she just let them flow. She raised her hands and touched his face which was also damp with tears. "Remember our vows, Brennan? In sickness and in health? For richer and poorer?"

Brennan saw Abigail smile as she tried to lighten the situation up more, but recalling their vows only made him weep even harder.

"We need to think about the kids. We made a commitment to them too by bringing them into this world," she continued. Brennan nodded and let out a huge sigh. Abigail went on saying, "We have to find a way to make things work."

"You're right," he agreed.

Abigail took the family photo that she was staring at earlier and gave it to Brennan. "We made something beautiful," she said. "We can't let it go to waste."

"I need to end things with her," he said with affirmation. "We need to get back to normal."

The two of them retreated to the second floor, and for the first time in weeks, shared a bedroom together. Brennan thought that it would be awkward at first, but it felt just like riding a bike. There was no awkwardness at all between them. The two of them just lay there with Abigail resting her head on Brennan's chest. When he knew that she was fully asleep, he grabbed his phone and texted Charmaine. "Let's meet for lunch tomorrow," he wrote. "Need to see you."

The next day, Brennan planned to meet Charmaine for lunch at a French restaurant within town. He was nervous about meeting her and decided to practice his speech while he was driving over to her. He planned to open the discussion by telling her that their relationship had really taken a toll on his relationship with his kids. Brennan thought that Charmaine could never fault him for breaking their romance up because he wanted to be a better father to his children. He wasn't comfortable with using his kids as a scapegoat because it all felt so cowardly. But it also happened to be the truth, so he knew that he would sound convincing.

Once he arrived at the restaurant, he saw Charmaine already seated at a table in the al fresco area of the restaurant. She forced a smile once she saw him, but he noticed that she had a look of anxiety on her face. He smiled back in an effort to make her feel more at ease, but he didn't know if that had any effect on her. "Hi," he said as he leaned in to kiss her. "How are you doing?"

"It depends," she responded. "Brennan, we have to talk."

Brennan thought that Robert had probably told Charmaine about the letter he sent Abigail. He also assumed that Robert might have threatened to leave her.

"What's up?" he asked.

She took her phone out of her bag and browsed for a while before handing it to Brennan. He saw a picture of Charmaine in her bathroom with a white stick in her hands. Brennan realized that it was a pregnancy test.

"Swipe left," she told him.

Brennan swiped on the screen and saw a closeup image of the pregnancy test indicating a positive result. His jaw fell in shock as he stared at the image on the screen. His eyes darted towards Charmaine who had a look of concern on her face.

"I missed my period last week, and I started to grow suspicious," she said. "I took that test last night."

"You're pregnant?" he asked.

"I'm pregnant."

Brennan leapt out of his seat and lunged at Charmaine to give her a hug. He kissed her on the lips and hugged her tightly again. He was so happy to learn that Charmaine was pregnant, and his heart was racing with excitement. Suddenly, all of that positive energy was zapped out of him when his thoughts returned to the very reason he was there in the first place.

"Brennan?" asked Charmaine. "Can you believe it?" She was all smiles and had tears in her eyes.

"No," he said as he started to tear up himself. "I can't."

Chapter 52

Abigail

ABIGAIL WAS IN high spirits all day after having talked to Brennan the night before. She had been through an emotional whirlwind on the previous day, and now she felt like she was walking on a cloud. She had just finished picking the kids up from her mom's house and had helped them settle in back at home. Both Amber and Riley were still feeling pretty tired from all of the fun they had with grandma. Abigail helped them go to sleep a lot earlier than their usual bedtime before she went back downstairs to wait for Brennan.

Brennan came home during the usual time after work, and Abigail was already seated at the dinner table with the roasted chicken she had just prepared. She even popped open a bottle of wine because of how high her spirits were. However, all of her positivity quickly dissipated when she saw that Brennan was very pale and his face was devoid of all the energy that he was exhibiting before he left her that morning.

"Brennan?" she asked. "What's wrong?"

He was taking deep, heavy breaths as he loosened his tie and took his seat at the table. "I met with Charmaine today," he said.

"And?" she wondered. "How did it go?"

"I was there. I was ready. I had rehearsed my speech to make the breakup go as smoothly as possible," he explained. "I wanted to rip the Band-Aid off and be done with it."

"Right. And what happened?"

"Well, I was just about to sit down and start my speech. Then, out of nowhere, she tells me that she's missed her period. She'd been late for several days."

Abigail's heart sank. She already knew where this was going, but she needed to hear it from Brennan himself. In her mind, if he didn't say it, then it wasn't going to be true.

"She's pregnant," he said. "She's pregnant."

The two of them stayed silent. Abigail stared out into the blank space for a few seconds while Brennan waited for her to say something.

"And it's yours, I assume?" she asked.

"She hasn't been with anyone else but me," he confirmed.

"And she plans on keeping it?"

"She does."

Abigail felt her eyes start to well up and a lone tear fell when she blinked. "You've really messed this up for us."

He said nothing as he watched Abigail cup her face in her hands and cry. She let out a huge scream that was loud enough to be heard all throughout the house. "So what are your plans now, Brennan?"

"I don't know. It's my child, and I guess it's my responsibility to take care of it."

"Okay, but what about the children that you already have? Don't you have a responsibility to take care of them too?"

"Of course, I'm still going to be there for the girls."

"Oh no. I'm not going to put the girls through the

trauma of having a dad who splits his time between two families. They deserve more than that, Brennan!"

"What do you want me to do? What am I supposed to do?"

Abigail didn't say anything for a while. She had her hands on her hips looking Brennan in the eyes and saying, "Choose. You're going to have to choose."

"What?"

"Choose. It's her or us. If you choose her, then I'm going to fight for custody of the kids, and we both know that I'll win that battle," she said. "Or you convince her to not have the baby or let her raise her child on her own. Sever all ties with her and be a part of this family — your family."

"Let's be reasonable here," he pleaded.

"I'm done with reasoning, Brennan. I'm not going to force you into anything. Those are your choices. Those are my terms," she said. "It's either you go for the family that you already have or you go for that woman. The choice is yours."

Chapter 53

Brennan

BRENNAN DODGED CHARMAINE'S phone calls over the next couple of days. He had a lot to think about. Abigail wasn't speaking to him either, and he was back to staying in the guest bedroom. Brennan knew that he needed to come to a decision, but he still hadn't thought it through. It was only when he was lounging on the living room couch watching television as he tried to get his mind off things for a while when he discovered what he truly wanted. He peered over to the side table and saw the picture of his family at Disneyland again. It was then that he realized what he wanted. He knew that he wanted his old life back and that he wanted to be as happy as he was in the picture. Brennan picked up his phone and told Charmaine to meet him at the park that was near her home.

"Oh, a date at the park," she said. "How romantic. I'll see you in a bit."

"See you," Brennan replied.

It hurt him to know that she was blissfully unaware of what was about to take place. Brennan felt like he was on autopilot on the drive going to the park. He made sure to tell Charmaine to meet him there so that he wouldn't have to drive her back home after breaking the news to her. That would be too awkward for him to handle.

On the drive over, he once again rehearsed everything that he wanted to say. "I just can't leave my family," he repeated to himself. "They're my whole world."

He received a text from Charmaine just as he was parking his car. "I found a bench near the cotton candy stand. Do you know the one I'm talking about?" she asked.

"Yeah," he replied. "I'll be there in a few."

As he walked over to the part of the park where Charmaine was waiting, Brennan felt almost like an atomic bomb had just gone off in his mind. His feet felt like cement blocks, and every step he took was an absolute struggle. Brennan's heart was beating at such a rapid pace. He broke a sweat despite the chilly afternoon air.

Before he knew it, Charmaine was in his sights. He couldn't help but notice just how beautiful she looked. She sported a floral Sunday dress, similar to the one that she had worn on their first date. She was also wearing her signature red lipstick that Brennan had grown quite accustomed to. Charmaine spotted him walking towards her and waved. Brennan waved back and forced a smile He gingerly shuffled his way towards the bench as he tried to regulate his breathing.

Brennan took a seat beside Charmaine and gave her a hug.

"Are you okay?" she asked. "You look as if you've seen a ghost."

"I might have," he confessed. "How are you feeling?"

"I'm doing okay," she said. "The morning sickness should come sometime soon, but I haven't felt that yet."

"Alright," he said. "Good."

There was a long pause between the both of them. Brennan looked towards the horizon, and Charmaine broke the silence, "What's wrong? You're scaring me."

"Actually," he replied. "I need to talk to you about something. That's why I asked you here today."

"Okay," she said with hesitation. "Should I be worried?"

Again, Brennan didn't reply right away. He turned towards the lake and just continued to stare into space before taking a deep breath. Brennan closed his eyes and turned his attention back to Charmaine.

"You…" she said. "This is not a happy date, is it?"

"It's not," he answered. "It's also our last."

His eyes welled up, and Charmaine looked away herself. Her mouth was slightly ajar, and her eyebrows were bunched together. She opened her mouth as if to say something, but no sounds came out. She shook her head and stared down at her feet as if she were at a loss for words.

"I don't understand," she finally said. "Help me understand."

"Well," he replied while scratching his head. "This was never a part of the plan, Charmaine."

"To have a child with me?" she asked.

"Not just that," he mentioned. "Everything. Falling in love. Getting serious. The weekend getaways. The parties. Movie nights. None of this was supposed to happen."

"You selfish prick," she said. "That's so easy for you to say now, huh?"

"You're mad, and I get it. I understand," he said. "But I just hope that you can understand my side of things too. You're having a baby. My baby. And my wife's already told me that if I'm going to help raise this baby with you, then I can't be a part of their life."

"So?" she asked. "What's the difference? Why would you choose them over me?"

"Because they were always a part of the plan, Charmaine," he answered. "I know how cruel and insensitive that sounds. I know that I'm being selfish. But again, none of this was ever a part of the plan."

"How convenient for you."

"Is there any possibility that you would give this baby up?"

Charmaine's jaw dropped as she looked at him with an expression of utter disgust. She raised her hand and slapped him across the face. Then her eyes couldn't hold back the tears any longer, and they began to fall recklessly. She grabbed Brennan's hand and placed it on her stomach. Looking into his eyes, she said, "This is yours too, Brennan. This is your child too. How could you give up on it so quickly?"

She let Brennan's hand go, but he didn't remove it from her belly. He looked into her eyes and saw the face of a heartbroken woman, then he glanced down at his hand on her belly. In his mind, he could almost visualize the unborn child that was growing inside of her. "That's my child," he repeated. Brennan began to cry with her now, and the two of them just sat there and cried together for a couple of minutes, completely oblivious to the world around them. To Brennan, it was almost as if they were back on the beach, caught in each other's tight embrace. She leaned in and kissed him on the cheek. Then she planted another kiss on his lips. He kissed her back, and he was surprised at how good it felt to kiss her. He had almost forgotten. It was then he remembered what he was there for. He quickly withdrew himself from her and removed his hand from her belly.

Brennan gathered himself and took a look at the lake. The sun was beginning to set now, and the sky was changing into a soft orange hue. A flock of birds flew across the sky with their silhouettes painted against the backdrop of the setting sun. There were only a few people left at the park at that time. Some of them were running while a few others were walking their dogs. Brennan cast his eyes on the lake and saw the distorted reflection of the sky that stood directly above it. That's when the sight of what looked like a married couple with their kids caught his attention. The man and woman were walking along the paved walkway with their hands intertwined. Brennan also saw what he assumed were their two kids running in front of them. They were both girls who were dressed in matching dresses, but they didn't look like they were the same age. He couldn't help but notice how happy they looked, and it made him feel sad. Somehow, their happiness had reminded him of everything that he stood to lose.

He turned his attention back to Charmaine and saw that she was lost in thought as well. Brennan held her hand and that prompted her to turn her head towards him. He felt himself about to cry again, but he fought against it. He withdrew his hand from hers and closed his eyes. Brennan furrowed his brow, and in as cold a voice as possible, said, "I need you to get rid of this baby, Charmaine."

"What?" she asked. "Are you crazy, Brennan?" Her eyes were welling up again, and her voice started to break. Brennan saw that she was deeply affected by what he was asking her to do, but he convinced himself that he needed to stay stern about it.

"I'm not going to leave my family for you or this child," he went on. "And I don't want this child to have to grow up with an absentee father. It doesn't deserve that either. Be reasonable, Charmaine. Get rid of the baby."

"Who are you?" she demanded. She was completely crying again and looked to Brennan as if she were on the verge of breaking down. "It's like I don't know you anymore."

"Maybe you never knew me at all," he replied. "I need you to get rid of this child, and we must put an end to seeing one another. We have to go back to the way things were and forget that any of this ever happened."

"Cold," she said. "Cold, Brennan.

"Charmaine," he continued as if he hadn't heard her. "I need you to confirm to me that you're going to get rid of this child."

"I can confirm that you're a complete douchebag and that I'm sorry I ever met you," she said. "My husband is no saint, but I know for sure that he would never demand for me to get an abortion. You're absolutely despicable, and you're breaking my heart."

She stood up and was about to leave, then stopped and opened her mouth as if she wanted to say something else, but no words came out. Instead, Charmaine just stood there looking at him with tears rolling down her cheeks. She reached her hand out, and Brennan flinched because he thought that she was going to slap him again. Instead, she caressed his face and looked straight into his eyes.

"I don't know who you are anymore," she said. "The man I fell in love with is not the one I'm looking at now. But I have a feeling that he's still in there somewhere."

Brennan tried his best to keep himself from crying. He felt a deep urge inside of him that just wanted to reach out to Charmaine and lock her in a tight embrace. Instead, he hardened himself and removed her hand from his face.

"Let me know when you plan to get the procedure done," he said. "If you want, I can accompany you to the doctor. It's the least I can do."

"Unbelievable," she said. She looked down at her feet and took a deep breath. "I don't need you, Brennan. Whether I choose to have this child or not, I don't need you to be there with me. In fact, do me a favor and never get in touch with me again. I never want to hear from you again."

Charmaine stood there for a while as if she were waiting for him to say something. Again, he felt something inside of him that just wanted to reach out to her and hug her. He wanted to tell her that he wanted to be there for her, but he knew that he couldn't. Instead, he said nothing and merely nodded his head.

Charmaine shook her head in disgust and picked up her bag. "Goodbye, Brennan. It's been swell." She walked away and headed back to her car. Brennan watched the love of his life walk away from him with his unborn child. That voice inside of him resurfaced once more and told him that this was his final chance. It told him that he still had the opportunity to chase after her and the life that he wanted with her. But there was another voice inside of him that told him to stay put. He knew that letting Charmaine walk away would free him up to pursue the life that he's always loved with his family. So, as he watched Charmaine disappear into the horizon, he stood there as tall and as motionless as an anchor underneath a raging ocean. When he was sure that she was gone and could no longer see him, he sat back down on the bench and broke down, cupping his hands over his face and crying in disgust at himself.

Brennan sat there for a good ten minutes to just cry without caring about who saw him or who was judging. He couldn't bring himself to move. His muscles felt physically weak and compromised. It was almost as if he was paralyzed and had merely resigned himself to that spot by the lake. He looked around again and saw that it was nearly dark now. The sun was almost gone, and people were leaving the park.

He grabbed his phone and searched for Abigail's name in his contacts list. She picked up the call after just a couple of rings.

"Hello?" said Abigail's voice on the other line. "Where are you, Brennan?"

"I'm at the park near Charmaine's house," he said.

"Is she still there with you?" she asked. "What are you calling me for while you're with her?"

"No," he replied. "She's gone. She's gone forever."

"What does that mean, Brennan? Did you break up with her?"

"Yes. Well, she broke up with me. She told me that she never wants to see or hear from me again."

"And the baby? Is she keeping the baby?"

"I don't know. Either way, she doesn't want me to have anything to do with it."

Neither of them said anything for a while. They merely listened to the blank silence that was passing through the phone's earpiece.

"I think you should come home," she finally said. "Come home to your family."

"I would love nothing more," he replied. "I'm coming."

He hung up the phone and placed it back into his pocket. He took one last look at the sun and saw that it was practically gone now. Darkness had descended upon him, and the only sources of light were coming from the faint moonlight and streetlights that hung above him. He turned towards the spot on the bench where Charmaine was sitting just a few minutes prior and heaved a big sigh.

The next morning, Brennan woke up in his bed with Abigail at his side. To Abigail, everything had returned to normal. But to Brennan, there was still a heavy weight that lingered in his heart. He looked towards his wife and saw the woman that he chose. He saw the life that he had chosen for himself and committed to a long time ago. And yet, he also saw the face of the woman he knew he let down.

Brennan pictured Charmaine and their unborn baby in his mind. He saw her having to live her life without him as she raised their child together with the two boys that she already had. As soon as that thought crossed his mind, Brennan grabbed his phone and stepped outside of the bedroom. Abigail was still asleep, and he made sure to not wake her up.

As soon as he was out in the hall, he dialed Charmaine's number. He heard the first ring, and he felt his heart leap in his chest. Did I make the right decision? he wondered. Am I doing the right thing now by calling her?

Another ring. Still no answer. I have to know that she'll

be okay moving forward. The call rang again but ended abruptly. Brennan knew that this meant she ended the call. He dialed her phone once again, but the call wouldn't go through. He tried once more and got the same results. She's blocked me, he thought. That's when he realized the finality of his decision. Just as he was about to enter his bedroom, his phone beeped. It was a message from Charmaine.

Brennan glanced down at his phone and sighed at what he read. He stared at the message and reread it multiple times. It was a short text, but he had trouble grasping its contents. After he was sure about what Charmaine had meant by the message, he deleted it and shook his head. Brennan deleted Charmaine's name from his contacts and deleted all of the dating apps on his phone. After that, he decided to go back into the bedroom to lay down beside his sleeping wife.

Chapter 54

Charmaine

IT HAD BEEN three years since she texted Brennan to tell him to never get in touch with her again and to delete her number. Charmaine left Robert and moved to California with her two boys as soon as she could. Before leaving, the two of them had settled on her raising the kids herself and parting ways amicably.

She was sitting on the porch in her backyard as she gazed out onto the garden. It was a bright and sunny spring day in San Francisco. There was a cool breeze in the air that combated the stinging heat of the sun. The flowers in her garden were in full bloom as she took a minute to appreciate each one of them. On the table in front of her was a bowl of beautifully crafted pebbles that surrounded a large citronella candle which helped keep the bugs away.

In the yard were her two sons. They were now entering the teenage stages of their lives, and Charmaine knew what that entailed. She expected the two of them to eventually grow more and more distant from their mother the more that they aged. She realized that she needed to take in as many precious moments with them as she could.

Charmaine watched as the two of them played with their mini drones in their backyard, and she couldn't help but smile at how happy they looked. She knew that moments like these were fleeting, but she also knew that that was okay because of the other person who was sitting next to her at the table.

She turned towards her right and kissed the head of the handsome brunet sitting beside her on the high chair. He had a huge smile on his face with a steady stream of drool pouring down his chin. This little boy had orange juice stains on his shirt as he desperately tried to grab at the plastic utensils that were placed before him. "You're such a handsome little boy," she whispered to him. "Your brothers are getting older, but at least I'll get to have you for so much longer."

Adam had just turned two, and he looked a lot like his mom. He had inherited Charmaine's fair skin and soft eyes. Adam looked nothing like his brothers despite them having the same mom. "It's you and me, buddy," she said. "You'll always have me."

Charmaine glanced down at the citronella candle that was sitting in the middle of the porch table. Her eyes ruffled through the pile of pebbles until her sights settled on one particular stone that looked different from the rest. She grabbed it from the pile and examined it closely. It didn't look like it had undergone any industrial finishing and almost resembled any other typical pebble she could find on the street. She knew that there was nothing remarkable in the pebble's appearance, and yet she knew that she would never get rid of it. The more she looked at the pebble, the clearer the image of a beach and a man she once knew became in her mind. She felt her heart tighten and her eyes well up as she continued to study the pebble. Charmaine placed it directly in the middle of her palm and grasped it tightly as she closed her eyes to try to relive that fateful day at the beach in St. Paul where she had plucked this pebble from the ground herself. She could still vividly see the image of a man in her mind who held her in his arms that day. This was the same man whose face would envelope her thoughts everyday afterward. She also saw this man whenever she looked at Adam because the two of them bore a striking resemblance with one another. As Charmaine sat on the porch that day, she was anxious about what her future would bring. But she knew that she could always rely on the past to give her a fleeting dose of love and happiness, albeit for just a moment.

Chapter 55

Brennan

IT WAS PANDEMONIUM in the Sutton household as Brennan, Abigail, Amber, and Riley were locked in an intense game of hide and seek. They had just concluded a round where Amber had successfully uncovered the rest of her family's hiding spots. It was all laughs for them as they tried to help Brennan crawl out from underneath the coffee table. "You're really good at this game, Amber," he told his daughter. "That was the best hiding spot that I could think of."

"You're really bad at hide and seek, Daddy," chimed Riley who was grinning from ear to ear.

"Take it easy on Daddy, girls," said Abigail. "It's not his fault that he's terrible at this game."

"Very funny, you guys," he said.

"You're it now, Daddy," said Amber. "Go outside and count to ten while we all look for a hiding place."

"No peeking!" demanded Riley.

"I won't peek," he said. "I promise."

Brennan shuffled towards the door as the three girls scrambled towards different parts of the house behind him. He went outside and was greeted by the hard pouring rain. It had been raining in Minneapolis all week, and he regretted not bringing a coat with him as he stepped out. Then, as he stood there in the pouring rain, he was greeted with a wave of melancholy that swept over him. The laughter and smiles he was exhibiting just a few minutes prior had now been replaced by a sullen seriousness.

As he counted to ten in slow agonizing beats, he reached into his front right pocket and pulled out a smoothed pebble. He stared at it and recalled the bright sunny day he had first gotten it at the beach. That day was a stark contrast from the hard rain that was pouring in front of him at that moment. He looked at the pebble with a deep longing and felt a tear stream down his cheek. Brennan quickly wiped the tear away and shoved the pebble back into his pocket before reentering his home to look for his family.

The End.

Printed in Great Britain
by Amazon

19801762R00192